STEALTH: MASON

EAGLE TACTICAL BOOK TWO

WILLOW FOX

SLOWBURN
PUBLISHING

Stealth: Mason

Eagle Tactical Book Two

Willow Fox

Published by Slow Burn Publishing

© 2021

Cover by Slow Burn Publishing

Image(s) used under license from Shutterstock.com.

All rights reserved.

CHAPTER ONE

Hazel

I didn't dare gaze into the eyes of the man who bought me. Thanks to my stepbrother, Nikolai, I belonged to Franco, his second in command in the mafia.

"Next week, you'll be my bride," Franco said, his teeth yellowing and crooked.

He grabbed my jaw and yanked my face closer to his for a kiss. His breath smelled of vomit. My stomach recoiled.

We stood outside his black sedan, the door open.

I was to go with him. I'd sooner starve myself to death. That was still a possibility after I went with the man to whom I was engaged to marry.

Bile rose to my throat, and I swallowed the burning acid as it slid back down. I kept my mouth sealed shut, but it didn't stop him from planting his thick, dry lips against mine. His tongue pushed at my mouth, rough and forceful, but I refused to grant him access.

The scum-sucking vermin could kiss the soles of my feet.

I wanted to kill my stepbrother but not before I took out Franco.

Franco's thick hand palmed my hair, his fingers tangled in my locks before he yanked hard, bringing my face to his. "Other girls should be as lucky as you."

My stepbrother was nowhere to be found. Typical. Sell me and move on, like I meant nothing to him. I was a piece of property. That was it.

Franco shoved me toward the back door of his sedan.

Oh hell, no. I had the upper hand now, with only Franco and his driver.

If I made it to his house, who knew the danger that awaited, how many men I'd be forced to fight or what other security measures would exist.

"Get off me!" I slammed my elbow into his stomach and stomped on his toes before kneeing him in the crotch.

His driver lifted his gun, pointing it at my head.

"Please, you'd be doing me a favor," I said. I'd sooner die than marry *him*.

"Don't shoot her!" Franco pushed the gun away from the driver, lowering the barrel.

I pulled back my fist, landing another blow, this one to Franco's face before his hand yanked my hair and slammed my head into the side of the car.

The world spun and nausea swept over me.

He shoved my body into the back of the vehicle, slammed the door shut, and stomped around to the front passenger side.

"Don't puke on the interior, bitch."

The car engine started.

My vision blurred, but I felt for the door handle and gave it a hard pull. Damn child safety locks. It didn't open.

Roar.

I flew back against the seat as the driver slammed on the gas. The tires squealed, and my nose tickled with the scent of burning rubber.

The skyline grew smaller in the distance as we tore out of the city.

Where the hell were we going? Where did Franco live?

"Where are you taking me?" I rubbed my eyes, confused and tired. The blurred vision was getting better, but I still felt like I'd been run over by a car.

"Home sweet home, darling. We're going to Russia."

Russia wasn't my home.

I'd never been out of the country.

My fingers stroked the white gold locket against my neck, the only token of my mother that I had left, a gift from my deceased father.

PROLOGUE

Opal focused on the pedestrians strolling on the Boulevard du Montparnasse, most of the locals walking with what struck her as a Parisian air of indifference. It lacked the frenzy she felt in New York where she could often imagine the dollar bills dangling like bait on a hook in front of people rushing from their offices to appointments. Not that the French weren't just as interested in making money, but they disguised their avarice with their love of fashion and food. To foreigners it seemed as if nothing else concerned the French.

She was sitting at a corner table on the sidewalk patio of Le Select, a table that her waiter swore had been Picasso's favorite. He obviously was too young ever to have seen the great artist, but he had also confidently assured that he'd also served Henry Miller, Hemingway and F. Scott Fitzgerald and spoke with the authority of someone who had truly been their waiter. There it was, that certain pretentieuxeuse that especially annoyed the Americans. Many of the tourists she met arrived in France so eager to confront French arrogance that they immediately became defensive. Poor things, they simply had no sense of humor, Opal mused and sipped her café au lait. One thing she had learned from all her travel was you had to have a sense of humor. Nothing brought the pompous down to earth faster than mimicking their pretention. They then almost immediately stepped off whatever stage they had climbed on.

Her current lover, Don Roman, at times possessed self-confidence bordering on pompous. Normally, that usually would have irritated her enough to end the relationship quickly. She had never ended one any other way. But he nonetheless intrigued her. Simply put, he presented a challenge and it had been so long since any lover had. She felt a need to keep prodding to understand him. Often, she invested so much of herself in a lover so quickly that in a day she practically knew his life story. She felt in fact unsafe to be with anyone who was too much of a mystery and Don was. So she tried to tinker with his emotions and his behavior analytically. In this way she resembled a computer technician studying what new stuff hackers were doing. Like him, she felt a need to be prepared for any new deviant technique.

Give the Devil his due, she thought. Don not only had good instincts, but more wisdom than most of the many men she had met. For her it was rare to find a date who was subtle and agile. Most lacked the patience and wanted instant gratification. And they revealed their intentions with childish awkwardness as if they had neon signs in their eyes flickering with lust.

Early on in her life, Opal recognized that her deepest flaw was boredom. The most dangerous expression in her ever growing philosophical thinking was *Been there, done that*. It was sort of summed up in Samuel Johnson's comment that *when a man is tired of London, he is tired of life*. She felt the same way about most beautiful and interesting places she had been. And especially felt that way about her romances.

To her having a new lover had to be like having one for the first time or what good was it?

What first had recommended Don Roman to her beside his good looks was he so much more than a bon vivant. Don turned out to be wise about the wealth he had inherited and so very careful about leaving clues to his travels and expenditures. It clearly had become second nature for him to reveal little about himself. He would shift from one facade to another to keep her off-balance. He was good at it; but not as good as she was at detecting it. Their affair in a way resembled ping pong.

"If you had ever gone into acting," she once had told him after they made love in her loft apartment in Barcelona, "you'd be an Academy Award or nominee. Yes, you make love like someone in a movie, and your words are worth memorizing."

"Not a winner? Just a nominee?" he asked, showing not an iota of embarrassment or offence. And when it came to shrugging off a criticism, he could be ice.

"Si, un ganador," she replied. She always spoke some of the language of the country where they were. "I go only with winners."

And Lots of laughter always followed, something she insisted on, always lots of laughter and kisses, warm touches, holding onto each other everywhere. She had a fierce need to be in love, and to have an all-consuming longing for whomever whenever they were apart. And the lovemaking had to be fiery to be worthy of her and she was always striving to dig deeper.

When do you realize you're in love and not in a dalliance? Could she ever be that head over heels? Was her pursuit of it another tragic flaw? She knew the adage: *When you stop being skeptical, even cynical, you lift the lid of your coffin.*

None of her previous relationships had ended well. That realization was here beside her right now, intimidating, haunting, as she anticipated him coming up the boulevard any moment. She so lost thinking about it that the poor adoring young woman standing beside her with her just as excited girlfriend had to repeat her request with a little more urgency.

"Please, si vous plait, your autography, Madame?"

"What? Oh," she said.

The latest copy of Vogue was opened to her page, her picture modeling Cavalli's newest dress. With her characteristic flair, she seemed to magically inscribe her distinct Opal. Unlike other celebrities, she made sure to date her signature. It was, after all, historic.

"Merci, Madame. Vous etes encoure plus belle en personne."

"Merci," Opal said. *I really am more beautiful in person,* she thought. It was always difficult to be modest, but she could be so when it was necessary. Her smile, unpretentious or not, was captivating. They practically fell over a chair thanking her and backing away before turning to hurry off to prove to their friends that they had met her, one of the world's most impressive and highest paid models. Vogue was only one of dozens of magazines that featured her in one way or another and just this week there was the international commercial for the goat's milk crème that sold for a price suggesting it was more liquid gold than anything else.

She turned to the boulevard and again scoured the groups of people ambling along, most talking and laughing and some, the first time visitors, visually gobbling the architecture of arguably one of the world's top five beautiful cities. On a bright spring day like this, the streets glittered. For a few moments because of the way the sunlight played through trees and buildings shaping shadows, it looked like people were walking over stained glass windows. Images like that often merged and reshaped what she was observing. There were so many now that even her vast vault for memories was becoming saturated. A little amnesia was in order, but how do you complain about living too long and seeing too much?

Although she would never reveal it, she was a little angry.

Don was significantly late. No man should ever keep her waiting. Almost all were at the rendezvous point early. She could feel the rage begin to boil. And yet, she still wanted him. Was this the first sign of some sort of breakdown, weakness?

I'm as anxious as a teenager, she thought. It frightened her. Could she be in love too deeply? Wasn't there always some disappointment? It was like living with inevitable failure on the horizon no matter what direction she took.

Too often lately, the sight of a couple walking hand in hand and obviously basking in the light of each other's eyes annoyed her, especially if they were elderly and still found satisfaction being together. What did they possess that overpowered wrinkles and gray hair? Could it really be that they never looked at each other without seeing who they were when the desire for each other was so strong that it nearly burst their hearts? What an idea: love caused youth to be frozen on their eyes. Why wasn't that ever true for her?

Oh be still my beating heart!

She sipped her coffee, her eyes on the people coming her way and then she spotted him behind four English tourists who were making sure they were identified as such by wearing the Union Jack, on their light jackets. Perhaps nothing about people interested her more than their nationalism. Their emotional ties to the Motherland no matter how small and insignificant an entity in the world market of nations fascinated her. They teared up at the playing of their anthems; they literally died in defense of their honor and often denigrated other patriots to express their sense of superiority.

What were countries after all but elaborate tribes? She shook the serious thoughts from her mind and smiled when Don spotted her and hurried past people, so fixed on her that he obviously heard or saw no one or nothing else but her. He actually bumped into people without realizing it.

That pleased her. Whether she was letting her guard down or not, she believed he sincerely appreciated her for more than her physical beauty. He reached deeper into her and feasted on her unique vision, the richness of her emotions and the intelligence in her conversation. There was respect and not simply desire. She believed that no matter what, whether it was age or some scar or other injury, he would love her just as intensely. It was the romantic in her that convinced her of this, of course, something she had to smother when it got too strong. "Mon cher," he said. "Sorry, I'm late."

He kissed her on both cheeks and then on her lips. "Dare I ask why?" she saidwith not a suggestion of a smile. She had met less than a handful of men who could withstand the intensity she projected when something troubled her.

"You can ask, but dare I tell you?" he asked, hoping his humor would lower the temperature.

She held her rage for a moment and then softened her expression.

"Another secret insider trade deal?"

"Maybe."

He sat as the waiter came hurrying to them. Don looked as relieved as someone who had just escaped a hanging.

"Cappuccino, si vous plait," he said.

It was late spring but still a little cool as the breath of winter receded reluctantly. He wore a class blue seersucker suit with a red tie and white shirt. His shoes were Burgundy antique calfskin with two tone laces.

"Can I say that you pay more attention to fashion since we met?" she said sitting back and looking down at his shoes. "Edward Green Inverness Wingtip Bals? Do you put those on your expense account?"

"Everything can be a tax write-off if you're creative," he replied, leaning over to whisper. "The truth is that deep down, I'm just a small town farm boy. Didn't get a pair of shoes until I was twelve."

She laughed and reached for his hand. He did have charm and he was fixated on her with the adoration she expected but still enjoyed as she would if it was for the first time. For a moment all they did was stare at each other and hold hands like two heart-sick lovers. Time to say something clever, she thought, never wanting to be taken for granted.

"I think I can readily testify to the adage *absence makes the heart grow fonder,*" she said. "Every time we're reunited, I see more of you."

"More? Have I gained weight?" He feigned a wounded ego, but looked a little frightened, too. Were his secrets exposed? Had she had him followed, investigated?

"Hardly. Frankly, I don't know how you stay in such perfect shape," she said, pretending to be suspicious. "Perhaps you're just a wealthy playboy after all with private physical trainers, private gyms and not this worldly, brilliant businessman you tell me you are."

"Oh? And how do you stay so beautiful? Is it all as natural as you claim? Or do you really have access to one of the world's most brilliant plastic surgeons?"

"Touché," she replied.

"What's the true answer?" he pursued. Was he serious? He wanted her to tell him?

"What's that line: *I can tell you but then I'll have to kill you?*"

He laughed.

"Maybe it would be worth it."

"Oh, it would be worth it. Believe me," she said. The waiter brought his cappuccino. There were some Madeleines on a small dish. He nibbled one and looked around.

She watched him study the pedestrians with that Je ne sais quoi expertise she couldn't quite figure out. He had an amazing awareness of his surroundings, no matter where they were or what they were doing at the time. Other women would have found that fascinating perhaps, but for her, it set off short electric surges of warning. He was behaving a little too much like her and she knew why she behaved this way. She was always looking for proof that she was being stalked, and not by adoring fans either.

When she studied him like this, she kept a soft smile on her face, hiding the pulsating tension flowing beneath the surface. Anyone watching would think of them as two lovers whose love only ripened in Paris, the garden of love. Hopefully, he would as well. The less on guard he was, the deeper she could penetrate him.

"What I simply meant with my compliment was I appreciate the depth of blue in your eyes, the strength in your mouth and the firmness in your jaw. I read beauty in men as well as in women, especially my stunningly attractive competition. I'm a bit androgynous that way."

"Only that way?" he teased.

She laughed.

"Time will tell."

He sipped his cappuccino and nodded as he became more thoughtful.

"How much time have we had together? With your schedule and mine, it's hard to keep track," he said.

"Are you reaching your allotted quota of minutes with one lover?" she asked.

He laughed, but it had the ring of a nervous laugh. "Hardly, although perhaps you will exhaust me," he said. "One of the better ways to die, n'est ce pas?"

He laughed, but again it wasn't pure amusement. He flashed a little fear. She sensed that and another alarm surged through her breasts.

"I count the hours," she said. "It's been the equivalent of

continuous two weeks, three hundred thirty-six hours. Do you want the minutes, the seconds, too?"

"No," he said laughing. "You make it sound like you have a meter running."

"Don't we all?"

He stopped smiling. She caught the way he perused the crowd of pedestrians again.

"Are you waiting for someone?" she asked.

"Always. It's the paranoid in me. Anyway, I've tonight and tomorrow until noon. And you?"

"I'm on my way to Singapore for a Charles Wan fashion show in a few days."

"One of these days I have to attend one of those fashion shows and watch you strut down a runway." He looked across the Boulevard, his eyes narrowing.

"What really is stealing away your attention from me, Don?" she demanded now.

"Nothing," he said. "I'm sorry."

She could sense how nervous he was. She perused the oncoming pedestrians more closely.

"I've made a study of you, Don Roman. I know when it's nothing and when it's something . . . possibly," she said. "Tell me."

He shrugged.

"I thought I saw someone I had seen when we were in Budapest," he said.

She turned to look, now more concerned about it herself. "Where?"

She looked at the crowd, sifting through faces, studying walks and hands, watching for anyone who was looking particularly interested in them, in her. Even if it was only someone following him, that someone would be following her. There could be no innocent suspicions, not for her, never for her.

"What, do you think?" she asked as she studied the pedestrians, "That the IRS is following you about Europe?"

"That's not such an exaggeration," he said. He looked relieved that she had come up with an explanation she might believe. Not a good sign, she thought.

"Don't tell me about it," she said placing her fingers on his lips. "I don't want to hear about the stock market, commodities, corporations and the like. There's nothing romantic about finding good investments for yourself and your business partners, legally or illegally."

"Must everything be romantic?"

"For me, yes."

He laughed, but the trembling inside him was practically roaring in her ears.

"Who is it, Don? Who do you think is following you and why? It's better that you tell me now," she said firmly.

He looked down at this cup. She was relentless and he knew it.

"I didn't want to tell you. I didn't want anything to get in our way. I thought I could handle it myself, but this guy didn't simply follow me here. He's been following me everywhere, threatening me with exposure. He knows things practically no one but me could know about my business. It's creepy, like he's inside my shadow."

Church bells inside her thundered loudly enough to shake the stone walls around them loose.

"What does he want? Is it money?"

"No. He's just a nutcase, Opal. I'm sure. Probably nothing more than a celebrity stalker who thinks he can get to you through me."

"Get to me? What does he want from me?" she demanded. "I sense it's not simply an autograph."

He hesitated and then burst into a reply like someone who wanted to confess and get it finished.

"He wants me to bring you to a party at his home tonight. He claims to be a big investor in some new clothing line and wants to get you to endorse it. Let's just forget about him," he quickly added. "I'm not worried. I've got my lawyers working on various cover ups. His threats won't amount to anything. I don't like being used to get to you."

"What did he look like?"

He shrugged.

"What did he look like?" she repeated with more insistence. "Dark-brown hair brushed back and down to about mid-neck, six feet two, broad-shouldered, a face that looked cast in granite, one of those classic Roman noses. Whenever I've seen him, he wears this pin-stripe gray suit and black tie. Oh, and he has a birthmark on his right cheek at the crest. It looked like a spot of dried blood. He walks with perfect posture, something like a military walk."

"Such detail. You have that photogenic of a memory?" she asked. His detail suggested that he had seen this man more than he claimed.

"This guy has a way of imprinting himself on my brain. To be honest, he's the stuff of nightmares. I'm sure he could teach Satan a thing or two about intimidating someone. I'll take care of it. Really. Don't worry about it."

"Okay."

She smiled. Her body seemed to go off alert, but of course she would be worried about it and it was wise to seem unconcerned. Nevertheless, her good paranoia rose to the surface. After all, she had a responsibility to more than simply herself. Her mind raced to remember every detail of Don and her first meeting. There was nothing to suggest he was planted in her way, but that didn't matter now.

Who was it who first told her to be aware when "Something is rotten in the state of Denmark? Someone who knew Shakespeare perhaps?"

"I'm sorry you made me tell you. Really. I'll handle it, Opal."

"If you did nothing that could be questioned, Don, you would not be vulnerable to blackmail. A lesson sometime painful to learn," she said, sounding like someone's mother now.

"It comes with making money," he replied. "I'm just a good capitalist. We have to bend the rules to make real money. Look at who became President of the U.S."

"Okay. For now I'm going to take you to a place where you will have no reason to be so concerned about making money for a while," she said. "My secret hideaway. Not even Interpol could find it."

He laughed.

"I knew from the first time I met you that I always would be in capable hands," he told her. "I'd be . . ."

"Safe as a baby," she said. "Allez."

The moment they stood up, her limousine appeared. Her driver, a dark-haired, dark-skinned South African man with a professional wrestler's build, moved amazingly fast and gracefully, to open the door for them.

"Thank you, Idra," she said.

Don put some euros on the table and followed her into the elegant vehicle. It had been customized so that there was black velvet on the sides. The bar in the limousine was built out of a rich mahogany.

"When you were a little girl, did you ever think you'd have all this?"

"Who says I was ever a little girl," she said, threading her arm through his and leaning on his shoulder. He kissed the top of her rich, ebony hair that she was wearing in a French bouffant and then she turned those mesmerizing gray eyes shaped like rich almonds and looked up at him with such desire, he felt his loins warm and the salty taste of love-making on his lips.

"You are magical," he said and kissed her.

"Yes, magical. I like that."

"I want to know more about you," he said. "I don't care how insignificant you think the details are."

"Why?" the voices inside her chanted. He didn't notice how she nodded like someone assuring another she was aware of the hatching danger. Whether he understood it or not, he had become a Trojan Horse. Her fortress was about to be breached, but she would send no signals to indicate she knew.

"What? Provide the details and ruin the mystery?"

"You are a mystery, in every sense of the word and I know mysteries. Sometimes, you seem so vulnerable to me, so much like an innocent little girl, and sometimes, I think you've lived ages and have illimitable wisdom."

"Perhaps I'm both," she said. "Will you be unhappy about it?"

"Since I've met you, the only unhappiness I've known is separation," he replied and they kissed again.

"You're quite the Don Juan for a stock market jockey."

"I have to be a Don Juan. You learn you have to romance money, too," he said.

"When you cherish money for itself, you lose the romance, mon Cherie."

"Another touché. At this rate I'll have to hand you my sword."

"Oh you'll do that anyway," she said and he roared. Then he held her tightly and gazed out the tinted windows at the Paris streets they were navigating. It was as if they were on a magic carpet. In what seemed to him to be moments, not minutes, they were heading out of the city.

"I can't keep track of all the homes you have."

"I'm not happy staying in hotels if I can avoid it, specially in what I consider hubs for my career such as Paris, London, New York."

"So instead, you buy a house, an apartment, even a house boat?"

"You of all people should understand. Invest in property, I was told."

"Who told you that, your father? Grandfather?"

"Why not my mother? Chauvinst," she accused. He laughed.

"Neither of us have talked much about our families," he reminded her.

How he was pushing to know more, she thought. He is purchasing his freedom and safety with the information he delivers, no matter how confident he pretends to be.

"Let's pretend we're Adam and Eve. There are no families yet," she said. Her eyes twinkled with that impish quality she could evoke at will. Sometimes, she had a dimple in her left cheek and sometimes she didn't.

How can you control a dimple? he wondered and shook his head.

"Maintain the mystery, huh?"

"Why rush into our pasts and endanger all the wonderful things we can imagine about ourselves?"

"Very good. Who can argue with that?"

His anticipation of their soon to be lovemaking was stirred by the memories of their last rendezvous. They had first met six months ago and only had rendezvoused a half dozen times since, but to him it seemed as if they had been seeing each other for decades. He felt absorbed by her. At night, alone, when he could relax, he saw her on the surface of his eyes. It was as though she transported herself and glowed in the dark no matter how far away she was.

He watched and mentally recorded the turns Idra made,

marking road signs along the way. He had no doubt that after only one ride, he could find his way to their destination again. She sensed his attention had gone elsewhere and turned his face toward hers to kiss him.

"Bored already?"

"Hardly. I was just admiring the scenery," he said. "Even if we were in the most beautiful places in the world," she said, "I would envy the sea, a mountain, and fields of lavender, anything that would steal your attention from me."

"You're that demanding?"

"And proud of it," she added.

He laughed, but out of the corner of his eye saw Idra turn sharply and head onto a side road that cut through a small wooded area. Another turn took them to a driveway running up a small knoll to a house that belonged more in Normandy with its second story windows arched at the top and breaking through the cornice and above the eaves. It was stately, formal with its steep hipped roof and square symmetrical shape. The windows were balanced on each side of the entrance.

The grounds were well manicured with Kelly green grass and tall shrubs. Despite still being early spring, the flowers looked mature in their blossoming, more like flowers in late spring or summer. There was a variety of Dahlias, Salvias and Echinacea. At the side of the house, he could see climbing rose Bougainvillea.

"It looks like a house that belongs in a fairy tale," he said as Idra pulled into the driveway. "It seems like another world."

"Now that you've arrived, yes," she said. "It will be part of a fairy tale."

He laughed and then was surprised at her eagerness. She was so anxious that she didn't wait for Idra to open her door. She pulled him along as she slipped out of the limousine.

"Come on. As Iago says, 'Happiness to their sheets.'"

He paused to look down the wooded road and then turned back to her quickly, afraid she had noticed.

"I know that quote. Othello? Senior high English lit. Did you see it recently?"

"No, but that doesn't matter. Shakespeare was a friend. I promised him I would always quote him."

Her laughter rippled. He looked back at Idra who sat as if he had been turned into a statue until he was again beckoned to come to life, and then glanced at the road again, now worried he had agreed to way too much.

"Are you coming?" she asked.

He felt like running in the opposite direction, but instead, he rushed to keep up with her.

They entered the house together. She held his hand, but tighter than he imagined she could.

He had no idea why he should have it, but he did: a growing suspicion that this time, after this rendezvous, it would be over. It was truly as if he could stream his life through the Internet, fast forward and see the final scene: Idra carrying his lifeless body out the rear entrance.

And when he turned to her now to find some mercy in her eyes, he realized it was absolutely too late. His imagination was overwhelmed. His eyes were exploding and inside, he was shattering like ancient glass.

1.

A full year later a similar stream of rage thickened Opal's blood. Her heart did not beat faster, however; it thumped slower in fact, more like a deep, African drum, every beat resonating through her bones.

"Who put this on my makeup table?" she asked in a soft, but firm voice.

Seated at the table and facing her mirror, she held up the gold tube of neon red lipstick. Her licorice black hair was tied in a chignon with a pearl pin shaped like a dagger jabbed into the center. The handle had tiny rubies and diamonds. Opal was one of the only well-known fashion models who insisted on doing her own makeup and hair. She was at the far end of the room, isolated the way a star would be, working in an invisible cocoon.

Normally, no one would have heard her amidst the din created by over fifty fashion models being dressed and primped to exhibit the new Henri Beaute designer styles at New York's St. Regis. A cacophony of French, Spanish and even Chinese was woven in with the English spoken. In the long dressing room with walls of mirrors and vanity tables on both sides, it sounded like a recording made during construction of the Tower of Babel. Faces were reflected in a wall of mirrors, an array of exquisite beauty. It was a fitting setting for women who spent most of their days and even their nights being photographed. It was as though they could live only through images of themselves. Without mirrors, they would wither and fade like flowers without sunshine.

And like Tennyson's *Lady of Shalott*, if they turned and looked at reality, they would die.

Every eyebrow was doubly checked; every blush reinforced. A rebellious strand of hair was instantly brushed into obedience. Hairspray fell like napalm. Models looked adoringly at themselves, but kept an eye on their competitors. A new, lucrative job could easily come from this one. The self-questioning was heard like short-wave radio transmitting into everyone's head. "Am I too heavy, too thin? Did I ruin the flow of my lines with that rouge? Is that a pimple?"

The fashion show was sold out and everyone knew that a number of those attending were there to see Opal almost as much as they were to see Henri Beaute's new creations. Whenever the door to the catwalk was opened, the music and chatter came pouring through in waves full of laughter, mumbled words and music. It added to the anticipation and excitement as if humanity itself like ocean tides had an ebb and flow with the draw of the moon. The noise seemed to mesmerize everyone. They looked frozen with anticipation and excitement.

However, Mary Plunkett, Opal's personal assistant, often with a nervous twitch in her lips, practically shook herself off her bones when Opal spoke. She had no trouble hearing her. She never had trouble hearing her no matter how far she was from her. It was as if she could hear Opal's words before they were spoken. Actually, she wondered if Opal could do that, transmit her thoughts to her. Nothing would surprise her.

With panic smeared over her face like someone realizing she was drowning, she spun around and, despite the tightness that had come into her throat, she closed her eyes, pressed her fists against her thighs and managed to squeeze out a desperate, "Mr. Beaute! We need you. Right now, Mr. Beaute!"

For a moment the cry put pause on all the conversations. Someone might have thought a mirror had shattered under the pressure of so much beauty. Faces turned in Mary's direction. Brushes and combs froze in mid-air. The momentary silence was as deafening as the din had been. Mary Plunkett still had her eyes closed, her hands clenched into small fists now pressed against her chest. The veins in her neck looked embossed as if her whole body would explode any moment. Everyone's had the same questions. What terrible thing was happening? What sort of crisis would occur this close to the start of the fashion show? Eyes darted everywhere. Everyone held his or her breath.

The fifty-two-year-old international French designer with a full head of blazing white hair that flowed into a pony tail had just finished doing everything but skin alive one of the hairdressers working on Demi Tom, a top French model flown in just for this fashion show. He was only about half dozen feet away. His plump, round face was crimson with dramatic rage. Everything he did was over the top, but somehow that was expected. Who in this business wasn't high-strung? It was practically a perquisite.

He turned and looked toward Opal who remained frozen at her table, her right arm stiffly up, her fingers holding the gold tube of lipstick high. Because of this posture and the diamond stuttered tiara, she looked like an au couture version of a sitting Statue of Liberty, draped in one of Beaute's new designs, an off one shoulder, sweeping pearl silk cocktail dress with dark rubies sewn into the bodice and into the waist. The skirt was mid-calf and uniquely wrapped, Beaute's signature touch.

Mary's eyes opened, but her mouth seemed to freeze in the shape of an egg. She looked struck dumb. Beaute's right eyebrow lifted and his left dipped. Everything on his face moved in one way or another. His lips twisted and turned and his nose twitched, all of which fascinated babies and young children, even some adults. It was truly as if his face could be reformed just the way they could reform a glob of clay.

"Mon deux, what now?" he moaned and dabbed his black silk handkerchief at the tiny beads of sweat popping out like pimples over his upper lip. He glanced angrily at the others to set them back at work and then hurried over to Opal, widening his syrupy smile to expose his tiny bleached white teeth while clasping his hands together as if in prayer. They looked like small pearls. An oversized diamond pinky ring in a gold setting reminded Opal of a big wart, especially on his ugly, fat fingers. It never ceased to amaze her that a man so physically unattractive could create such beautiful fashions.

"What's wrong, Cherie?

Opal turned ever so slowly as if she savored the tension and Beaute's anticipation. She stared silently at him a moment. Beaute's heart fluttered. He still believed no woman on any continent had Opal's exotic almond-shaped ebony eyes. They were set in a bed of creamy rich milk which was brought out even more because of her perfect blemish free dark-peach complexion. A reviewer had once written that she *radiated beauty and made everyone aware of his or her own imperfections.* Beaute thought that was no exaggeration. Everyone, even he, felt that merely being in her presence was a special experience. Charisma wasn't a big enough concept to encompass her powers.

Stately, with a figure that Venus herself would surely crave, Opal was, in Beaute's and most every designer's mind, absolutely the world's top fashion model. She had shot up through the fashion world like Old Faithful nearly eight years ago and what was amazing was she showed not even the smallest sign of any aging. She was like a movie star frozen on film, never to change. The image was imprinted as strongly on the brain as it was in the movie. There wasn't an eye able to drift from her when she did the catwalk.

Except for the click of cameras, the absolute stillness in the audience that accompanied her foot crossing over foot made it seem as if everyone had been transported to the Vatican. Photographers went to their knees to get a better shot, but they looked like they were preparing to genuflect. Some were even so mesmerized, they forgot to take the shot when she paused and leaned in their direction, each one thinking she was looking directly at him or her. The electric excitement traveled every vein and artery, riding on the surface of their blood.

"Who put this on my table?" she asked turning back to speak to him through the large oval mirror as she continued to hold up the tube of lipstick. Addressing him this way had the effect of diminishing his importance and relegating him to the status of some gofer assistant even though he was a top fashion designer and this was his show and he had hired her and would pay her top money.

"Oh. It's a new line of lipstick a good friend of mine has created. It's all natural and hypo allergenic," he said, desperately trying to make it sound insignificant.

Opal widened her eyes, seizing him in her gaze. He dabbed the sweat off his lip again.

"By now, Monsieur Beaute, you should know I don't wear anyone else's makeup," she said and put it down. "Mary, my lipstick," she called, holding out her right palm like some surgeon asking her nurse for a pair of scissors. Mary leaped into action, practically flying across the six feet or so to her side.

"Please," Beaute said. "Si vous plais, Madame." He knelt to whisper. "He's putting up half the cost of the show tonight and has already bought four new dresses. A small favor. When have I ever bothered you, asked you for anything special? Please," he pleaded. He reminded her of a street beggar on the streets of Casablanca recently. She always found an overweight beggar to be a living oxymoron.

"A close friend?"

"Well," he said smiling so hard his rubbery lips seemed to dip into his jawbone, "his money makes him a close friend, n'est-ce pas?"

She turned again slightly to give him a side glance of annoyance, but he was practically on his knees and Mary and two hairdressers were right on top of them, hearing it all despite his whispering.

The man has no pride, she thought, but then thought, why would he have in my presence?

She glanced at the lipstick.

"It's your color," he quickly added, seizing on the possibility of success. "I made sure of that."

He held his breath.

"Not quite."

"No, not quite. It's why it's unusual and why he'll know whether you are wearing it or not. He made a point of saying, 'I don't care how many of your models wear my lipsticks as long as Opal wears it.' He's a smart man. He knows how much influence you would have on his product's success."

"I don't need your or his flattery, Beaute. Someone once said, 'Sweet words are like honey. A little may refresh, but too much gluts the stomach.'"

"Oh, very wise, very wise. Please. All eyes will be on you, especially his."

She sighed, shook her head.

"I'll do it, but I'm not happy about your taking such liberties, Beaute. If I endorse anything, I am well paid. You should have cleared it with my personal assistant."

"Oh, I spoke with her."

"You did?" She turned to look at Mary Beth who was shaking her head vigorously.

"I'm sorry. This won't happen again. Never again," he promised, raising his right hand. Even his palms were sweating. "C'est sûr. That's certain," she translated for Mary, whose eyes were still wide with fear. Opal held her for a moment longer in her gaze and then turned away.

She started to put on the lipstick.

"Merci, thank you, merci," Beaute chanted, backing up and bowing as if she were the Queen of England and he was following royal protocol which demanded he never turn his back on her.

Opal nearly smiled.

Except.

Literally seconds after she put on the lipstick, her lips began to swell and she had a familiar salty taste come flooding into her mouth.

She cried out and dropped the tube.

"Oh dear, dear, dear," Mary Plunkett cried, clutching her left breast as if it might drop off.

Beaute turned and rushed back.

"What's in this?" Opal asked as she rushed to wipe off the lipstick. Mary hovered over her hoping to get the opportunity to do something significant, her hands moving nervously as she fed Opal one tissue after another. She was like a nurse beside a surgeon losing his patient to hemorrhaging.

"Nothing artificial. I assure you." He picked up the box, plucked his jeweled, feminine reading glasses out of his tuxedo's top pocket and recited the ingredients the way he might attempt to recite a Shakespearean sonnet.

"Stop," she said before he reached the end of the list. She put up her hand and then turned, her eyelids narrowed, her shoulders rising.

"Did you say . . . Hawthorn!"

"Oui. It's his special recipe, what makes it unique. He claimed it has certain qualities enhancing the color. There's no odor. He assured me." He placed his hand on his heart. "On my mother's soul."

Nearly knocking him over, she leaped out of her seat and hurried toward the bathroom.

Beaute gasped and looked at Mary, whose face appeared to consist of fragile china, her grimace cracking her cheeks and chin.

"What . . ."

Opal slammed the door behind her and locked it as quickly as she could.

It was almost too late.

When she looked in the mirror, they were already there.

Her two fangs.

Without exposing herself, Opal handed her dress through the slightly opened bathroom door. Only Mary was close enough to realize the difference in the size of Opal's hand. She had quickly taken off her gold and diamond ring before her fingers had swelled, but there was also a yellowish pallor and reptilian scale like appearance to her normally baby smooth, creamy skin.

Off to the side outside, Beaute was apologizing so profusely and loudly he almost overcame the thunderous pounding of Opal's heart, which as always rolled through her ears drowning out the screams of her victims. Right now, it was drowning out her own internal screams, a raging series of primeval cries that echoed through her bones.

How could she have been so careless?

This was a very close call.

It would take a few minutes to come down from her vampiric erection because hawthorn had caused it and not her natural hunger, over which she did have control.

"I can't go out there like this," she cried, her voice already too deep. "Give the dress to someone else."

She slammed and locked the door as soon as Mary had the dress.

"Should I send for a doctor?" Henri asked Mary Plunkett.

His eyes were already bloodshot with terror.

Now he pays attention to me, she thought.

"When you first suggested it, I told you she wouldn't like using someone else's product," she said, "but you wouldn't listen. I didn't know you had snuck it in like that. She thinks I gave you permission. Why did you lie?"

"Does she need a doctor?" he repeated with more impatience, his lips pursed and tight. He would not permit a model's assistant to chastise him.

"No. She'll be fine."

He looked at his watch.

"Mon deux. Look at the time." He looked out over the room to find another model to double up. He knew their damn egos would make it difficult, but he hoped one or two would see it as an opportunity to outshine Opal. And then he thought hopefully that he might not need one.

"Maybe she'll recuperate quickly enough. I can change the order and have her be the very last model, no?"

"She definitely won't recuperate quickly enough and she won't go out there unless she's perfect," Mary Beth said dryly. "You should know how good the cameras are nowadays. My mistress wouldn't permit a hair out of place much less a swollen lip."

Mistress, Beaute thought. Who uses such an expression for a model? Damn their egos. His facial features moved in chaos. He spun around for a moment, took the dress from Mary Beth's arms, and shot forward.

She watched him plead with Demi Tom who finally agreed. Then he looked back at her standing guard at the bathroom door and he raised his arms. He looked like he was threatening. Last chance.

She didn't react. He hurried away to make the necessary adjustments in the order and check on final preparations. The other models began to move out for their lineup.

Mary knocked gently on the bathroom door.

"Just stay there," she heard in a voice so deep it would have been unrecognizable if she hadn't heard it before.

She didn't move from the spot and watched the last model and her accompanying attendants leave. Finally, the fashion show was underway so the dressing area had emptied quickly. Everyone, every hairdresser, dresser, cosmetician, and member of Beaute's inner circle wanted to be out there.

"It's safe now, Madame," Mary whispered through the door. She had her forehead against it. "Everyone's gone to watch the show."

"Get my clothes and hand them to me," Opal ordered. Her returned voice snapping like a bullwhip. "We must leave immediately."

Mary hurried to gather everything and hand it through the now wider opening. Opal's fangs were completely receded. Her complexion was returning to normal. She seized the clothes and glared angrily at Mary.

"You fool!" she said and slammed the door in her face. Mary wasn't sure what she should do. She could turn and flee, but how far would she get? It was better to wait and plead her case. Surely, Opal placed great value on her service. She wasn't all that easy to replace. How many normal human beings would accept such a job, regardless of the pay? She had no real talent for anything and didn't have enough education to pursue a good career. Worst of all, she personified the word average. She was comely, so comely, she could easily go unnoticed and her figure leaned toward the chunky side, no matter what she did.

Mary saw herself as such a loser that there was little chance of ever accomplishing what she had accomplished otherwise. Look at the traveling she was able to do, the houses she lived in, the celebrities and rich people she had met and would meet. The money was actually the least of it for her. She had made mistakes and she had been threatened, but none were as serious as this one. Nevertheless, she wasn't afraid of the consequences. She would accept whatever Opal did to her and plead for forgiveness because to go back to her normal existence was as dreary as death itself.

She stepped back instantly and held her breath as the bathroom door opened and Opal emerged, nearly fully recuperated. Only others of Opal's kind would be able to see the subtle differences in her complexion, her eyes and her torso. Her shoulders were soft again as were the muscles in her arms and through her chest. She had returned to being the slight, feminine five feet eleven, 115 pounds stunning fashion model that adorned the covers of the most prestigious magazines and performed in commercials everywhere. Nothing suggested the powerful creature she became when she metamorphosed to feed and kill.

"How could you let this happen?" Opal asked. "I spent time educating you, Mary. You should have known the effect hawthorn has on me."

Opal spoke in such a reasonable tone that anyone else would think she was calm, but Mary could not only see the rage still fermenting under her skin; she could feel it. It was like static electricity, just low enough to keep her from jumping, but enough to keep her heart fluttering like a bird that couldn't lift off the ground or a branch and desperately needed to flee.

"I had no idea what was in the lipstick. I never imagined Mr. Beaute would do that. I didn't give him permission even though he was so insistent. I thought it was no longer an option because he acted like someone in a panic and seemed to forget about it himself. Everything was so disorganized this time. I didn't have a chance to tell you what he had wanted and didn't think it mattered since he stopped talking about it. I'm not surprised he went around me and snuck that on your table and then blamed me. You know how they treat me. Some of them look through me as if I'm invisible," she moaned, her chin quivering. Rattling all that off quickly had left her breathing hard.

"Don't start that self-pity thing, Mary. You fucked up big time. You should have warned me of the possibility."

Mary nodded. She knew arguing, rationalizing wouldn't get her anywhere anyway.

"I did fuck up. I'm sorry."

"I depend on you. I thought by now you understood all this. I can't be everywhere, see everything, and hear everything, especially when I'm in a fashion show or doing a television commercial."

What she really meant was especially when she was completely human.

Mary nodded and lowered her head. She prayed this wasn't going to become a Tyra Banks anger tantrum. However, if death were coming as a result of all this, at least it would be swift, she thought. She knew Opal could call up her great strength in a rage, swing her hand sideways and literally cut off someone's head. She had seen her do it. The only thing Mary had going for her was the location. There would be no way to explain her blood and her corpse in a dressing area for fashion models. Of course, Opal could make up a story and say some psychopath got in and went on a rampage.

Mary could easily envision the scene. Since she had begun working for Opal and had seen so many weird things, her imagination was capable of making huge leaps into the fantastic. She had nightmares that were so horrendous, she woke soaked in a sweat and had to change the bed sheet even in the middle of the night, and whether it was her overworked imagination or not, she often thought she saw strange creatures in the shadows no matter where they were.

"Get my things together. We're leaving before anyone can see me and ask questions. The press and their photographers will be all over me as soon as they realize I'm not going out there."

"You look fine now, Madame," Mary said.

"I look fine?"

Opal glared the glare that spoke volumes. Mary rushed to gather Opal's things. They were almost out the door before Beaute came running back.

"Ah, you are okay. Good, good. Of course, I'll see to it that you are paid, Opal. I spoke to Mr. Rosencranz and he assures me the products have been tested for allergic reactions. The amount of hawthorn is infinitesimal. He's dumbfounded, but very concerned and of course, apologetic. He offered to double your salary today and I took the liberty of accepting his offer on your behalf. I'll see that your manager receives it promptly."

"Rosencranz?"

"Yes."

"I never heard of such an entrepreneur on the cosmetics business."

"He's just starting out, building it up. He has lots of money. I think he is mainly in import-export."

"What does he look like?'

"Look like? Oh, he's a very good-looking man of about forty, forty-five, broad-shouldered, dark-brown hair," he said, moving his tongue slightly over his lips like someone anticipating a delicious dinner. "He has wide shoulders and a waist to die for," he added, practically salivating.

"Is he tall?"

"At least six feet two or three. Not an easy man to miss. He's has one of those classic Greek faces. Perhaps you know him after all?"

"Does he have a birthmark on his right cheek at the crest?"

"Yes. You know him? I didn't ask, but I think he's from South Africa, although it's difficult to narrow down his accent. Very interesting man. Charming." He smiled. "He wears a small gold earring in his right ear. I've never seen such rich gold."

"How long have you known him? Tell me the truth, Beaute," she added, focusing her gaze on him so intently, he though his skin was being pealed back.

"It's a recent . . . he came to me . . . just . . . a few days ago, but the money he offered. . . ."

"Didn't you mother ever tell you, 'Penny wise, pound foolish?' You lost my services out there. Just think of the public's disappointment and what a loss to your exhibition."

"Yes, I'm sorry for what happened to you."

"Be sorrier for yourself," she said, turned and walked out. Mary glanced at Beaute who looked devastated. She could offer him no solace and didn't want to anyway. It was all his fault for not giving her the respect she deserved. When she had said, "No," it should have been "No." If he had respected her, she could have prevented all this. She shot a look of disgust his way, trying to emulate Opal's expression of disgust and then hurried after Opal, carrying her bags, even attempting to imitate her walk.

Idras was nearly asleep behind the wheel, but something woke him. It felt like an iron pipe jabbed in his ribs. Once he saw Opal emerging, he nearly leaped out of his own skin to rush out and around to open the door. Why wasn't she in the show?

Opal slipped in quickly and immediately went to her smart phone. Mary handed the bags to Idras and got in after Opal, who sat all the way across from her in the stretch limo. Mary assumed Opal would want to go directly to her East coast residence in Westport and told Idras so. She hoped, no prayed, that wasn't another mistake.

"I told the driver we're going home," she said. "Is that all right?"

Opal barely nodded. She used speed dial and brought her phone to her ear.

The private line in Dave Crowman's office began to blink. He was talking to Director Palmer Michael, not someone he would normally put on hold, but there were only a handful of people who called the private line, and all who did knew it was to be used only in dire emergencies.

"My PL's ringing," he explained when he interrupted. "Go to it. Call me tomorrow afternoon unless there's an emergency I should know about immediately."

"Will do, Sir," David said and ended his conversation with the head of the CIA. He lifted the receiver of the private line and said, "Crowman."

"Ugarte?" Opal said. She was absolutely positive that was who Rosencranz really was.

"Pardon?" He knew who she was immediately, of course. There was something in her voice, some unique tone that actually sent a shiver down his spine.

"Ugarte, Ugarte, don't you know the name?"

David Crowman shook his head as if she could see him. Sometimes, he had the feeling she could, even from a few thousand miles.

"Not familiar," he replied.

"He's on my list if you bothered to look. Twenty-five years ago, he tried to stake me in Eze, France and last year followed me to Paris and tried to penetrate my defenses through a Trojan Horse. I told you about that and explained what he was, what they were. I made all that perfectly clear. He's in New York. It could complicate the hit on the Yemen ambassador."

"How did he come into contact with you now? Aren't you at an important fashion show?"

"He's supposedly selling a new line of cosmetics, all made from natural ingredients. He talked Henri Beaute into giving me a tube of lipstick that contained an ingredient poisonous to me. It was design to expose me and then you know what would follow. The least of which is I couldn't complete the mission."

"I can't see how anyone could possibly know about that. Except for you, Sean and myself, that is. No, The ambassador from Yemen?" He laughed. "I can't imagine he would have realized anything, especially this. He hasn't the brains or the talent to suspect someone like you. Good bureaucrats who don't rock the boat always get promoted first," he added with a shrug.

Crowman had a personal distaste for career diplomats, no matter who they were or what country they represented, even the United States. Maybe that was why he didn't even have the slightest ping from his conscience when he ordered a hit on one of them, consul, ambassador, or secretary.

She was silent a moment.

He's the one wondering how these unimaginative men get promoted to these positions? She told Sean Waters how little she thought of Crowman, forming her impression five seconds after he had brought the man to meet her.

"No one in my world gets promoted without reason or merit," she told him.

"Someone must have alerted him," Crowman said. "But I don't understand how he would know how to get to you through whatever effective poison. The guy practically needs a GPS to go to the bathroom in the embassy."

"No, Mr. Crowman," she said. "No one alerted him. Ugarte is does not work for the Yemen ambassador. He could care less about nations and politics. I'm talking about someone four hundred years old," she said, not hiding her impatience and disgust. "I'm talking about a different tribe of creatures. You ignore things I tell you as if you think they're all myths, despite what you know about me and what you've seen. Embrace it all or don't embrace any of it."

Crowman swore that it felt like she was literally snapping at him through the phone. Her teeth were millimeters from his earlobe.

"Of course. Sorry. Got a little confused."

"I'm heading home," she said disgusted. "We'll talk in a few hours and decide whether or not tomorrow night's still a good idea for this assignment. There might be a news bulletin about my not appearing on the runway and that might bring up some new suspicion."

"Yes, of course. Are you all right? I mean . . . no one saw anything or . . ."

"Don't you think I would have mentioned that immediately? All would be over between us."

"Yes, of course. Certainly. I'll make sure Ugarte's name is on the list."

"I already told you it was. Shouldn't I know who is and isn't on my own list?"

If only she could reach Sean, she thought, but he was on an assignment somewhere in Taiwan and she didn't want to alarm him. "Of course, I merely meant . . ."

"You need to get this whole thing together much more efficiently, Mr. Crowman. The consequences could be quite serious. For all of us," she warned. "We don't leave tracks behind us that anyone could follow and we've been successful at that for centuries. Don't you remember what I told you once? The greatest trick the devil pulled on mankind was convincing them he doesn't exist. Well, we've copied that from his playbook."

"Yes, yes. I'll wait for your call. Whatever you decide," he said quickly.

The irony of her warning him considering where he worked and what he did was never lost on her and at least added a touch of humor. She would never forget the first time she met Crowman. It was clear to her that if Sean weren't one of Crowman's best agents with an impeccable record, he wouldn't have given any credence to anything he had said, and certainly not gone along with the secret introduction. When Crowman realized who and what she was, he looked like he could actually melt. He couldn't wait to get out of the room. Even when he saw her recovered, he looked terrified. But he wasn't a complete fool. He realized what he had in her.

She laughed to herself recalling that first meeting and how his hand trembled when she took it to say goodbye. Even agents and officers in the CIA had nightmares.

After Opal ended the call, Mary Plunkett mistook the smile on her face for forgiveness and breathed relief.

"You," Opal said as she put her mobile back in her purse. "Do you realize what would have happened to you if I were revealed? Where is your own sense of survival?" Opal shook her head. "I can think of no other creature on earth beside you mere mortals who has your blindness when it comes to that. Do you think it's merely good luck that has kept me alive all these years? Hasn't anything I've said or done rubbed off on you? At times like this I wonder if I have been as stupid as mere mortals to have taken you into my confidence."

Opal narrowed her eyes.

"You realize, I hope, that I cannot simply fire you and send you on your way, don't you? I can never do that now. Your fate is sealed with mine."

Mary tried to answer, but she couldn't even swallow. She embraced herself and curled in the corner of the big, black leather seat as if she were an intimidated puppy. She didn't dare cry.

Opal's eyes didn't seemed to drill right through her. She held her breath. She couldn't pray for herself now. It was far too late to find forgiveness.

I've sold my soul to the devil, she thought, *and there are no refunds.*

2.

Opal leaned back and closed her eyes the rest of the way home. The memories began to unreel on the insides of her eyelids. Six months ago, agent Sean Waters had flung open the door of the Paris hotel suite she was in and, not realizing it was she standing there in the shadows, had begun to fire his pistol through a silencer. The bullets went right through her, but her body closed the holes as quickly as they were made and there was no bleeding whatsoever. When she didn't fall, he turned on the lights and saw her standing over his target's body. He knew he hadn't shot him. What was this?

Not five minutes before, she had brought her victim to a state of acute anemia which triggered a heart attack. She had met him at the hotel bar or more accurately, he had met her. The moment she had seen him enter and look around, she knew he was an easy target. He looked at every woman lustfully, regardless if they were with another man. There was such a thing as sexual greed. She made her way through the ages depending on it.

When his panoramic gaze had reached her, she hooked him with a slight turn of her left shoulder. She was wearing that one shoulder black cocktail dress with no necklace. Her bare, now caramel shaded skin exploded visions of her nudity on the surfaces of every man's eyes, but especially the target's. He looked like his body instantly softened into a pliable blob of flesh, boneless, practically pouring in her direction. She continued reeling him in like some helpless fish. He bumped into a chair at one of the small lounge tables, nearly causing a man to spill his Cosmopolitan, but he barely paused to apologize, a sign of his arrogance.

She shook her head, smiled, turned away and waited for him to reach the red cushioned seat beside her on her left. He was practically breathing down her neck when he slipped onto the seat. Slithered onto it was more like it. It was as if the air around him had been greased for his reptilian movement.

The bar counter was a hard, see-through glass that revealed a stream of rainbow colored liquid floating from one end of the horseshoe structure to the other. The wide variety of wine, whiskey, vodka, gin and champagne was displayed on small, individual shelves in the white marble cabinet with streaks of red running through it to match the cushioned bar stools. To her it looked like blood and had the same effect that displaying realistically reproductions of choice meats, vegetables and fruits had on potentially starving pedestrians visually gouging on them through a restaurant store-front window. Her mouth watered.

"Don't I know you?" he asked. Pathetic opening line, she had thought. She had literally heard it a thousand times.

"We all know each other from some place or another," she replied, not looking annoyed or put off. In fact, she gave him a soft, sensuous smile.

His eyes brightened. She could read his thoughts easily. Could he be this lucky and so quickly? Perhaps she was a high-priced escort. He hated paying for it, especially those exorbitant prices some of his associates eagerly shelled out. They had no confidence, he thought, and a few were too ugly to attract a black widow spider.

"May I buy you another drink?" he asked. That was an okay small investment.

Of course, she had anticipated it. She always kept the drink she had ordered just a swallow from being totally consumed. Everything about her seduction was carefully planned, down to the way she stirred her drink and then sucked on the glass stirrer. It wasn't difficult for them to imagine her lips on their dicks, their heads thrown back as they anticipated sexual ecstasy beyond any possible expectations. She was the ultimate, the dream fuck, that image just inches from being captured. Until now.

"Please do," she said. "Thank you."

He signaled for the bartender with such urgency one might think he was a desperate alcoholic.

"Whatever the lady wants," he said. "And a double single malt for me."

The bartender looked at her and then at him. It was almost always this way, the bartenders across the face of the civilized world wondering why in hell she would encourage any man so physically inferior to court her. He shrugged and got her the drink. He hadn't recognized her so he, too, suspected she might be a high-priced escort. Whatever, it helped his bar business and brought in great tips.

"So really, how do I know you?" he had asked. He was surely wondering how he could have ever forgotten that moment.

"I'm in your dreams," she had said smiling. "You meet me practically every night."

She always played conversation like a parlor game, each sentence lined with erotic suggestions, images, and promises. Most men got hard in minutes if not seconds. The conversations, the music, any other sounds around them fell back. It was only her voice they could hear.

This man had seemed immediately uncomfortable with his growing erection, especially when she ended a comment by putting her left hand on his right thigh. She kept it there just a beat or two longer than he had anticipated. She remembered how desperate he had looked. It was as if he was imprisoned in his own clothes and longed to be naked.

She really had told him nothing about herself, kept herself mysterious and exotic. He had enjoyed the wordplay and the cleverness of her responses. He drank quickly, nervously, his eagerness making him look a bit foolish, but he could sense he was about to score a major assignation. When he had started to sip his third drink, she casually had remarked about how crowded and noisy the bar was getting.

"It gets difficult to think," she said looking back at the other patrons as if they were mere riffraff.

"Can I take you to dinner tonight?" he asked.

"Maybe I can take you," she had said. If he only had known what she really meant by the seemingly innocuous suggestion, he might have saved himself. Instead, he had brightened as if she had just pressed the right button, pulled the lever that would cause him to open his mouth like a slot machine and regurgitate his life into her waiting hands.

He had looked speechless, actually pathetic, she recalled. "But it's early. Are you staying here? Some of the rooms have extraordinary views of Paris," she said. She imagined which suite he had taken, which would surely be one of the more expensive.

"Oh mine does. It's a suite looking out on the Eiffel Tower."

"How fortunate."

"Care to see the view?" he had asked, holding his breath.

"I thought you'd never ask," she had said.

He nearly tripped over himself getting off the barstool and had to remind himself to pay for their drinks and impress her by leaving the bartender a sizeable tip. He tossed his money without his usual penurious care. She had captured him completely when she had taken his hand. He straightened his shoulders, suddenly wanting to brag about his conquest through his posture and haughty smile. They moved gracefully between tables, thanks to the way she glided when she walked. She didn't know who she was or he would have realized why people were staring and why she moved with such grace.

She smiled to herself remembering every little detail. It never ceased to amaze her. Her victim thought he was so charming and attractive that even a woman like she was would be clay for him to mold. She let this one believe anything he had wanted to believe, still clinging to her hand when he had led her to the elevator, kissed her and then brought her to his suite. As soon as the door had closed behind them, he was at her like a starving peasant, clawing at her clothes, pressing his mouth to her breasts, and practically carrying her to his bed.

Enough was enough. She recalled how her body hardened and rushed into its favored form so quickly that she hardly had time to take a breath herself. He was frozen in shock. She lifted him to make her feeding more comfortable. He wiggled like a baby, helpless, his cry muffled by his overwhelming fear. He was choking so quickly on his own saliva that she was afraid he'd die too soon. His eyes went back. He kicked, he pleaded and he then he had died as smoothly as she had anticipated.

Moments later, there she was in that Paris suite standing over her victim's body, wiping the traces of blood off her lips with a perfumed silk handkerchief the playwright De La Manet had given her in a solid gold case when they had gone to dinner after the production of his musical comedy in Paris easily eighty years ago. She was quite the femme fatal back then and yet had far less of a public persona. The fashion modeling gig occurred to her only eight years ago, but she had to admit, it was a wonderful distraction and she had always craved the adoration. Only the cleverest of her kind invented personas that enabled them to be more outgoing and visible, but as far as she knew, none had done it as well as she had.

She paused on that delicious night when she had heard the lock being manipulated. She had just come down from her ascension and was preparing to leave the hotel room. Even though it wasn't too late to flee, she didn't move. She realized instantly that someone else was attempting a surreptitious entry. Why? Her curiosity had outfoxed her sense of danger, ordinarily a potential fatal mistake.

But this was going to be anything but ordinary.

Sean Waters flipped the light switch. For a moment he thought he had walked into the wrong room. He had seen only that shadowy figure and had fired. That was not like him, not like him at all. Something triggered a fear he rarely experienced.

Normally, he would have taken her out quickly even when he had realized she wasn't the target. Whenever any of them were sent on an extraction, it was an unwritten rule to take out any witnesses who could identify you, but her beauty made him hesitate. He was also pretty sure he had hit her with each of his shots, but she seemed untouched. He was amazed and puzzled at her apparent lack of fear.

To his credit, Sean regained his cool quickly. He looked down at the victim and then, he closed the door.

"Can I help you?" she asked, brushing back her hair and wiping her lips again. Funny, she thought as she remembered every moment, how unafraid she has been. Here she was caught with her hand in the perennial cookie jar.

He approached slowly and looked more closely at the dead man. There were no signs of bullet wounds, no trauma of any kind.

"What happened to him?"

"I think he got a little too excited and had a heart attack. I was just about to check when you broke in. Are you a burglar?" she had asked with just a hint of amusement at his reaction.

He glanced at her and then knelt to feel the man's pulse and check his eyes. He searched his body for any stab wounds or any other wounds he might have missed. There were none.

"No, I'm not a burglar. Is this something that happens often to you and those you escort?" he asked, still kneeling.

She smiled to herself. He thinks I'm a call girl. He doesn't know who I am.

"It has happened before," she said. "I might be what they used to call a femme fatale."

"I'll bet." He rose and studied her. "I'm sorry I opened fire. I could swear I hit you."

She turned and looked at the wall behind them. There was evidence of two bullet holes.

"Looks like you completely missed," she said.

He shook his head.

"That doesn't happen often." He observed the angle of the bullet holes. It really didn't appear possible. She was still in their pathway.

"Lucky for me it did," she said.

"I'm sorry about that," he said, screwing off the silencer and putting it in his jacket pocket.

"Missing me?"

"No," he said smiling. "Shooting before identifying. It's quite unlike me, but in the dark, you looked . . ."

"Like a man's silhouette? I've been called many things, but not that."

"Yeah, I bet. Anyway, sorry. Believe me, it's not my M.O. to miss."

"Oh? I'm not sure what to make of that. Should I be insulted that you tried or happy you failed?" she asked, making it sound hypothetical. She kept her eyes fixed on him.

He had returned the pistol to his shoulder holster and continued to smile at her. She had intrigued him. Despite what had just occurred, she didn't look angry; she still didn't look frightened, and now that he realized it, she hadn't even screamed.

"I'm not sure yet," he said. If anyone knew how he was flirting, not only with her, but with angering the agency . . .

"So, you're not sorry about nearly hurting or killing me as much as you are about messing up your statistics? Is that it?"

"It did come out that way, didn't it? Sorry again, although . . . it doesn't look like it bothered you much. You don't even look shocked or surprised. How come? Or do you get shot at often?"

What a strong, manly face, she had thought, what firm lips, how perfect a nose and those eyes! They were so deep blue, truly vintage blue, aged like good wine. They could be eyes belonging to one of us. How perfectly his tuxedo fit him, clung to those strong looking shoulders. One sniff told her he had a nearly perfect proportion of fat to body content. He was, in short, a prime specimen, the filet mignon of men. Remembering all that brought a salty, delicious taste to her lips even then.

Fortunately for him and, she came to believe later, for her, she had already fed. Her appetite was satiated. She was back to being just Opal Stone.

"It's all happened too quickly for surprise. Someone you didn't like?" she asked nodding at the corpse again.

"Didn't know him well enough to not like him, but what he represented and did is quite abhorrent to my superiors.

How about you? Were you his girlfriend? I know he wasn't married. Do you work for him?"

"No, we met just a short while ago actually."

"I had that feeling."

"Oh? Why?"

"You're not showing too much grief. I'd say, you border on complete indifference."

She shrugged.

"I'm not sure I would have shown much grief even if I got to know him better and longer."

Sean had laughed at that. She smiled, looked at the body and then at Sean.

"Considering your preparations for this, I have the feeling you already knew I wasn't very involved with him. Sometimes, you get to know the people you're going to kill more than the people you like, am I right?"

"Got to be careful nevertheless. So, how do you know all that anyway?"

"Just common sense. What are you? A hired killer, a hit man?" she asked, flirting with her eyes and restored feminine shoulders. She didn't need a mirror to tell her that she had returned. When she had control, she had complete control. That was and remained the essence of her power.

"Hired killer? Of sorts, I guess. Do you know who he is, at least?"

"He claimed to be the Liberian attaché. We met at the bar here."

"That's who he is, but he's actually Hezbollah. Under-cover, of course. We decided we had to take him out sooner than later."

"We? Oh, so you work for your government?"

"Yes?"

"Israel or the United States or whatever?"

"Maybe all, including whatever. What country are you a citizen of?"

"Presently, a citizen of the world," she had said smiling. "I have multiple passports. Are you FBI, CIA or something?"

"Something," he said. "The letters are interchangeable just like your passports. Well," he added looking at the body. "This actually saves us a lot of work. You must be quite the femme fatale. Deadly kiss or what?"

"We didn't get far enough for any or what," she said and he smiled.

"You're a pretty cool cat."

She shrugged.

"I've seen a lot worse in my lifetime than a man drop dead of a cardiac arrest."

"Really? I'd never guess that."

"However, I would very much appreciate it if I'm not involved with what follows here."

"I'm convinced. Well, I can take you back to the bar and buy you a drink. I owe you that at least."

"They do have a beautiful bar here," she had said. "I didn't get a chance to experience it as much as I would have liked. Our dead terrorist was a little too eager to show me some extraordinary view of the Eiffel Tower."

"I'm surprised you fell for that old line," Sean said gazing around the suite. "The old spider web. He had you here, but could not close the deal." He looked at her. "I'd say that was too bad for him."

"Yes, too bad."

He had started out, paused to open the door and stepped back. She remained by the body at her feet. She knew in her heart that he wasn't just going to walk out of her life.

"You're not just leaving him like this?" she asked. "I'm sure they have turn down service."

"We have the proper turn down maid service. No worries. And I promise. No one will attach you to any of this. I'll see to that. Please," he said, stepping farther back with a small bow. "Let me help you escape notice," he had added.

"Merci. Un tel gentleman. Et killer trop."

"So you're French?" He noted that her accent was perfect. "Among other things. Many other things," she added and he laughed.

"That's good," he said. He closed the door behind them and walked her down to the elevator.

"It's good that I'm many other things?" she had asked when they paused for him to press the down button.

"Sure. This way it will take much longer to get to know you."

She smiled. Witty, clever, handsome and manly. Ordinarily, they don't come this well-wrapped, she had thought and still did.

"You have that much time to spare?"

"I'd be a fool to say no."

She laughed and now she remembered thinking that not even her Prussian count had this man's poise.

The elevator door opened. He gestured for her to enter first.

"I'm Sean Waters," he said.

"Should I tell you my name?" She actually had been a little surprised he didn't recognize her. She wasn't sure if she liked that or not.

"It's a first step. Gets me in the door and again, don't worry about what just occurred. You weren't there so your name's in no danger."

"Opal Stone."

He thought a moment and then smiled as he realized who she was.

"The model?"

"So you've heard of me? I was about to consider firing my press agent."

"Honestly, I thought you looked familiar. I was going to ask you back there if I knew you."

She laughed.

"How many times have I heard that line?" she asked herself aloud.

"I'm not a follower of fashion, but my sister works for De La Rega in New York. She introduced him to me last month. She manages his operation over here," he added.

"I did his show last year in London."

"Small world," he said. "We know some of the same people."

"Yes, especially if you add a certain terrorist attaché lying on a hotel room floor."

The elevator door opened.

"Are you sure you want to do this?" she asked. "You're under no obligation. I have no interest in exposing your mission. As you now can imagine, it would do me no good professionally."

"Believe me, this has nothing to do with my mission or should I say that mission," he added. "Now I have a new mission."

She laughed.

"Which is?"

"Getting to know all about you."

"Well, since you put it that way, I have a new mission as well," she replied. "I'd like to get to know all about you, too."

She remembered that there was some note in her response that raised his eyebrows, triggered some small alarm. He couldn't survive in the world he was in if he was too revealing. Everything he knew and all his training told him he should be quite cautious, but, he had put his arm through hers and said, "Shall we enjoy our good fortune to have met like this?"

"Oh yes," she said. "Absolutely. Enjoying good fortune whether it's been mine or someone else's has always been a prime activity for me."

"Don't stop now," he said.

She had no intention to stop, at least for a little while. After that, as her friend Shakespeare had written, "There are many events in the womb of time which will be delivered."

3.

Reminiscing like this calmed her on the way to her East coast home. Her pulse slowed and every part of her relaxed as it all replayed, word for word, gesture for gesture. She was amazed at herself, at what she was capable of doing to her own body and mind. To store what was a thousand, probably ten thousand times what a mere mortal could store in his brain never ceased to impress her. Was it wrong to be so enthralled with yourself? She was surely the paradigm of Narcissistic creatures. Shouldn't she worry about that? She knew what happened to Narcissus.

Right now, even though she didn't want the reminder, she could see Ugarte, who had just tried to surreptitiously harm her through the hawthorn, coming at her twenty-five years ago as if it were yesterday. It was that vivid in her mind. She could easily recite the time and the temperature.

It was summer. Days were much longer. She was having a wonderful time on the Riviera. She had taken a lover there, spending a romantic weekend in Eze, a beautiful mountain village overlooking the Mediterranean. The view from their hotels balcony at the Chevre D'or took her breath away. Matter of fact, it did every time she had been there. She understood early on that to be immortal meant to never take beauty for granted.

In fact, she had been thinking how it mattered where she was when she made love, especially if it was not a feeding. She was usually never oblivious about her immediate surroundings and how the sweet perfume of flowers, the rich scent of the salty sea or the aroma of freshly cut grass could heighten her sensitivity. Sometimes, the men she was with were so intent on their orgasms, they missed the whole point of the journey. Fortunately, the man she had been with then, a captain on a billionaire's luxurious yacht docked in Monaco, was a good lover, good because he didn't rush. She had sensed he would be so from the moment he had started a conversation with her at the Café de Paris.

"Making love to you is like sipping fine wine," he had said. "You don't gulp."

She liked that. When he had suggested they spend the rest of the day and the night on the yacht since the owner had gone off to Saint Paul de Vence for two days, she considered it even though she was worried she had spent too much energy since the last feeding. That was all that made her hesitate. When a man was such a good lover, she had the closest feeling to a conscience she could have. Maybe, just maybe she would spare him. Most of the time, she had the power to turn it off or on and simply kill to taste. It was ordinarily the gourmet in her, but not if her body demanded the nutrition. Was there still enough time to love and leave him untouched? Unfortunately for him, she wouldn't know until moments before it was time to either stop or start. Her body would take over. Ironically, in that sense, she was a victim of the affair, too. Whatever mercy there was would either take control or retreat for her as well as for him.

At the moment however, she had stepped out to take a little walk and observe the tourists on the cobble stone walkways, jabbering excitedly in German, Italian, French and Russian talking about the arts and crafts, the pizza or the fashions displayed in small shop windows. Some narrow streets had captured the sun and some were keeping it at bay. Shadows were deeper there, providing cool air to wash away the heat if only for a few moments. She thought to take a dip in it and return to the hotel. School girls ahead of her chatted like excited sparrows. Laughter rolled down in gentle thunder from the shops and cafes above. One could easily forget the rest of the world existed.

Rarely was she this distracted. Ugarte might have sensed that. She should have been aware of how long he had been waiting for his opportunity. He had swooped down from the roof of the building housing the shops she had approached on one of the narrow streets and almost the moment she had stepped out again, hurled a wooden spear at her. She sensed it in time and pulled back. It missed by inches. He just looked at her for a second, the disappointment fermenting on his ugly face, the surface of which exploded in small pox boils, and then he was gone over the edge of the precipice before she had a chance to respond.

It wasn't his first ambush and she never believed it would be his last. Their paths had crossed four times since then, including the time in Paris when he had tried to employ a Trojan Horse who would distract her long enough for him to get the advantage and get past her fortifications, physical and otherwise. Each time she had managed to slip away or escape an assassination attempt, but he was never deterred. She recalled how angry she was at herself for not sniffing him out and not pursuing him in Eze.

She would have metamorphosed into her bat form and gone over the edge after him, but her lover stepped around a turn a moment after the entire event had ended. He didn't see the spear lying against the wall so she pretended nothing unusual had occurred.

The sight of Ugarte's deformed body floating out over the ocean, those white wings extended so that he looked like a small cloud, lingered like a painful headache for a while, threatening to end her romantic escapade, and then finally she had packed it away, had buried it under other unpleasant moments. Despite how well she had done over the centuries, the happier recollections she had housed within her, she had more than enough of the ugly ones to weigh on her as well.

She kept them all in a graveyard of near blunders, disappointments and unfortunate accidents. They resembled tombs in New Orleans, above ground, but sealed tightly. She could open a vault at will, but just as quickly shut it in for decades. The skeletons of her victims rattled from time to time, but never gave her any pause.

Right now, to help push the ugly memories from her mind, it was surprisingly wonderful to think about that first date with Sean in vivid detail. But then again, everything about him was surprising. Considering what she had seen and done in her life, surprises were rare diamonds. Who could blame her for doting on them? She loved to visit and revisit her most beautiful memories. It was as if she were in a movie theater with infinite great films available at her beck and call.

Maybe she was getting soft in her old age, (couldn't she call it 'ancient age?'), but she really missed Sean whenever they were separated, either because of her fashion modeling schedule or his assignments. She couldn't remember this longing attached to any of the others when she was separated from them for long periods of time, at least, not to this extent.

Early on she realized that she continued these CIA assignments mainly because it helped her feel closer to him. She knew how much it pleased him that she was doing the work and that he had discovered her and brought her into it. She imagined it caused David Crowman to respect him more, not that he couldn't have earned the respect himself. Of course, helping him gain that admiration from Crowman really wasn't important to her. Often, she thought it wasn't important to him either. Crowman wasn't someone she saw as essential to please, regardless of his position and power.

No, the motivation for what she was doing and what she had permitted him to arrange was simply to make their relationship stronger. Regardless of the outcomes, his patriotic talk, the concept of the ends justified the means when it came to doing what was just and good, she felt certain that his love for her, his need to keep her, was his true motivation as well.

"We make a great team in all respects," he was fond of saying.

For her, someone who had worked, if she could call it work, alone for centuries, it was odd to think of herself as part of anything beside her own family, as she sometimes called them, and even that wasn't much of an alliance. They did little to assist or comfort each other. It was weak to seek help. If you couldn't survive out here on your own, you weren't meant to survive. It was their version of Natural Selection.

Sean struck her as someone who had good survival instincts, despite the dangerous work he had chosen or maybe because of it. What Opal enjoyed about Sean that night they had first met was how calm and cool he had remained, even afterward in the hotel lounge when the previous events had settled and realizations were rising to the surface. They had decided to take a booth rather than sit at the bar.

She recalled how the bartender looked at her and nodded his approval. This was a man good enough for her. He was glad she had gotten rid of the previous one and rather quickly, too. If only he knew how she had done it, that smile would shatter under the explosion of a primeval scream. She couldn't help from being pursued by those grotesque images, something she had learned to endure and accept. But she had quickly cast this one off so she could smile and focus on Sean. He deserved her full attention, and now, she required his. Decades of exploring men, their psyches, made her gaze surgical.

"You're not only undressing me with those beautiful eyes of yours, you're giving me a Kat-scan," he said after they ordered their drinks.

"Well, you say you work for the government, but how do I know you're really not some hired hit man? I'm simply remaining cautious."

"I'd have taken you out upstairs, wouldn't I? Those guys don't want witnesses."

"Oh, and you government types do?" He smiled and shrugged.

"It's frowned upon," he admitted.

"Thought so," she said.

"Well, I didn't do anything anyway. Thanks to your charms or something, the guy was stone dead before I could do anything. So what did you witness? You're the one who appears to be dangerous here. Whatever you did hastened his death. Maybe you hypnotized him with those beautiful eyes of yours and stopped his heart."

"Aren't you afraid of the same fate if you go any further with me?"

"I can think of far more horrible ways to go, and besides, I've been with some women who easily were dangerous to men with or without heart problems. However, few, I might add, if any of them, would short out pacemakers as quickly as I imagine you might. You're quite beautiful. I'm sure you hear that constantly."

"No woman can possibly hear that enough."

She remembered now how she had recited the same line so many times before that it had become unfortunately rote, a line in a play. Yet, going through the dialogue with Sean had felt different, felt original.

He had nodded, but not like most men had. He looked like he was above anything trite.

"However, it does make me curious as to why someone like you would want to be with someone like that. He didn't look particularly handsome. If anything, he was borderline ugly and I can't imagine you needed money."

"The bartender agrees with you."

"Oh." He looked at the bartender who nodded and smiled without knowing what they were saying.

"He was nearly in tears when I left with our terrorist."

"So what was it about him that attracted you? If I might ask, that is? It would help me, too, to know," he added quickly. "How would that help you?"

"I'll see if I can dig up the same magic quality he had."

"Oh, I think you have some of your own. No worries. He did strike me as being hot blooded, however, but I wasn't exactly satisfied with his passion so I wouldn't offer him as an example of anyone particularly desirable."

"Hot blooded?" He nodded. "I can be hot blooded." She laughed.

"I bet you can."

Their drinks came.

When she remembered the scene now, she especially recalled how pleased she was with the way he had stared at her. Very clearly, he had moved from suspicion to appreciation and wanted to stay that way.

It was all written in his smile. She could hear his thoughts: *Everything about this woman is mesmerizing and not simply sexually.*

She had felt it then as she felt it now. She had captured his imagination, rounded up every fantasy he ever had and corralled them. The movements in her face, the light in her eyes, and that complexion that looked naturally photo shopped all reduced him to a love-sick teenager. She could smell his hormones raging and like all the men she had met and seized with her beauty and wit, he wondered how much longer she would give him the time of day. Was he enough to hold her attention, even after what she had witnessed?

"So, what are you doing here in Paris? Some sort of fashion show," he asked.

"I had a show at the Spanish embassy last night. A new young Paris designer. Interesting work. He married some modern concepts with some nineteenth century ideas."

He nodded, but it was clear to her, however, that he had no idea what that meant.

"Any pictures in newspapers or magazines?"

"There will be. Why? Fashion suddenly interests you?" she asked, a wry smile on her lips.

"I'd say everything about you suddenly interests me. I don't keep up with it even though my sister is in the business, but a good look is a good look. Of course, now that I've met you, I'll be looking at those magazines with much more interest."

She widened her smile.

"I do that to men, get them interested in things that they otherwise thought boring."

"Not a surprise. Too much flattery or not, I can't help but repeat that you are one beautiful woman."

His demeanor changed, drifted away from the admiring lover and back to his professional persona.

"It actually annoys me to think of you with that dud upstairs. C'mon. It can't be his hot blood. Give me something else," he pleaded like a little boy. "I hate the unexpected and I hate illogic."

"What would please you?" she asked. "I'll make it work."

He shook his head, sipped his drink and widened his eyes with a new thought.

"Are you a spy, too? Perhaps you're a double spy. Should I be worried that I'll be cited by my boss for stupidity?"

"I suppose I do have a great cover for a spy. I travel to most of the world's capitals, mingle with some very important and powerful people and I'm a quick study. Does it pay you well? I'll consider it."

"I'm no bounty hunter. I'm just a poor government official."

"Isn't that supposed to be "Only a poor corrupt official?"

"Huh?"

"*Casablanca*. Humphrey Bogart? Ingrid Bergman?"

"Oh right. I think I saw it when I was twelve," he said. He took a bigger sip of his drink. "Now you really do have me wondering if my boss will cite me for stupidity. After all, I took a spy out for a drink after I shot at her. How does that look?"

"Someone in his camp, so to speak and you merely caught us planning some attack? Go on, visualize it. Don't limit your imagination. Someday, it might save your life."

"I have the feeling it has already." He sat back and studied her. "The thought is becoming more and more credible, I suppose, even though you showed no sadness over the creep's death. On the other hand, good agents and ruthless terrorists wouldn't."

"I see. So I was right. Even though you know who I am, nothing would surprise you? To survive you cannot trust, nor can you accept anything innocuous. You're a man who walks about with his finger not far from the trigger. You probably sleep with one eye open and have your weapon beside you when you take a bath."

"You could say I'm something like that, yes." He took another sip on his drink. "Don't worry. I don't expect you to confess this easily however."

"Is that another compliment?"

He laughed and looked around. Then he paused. She glanced to her right and saw someone in the doorway nod at him.

"Maid service over?" she asked without even turning to see what had caught his attention.

"Am I that obvious?"

"Maybe only to me."

"Not much to clean up thanks to you."

"As long as you're the only one who gives me credit," she said.

"I'll give you whatever you ask for," he had said.

She remembered her smile, her confident smile. He hadn't known it then, but he definitely would give her anything she asked him to give her. She recalled how delightful that had made her. She wanted him in her magnetic field. There was definitely something special about him, something that had made her a little reckless, but being a little reckless was the only way to get herself some real titillation, some real thrill anymore What, after all, was left to do that she had never done? Nothing, except one thing: toy with her true identity, with betraying her own kind. Where else could she find any risk? Certainly not in driving too fast, drinking too much, or walking in an area particularly dangerous, even Middle East dangerous.

"What if I told you that if I did confess, you might pay the ultimate price?" she had asked sitting back to observe every movement in his face. Could he be frightened away, discouraged? How much of this bravado was a result of his training?

"I can tell you but I'll have to kill you afterward?"

"Something like that."

"I take that risk almost every day," he said with a shrug. "I don't exactly work in a library."

She finished her drink again and looked at him over the edge of the glass. Their eyes locked and for a moment she felt the old but familiar thump in her heart that usually brought her back to those early adolescent days. Why doubt the feeling? Why, she often asked herself, can't her kind experience love at first sight?

"What if I told you, I was a vampire and you had come in just after my kill?"

He laughed. She had expected nothing less or more.

"Is that the best you can do in the way of a confession? You disappoint me."

"Go with it. Humor me. Be a CIA agent. Analyze the possibility."

"Okay. Well, first, the dead guy had no wounds, no trauma. Aren't you supposed to bite him on the neck, get to that artery?"

"I did."

"Well, what did you do, come up with some miraculous first aide moments before I entered and whip clean away any signs of spilled blood?"

"Maybe you don't really know enough about vampires. We have our ways to cover our work. What you read in the comics and see in Hollywood horror movies is pure distortion. In our saliva is a healing potion. It closes the wounds. I can even heal a cut on your hand by licking it."

"Really? Now I am confused. I grew up with images of bloodied necks."

"Yes. Would you be surprised to learn that we enjoy, even encourage all that? It helps keep us . . . incognito. The more fantastic we are made to be, the more ridiculous the vampire lore, the safer we are."

"As I said, nothing would surprise me," he said. She remembered she was startled a little. He looked like he believed that to be true. What if she couldn't shock him?

"Is that right? I guess I have my work cut out for me then, rather than vice versa."

He laughed and then grew serious.

"I should explain this apparent coolness I'm exhibiting to your fantastical confession. There is a division in my agency that concerns itself with the paranormal, phenomenon not easily explained, UFO's, psychics, remote viewers. In my line of work, I have got to keep an opened mind. Even though," he added leaning toward her, "I have yet to see one concrete example of any of it. We have to sit there and humor the lunatic fringe, a fringe every organization has in one way or another."

"I see."

"Now you look like the one surprised," he said. "Maybe a little disappointed, too, at my not being so easily shocked."

"Maybe I am, and maybe, it's refreshing to finally face a real challenge."

"Is that touché?"

"Could be, for now."

"That's a relief. I don't want to fight to the death with a vampire. Odds are not in my favor."

She finished her drink. She remembered warning herself to stop when she could, but she had something defiant working in her that night, something she couldn't resist. Of course, now she was glad that she hadn't.

"What now Mrs. Dracula?" he asked. She remembered he did have a look of expectation, a hope that they simply wouldn't part and forget.

"I have a home outside of Paris, but I have a little pied a terre in the Fourth Arrondissment. It's closer. Care to take me back and find out what now?"

"Why am I so lucky tonight? Someone does my job for me and I meet a woman who is arguably one of the world's most beautiful women inviting me to her home."

"Call it just fate," she said. She had decided to offer a warning, maybe the final one. "Perhaps you're not so lucky. I just might be telling the truth and you're about to become my next meal."

"Now there's an invitation few women extend to me. How can I pass it up?" he asked, widening his smile.

"Okay, Mr. Bond or whoever you really are. When you come in for that perennial nightcap and we get hot and heavy, won't you worry when I attempted to kiss you on the neck? I could nip you just to test your resolve and you could run out of the place looking like a frightened rabbit."

"Hey, at one time doctors were known as leeches, weren't they? What's a little loss of blood once in a while?"

"Unlike those doctors, it's possible I won't stop once I start. There's that need to satiate my need."

"That still sounds pretty sexy. Besides, what if I tear off the leg of a chair and use it as a wooden stake? I just told you that we top agents are trained to be ready for any eventually, fantastic or otherwise." He paused. She had lost that wry smile. "You look worried. Are you changing your mind about inviting me to your place?" he asked. Now he was worried. "What? Are you giving up so easily?"

"How do you know that sort of thing would work? I just told you we deliberately encourage exaggerations and fantasy."

"I don't, but I thought I should sound informed. Does any of it work? Showing the cross, tossing garlic, and checking the mirror to see if you have a reflection?" he had asked. "Oh, wait. I'm afraid your fantasy is over. One thing I know you models do for sure is look in a mirror."

She didn't respond.

"Of course, now I'm forced to return to the idea that you were working with that creep and he just happened to have heart failure. Help me out here, will you? I was so looking forward to seeing you pied a terre. And more, of course."

She remembered thinking why not try the truth? What's a better test of someone than confronting him or her with the truth?

"Actually, wooden stakes are the only real threat in the list you described. There is also hawthorn which has other results, more detrimental to whomever happens to be close by than to me. I would recover eventually."

"What's it do to you?"

"Let's say, it brings me out of the closet."

"Hawthorn?" He nodded, thinking. "It's an herbal supplement, isn't it?"

"I've seen that in health food stores, yes," she said. "I don't even touch the bottle. Some might have spilled out."

"Hawthorn," he continued, thinking more about it, "is a shrub that bears white flowers and red berries. But they have vicious thorns as I recall."

"And those thorns have been rumored to be what was used to weave the crown put on the head of Jesus before he was crucified," she added.

He laughed.

"I get it . . . wooden stake, wooden cross . . . hawthorn and Christ's crown . . . very symbolic stuff. It all sounds quite intimidating."

"Still not scared off? You've seen one of my victims, witnessed my lack of any fear of you, and I've given you more information than you could get in training with your so called lunatic fringe."

"Look, it's simple," he said turning his palms up. "You're the most fascinating woman I've ever met, not that I have a string of them in my past. I'm pretty sure any man would agree.

My parents always thought I was too curious for my own good. It got me into plenty of trouble when I was younger, but also led to some pretty good things, led me to where I am now."

"I see. You sound convincing. I believe you're not terrified. So what do you say to my invitation?" she asked. "I'll risk your turning one of my chair legs into a wooden stake."

"So you admit we'd both be taking a chance?"

"Yes. It's time to stop the verbal tennis. Shall we?"

He tossed some money onto the table and sprung to his feet so quickly, she couldn't stop a laugh. She laughed now, remembering.

"You don't have to ask me twice."

He offered his hand and then pulled back as if she had stuck him with a pin.

"What?"

"I just realized something. What happens to you when the sun comes up?"

"You'll have to wait to see," she replied. "Although, I'm not sure you'll be at my place long enough to find out."

"Wow," he said pretending a chill.

They started out and she looked back at the bartender. He was smiling from ear to ear, partly in appreciation, but mostly envy.

"Don't you have to make a report first?" she asked. "I'm sure your superiors will have questions about no wounds, no blood."

"I'll tell them it was a stroke. A stroke of luck," he added, "which apparently is continuing."

She laughed. What a delight, she remembered thinking, and right after I have fed when I feel the sexiest. This is truly serendipity.

4.

Twenty minutes later, they were naked in her bed. He was everything her senses promised he would be, the closest human being nearly matching her male counterpart, firm, insatiable, with extraordinary sexual endurance. For the first time in decades, she experienced multiple orgasms. One actually came close to riling up her inner self. She felt her fangs nudge at her gums and took deep breaths to keep herself from ascending.

Their kisses were special, too. He didn't pull away when she sucked on his mouth, licked his tongue and nibbled gently on his lips. After he came, she waited and fondled him again until he had hardened and returned. He rode her as hard and as passionately as she responded. She was surprised at how hungrily he kissed and licked her nipples, nudged her breasts and brought his lips to her neck. If she didn't know better, she would have believed he was raised by a vampire. He didn't run out of breath. There were moments when she felt as if he wanted to envelope her body, absorb it into his. Sex wasn't sufficient. What pleasure he could give, and of course she had many lovers with whom to compare.

Afterward, they were both silent, both mentally reviewing what they had just experienced together.

"Where did I just go?" he asked.

She laughed. He was amazed at himself. She wondered if he would realize that she had brought out all the man in him. She had done that with many men, but Sean had more of the natural raw material to develop. No matter how deeply she had reached into him, there was still room to travel.

"To the farthest limit of your imagination, I'd say."

"Not yours?"

"Close."

He propped himself on his elbow and looked down at her. "I don't care how often you hear it. It's no exaggeration to say you're the most beautiful woman I've ever been with."

"I told you. A woman never gets tired of hearing that."

"Wait. You don't mind me calling you a woman, do you? I mean, since you claim to be a vampire, I'm not sure what . . ."

"Shut up, you idiot." She raised her head to kiss him. "When I'm with you, I'll always be a woman."

"That's reassuring."

"Unless you piss me off," she added and he laughed and fell back to his pillow. "Or, as I told you, you feed me some hawthorn."

"Worry not."

"I'm not the one who needs to."

He laughed again, but now with a note of caution. She heard that note clearly.

"Thinking you were a bit too curious this time? Pushing too hard with your half-joking inquiries?" she asked.

"No regrets yet. In old movies, we're both supposed to smoke a cigarette now, you know."

He lay back again.

"All those actors are dead, many of lung cancer," she replied.

"So you vampires practice healthy living? Is that why you look so good?" he asked, reaching around the pillow to stroke her hair. "And feel so good?"

"Don't you know we vampires don't suffer from any of your maladies. We never get sick; we never get old."

"Well we can't get married then."

"Oh?" She sat up. "And why not, pray tell?"

"Not that I wouldn't want to. It's just this little phrase in the marriage vow . . . *in sickness and in health . . . 'til death do you part?* Easy for you to go and say I do, but what about poor me? I'll be in some old age home being visited by a woman who looks like my granddaughter. Not exactly a recipe for a happy future together."

"Unfortunately, I can't help you there. Contrary to your folklore, we don't turn human beings into vampires. You're stuck in your mere mortal existence."

She lay back again.

"Well, then how do you get new little vampires?"

"We don't, not in the sense you mean," she said. He sat up again.

"Well, how does the population of your kind increase?"

"We evolve. I can't explain it as a birth really. We're out there, developing. All I know is the population is relatively stable, but I can't tell you exactly how many there are or where they all are most abundant."

"Evolve?"

"Let's see you don't know what you are and suddenly, as you grow older, you feel like you're shedding your skin, your body, and becoming . . . it's truly amazing. We never feel anything like it after it's happened."

He held his smile but shook his head.

"What?"

"You must have practiced this question and answer session many times," he said.

"Oh? Why do you say that?" she asked. She had never gone so far as to discuss herself with any man.

He turned to her and leaned on his elbow as he gazed into her face like something looking into a bowl of diamonds.

"You have an answer for everything."

"Maybe you just haven't asked the right question," she said "Okay. I'll keep trying. Do you chat about your delicious conquests, compare notes or blood types or anything? For example, does any particular nationality taste better than another?"

How she was tempted to stop his joking. She couldn't hide that thought, but he misread it for annoyance.

"Don't get upset. I am just curious again," he said, raising his hands.

"Who on the face of this earth is pure this or that beside some unadulterated Eskimos, and they're getting harder and harder to find thanks to the pollution of climate change?"

"Makes nutritional sense." He thought a moment. "Did you have parents?" he asked. "Someone must have been in charge of your growing up or did you just appear one day in this beautiful body?"

"You sure you don't want to stop this inquiry? You're not afraid of going too far?"

"Well, I did say I want to get to know you and you gave me reason to hope I would."

"Not completely in one night," she said.

He smiled gleefully.

"So there's going to be a second?"

"And a third," she said. "If you can take it, last that is. You could run out of testosterone. Male embarrassment when it comes to sex is far greater than female, thus Viagra and the horror of erectile dysfunction."

"I'm not afraid. I love a challenge." He beat his chest and she laughed.

"I notice men often revert to apes."

"Ha ha. Don't knock apes. Some of my best friends are apes."

He got up and went to the window. How she enjoyed a well-built male body, something harder and harder to find these days. She reminisced about the Greeks she had known on the islands. There was so much choice meat. She wallowed in masculinity back then. There were never enough of them and she never tired. Even their teeth were good when they were young with tight bodies and eyes like sparkling diamonds.

"This is a beautiful apartment, great view. That's Napoleon's tomb out there. I love being assigned a job in Paris. At least I can get something good to eat afterward or take a stroll and be constantly in awe of the beauty."

He turned around.

"Don't laugh. It helps. I appreciate it especially after meandering through some slum in Egypt or Santiago."

"Then why do you do it? Why not settle into an easier profession?"

"Become a dentist? It's a little late. I suppose I could get an instructor's job eventually, but the thought of it even bores me to death. I live on the edge and like Hemingway wrote, that's when the bullfighter feels life the most, facing impending death. And besides," he said, "I'm doing something for God and country. Patriotism justifies almost anything."

"I only know it as the last vestige of a scoundrel," she said.

He grimaced.

"Samuel Johnson," she said. "I heard him discuss it in a pub."

He laughed, but she didn't even smile.

"Not just your patriotism. All that government intrigue is boring to me. Democracy is too much of a burden. I had my best times in countries where there were monarchs. Dictatorships are well organized, but dull. Give me the pomp and circumstance of royal courts, the clothes, the traditions, the grand ballrooms and parties any day. If your leaders have grand parties, your people bitch about the cost to the taxpayer. How droll."

"Not droll to the taxpayers," Sean said laughing. "Monarch? Pomp and circumstance of royal courts? Okay, so if you're a vampire, and you heard and knew great writers, how old are you? Am I to believe you knew Moses or something?"

"No, not that old."

"So? How old? I know a woman's not supposed to reveal her age, but in your case, there should be an exception, don't you think?"

"Are you trying to determine if I'm crazy now?"

"Frankly, my dear, I don't give a damn. I'll take you in any shape or form."

"I wonder."

"So tell me your age," he insisted, approaching her.

"Take a guess."

He drew closer and studied her as if there was a way to tell her age. She didn't have a gray strand nor even tiny wrinkles at the corner of her eyes. Now that he was giving her this close an examination, he paused. She can't be much more than her mid-twenties and yet . . .

"Two hundred years old," he declared, hoping she would finally be upset with the game and would tell the truth. What woman would want to be described as two hundred years old? They hated thirty these days.

"Sorry, two and a half times that," she replied.

"You don't look a day older than two hundred. You must have known Ponce de Leon."

"His theory was amusing. And you're in what, your thirties?"

"Now we're getting to a solid subject, me."

He slapped his hands together and sat at the foot of the bed.

"I will now illustrate being truthful and hope it rubs off on you. I'm thirty-four, unmarried, unattached, a former Navy Seal, born to well-to-do parents in Bethesda, Maryland. My father was a general surgeon and my mother ran a regional newspaper. I have one married sister who lives in Westport, Connecticut. I already told you what she does. Her husband is a real estate attorney and they have three children, two boys and a girl."

"Really? Westport? I have a home there, too, but I don't go out and about so I don't know anyone there."

"Well, now you know my basic bio. Figured you vampires had ways of finding it all out anyway."

"Hardly. I don't have any organization behind me, especially compared to what you have. What you see is what you get. I'm a lone wolf loosely tied to a species so underground that it's practically invisible."

"As I've been saying like a broken record . . . I like what I see. You might as well stop trying to discourage me and deal with the truth. You can even confess to being a double agent. We'll work it out."

She leaned back against the pillow.

"All right. Let's review. You find me with a man dead at my feet. You accept my story that he died of a heart attack when confronting me sexually. You're confused as to how a world class fashion model is found with a rather bad looking, creepy terrorist type, and you keep your cool, trade humorous lines for humorous lines and make terrific love."

"Go on. I like the compliments. I get so little because everything I do is clandestine. I am quite unappreciated, except by some bureaucrats who also appreciate a better smart phone."

"You're right. They are compliments. I'm pleased. It's been a long time since I met a man with a real sense of humor, someone who wasn't making jokes to cover up his fear or trying to amuse me and convince me he's special when he's classic mediocre."

He folded his arms across his chest.

"I'm not exactly in a state of fear, but how do you know whether I am or not? I'm trained to hide it. Actually, I trained to hide everything."

"I have better basic instincts. However . . . tell me, how are you really going to explain what happened to your target tonight?"

"As you said . . . simple. I looked at the body. Heart attack. I won't mention you, don't worry."

"You convinced me with your love making. Otherwise . . ."

"Otherwise what?"

"Let's stop this," she said reaching for him. "We have a good thing. Let's leave it as it is."

He pulled back.

"Don't you know I'm also trained never to leave things as they are. Continue your review. So according to you, Mrs. Dracula, what is the real scuttle butt? Why did he die?"

She sat back, thought and then shrugged. "I don't know if they'll be an autopsy."

"They're won't. They're won't be a funeral either unless you want to consider a tub of acid a coffin."

"Well, then you'll have to take it on faith," she said.

"After I drew blood, he suffered severe anemia which brought on heart failure. You know the biology, I'm sure."

"Yeah, but that's boring. I was hoping for more detail, a dramatic struggle, something like in the Dracula movies."

"Aren't you really wondering about those shots you got off? You really don't buy the story that you missed me?" she asked.

His smile wilted.

"Yes, that does disturb me a little. What's the explanation?"

"Bullets, knifes, swords pass through us."

"What about silver bullets, crucifixes?"

"Folklore. It's only the wooden stake that's lethal . . . anything wooden that pierces us. Your bullets hit me in that hotel room, and passed through, but the wounds closed and healed instantly."

He shook his head.

"What if it was all true and now you knew it? What would you do now if you were me?" she asked.

"What would I do if I were you? Don't know, but I can tell you what I wouldn't do as me. I wouldn't run out to sell the story to some news rag," he said.

"Don't ignore my question. You know how important it is for me to remain incognito. So what would you do? You'd have to do something."

"You sound worried?"

"Not really for myself, but tell me anyway," she said, propping herself up on her elbow and looking very interested.

"I'd suppose I'd kill me with that anemia thing you mentioned and have someone who works for me put my body into the acid barrel too. But, if you didn't want to kill me and I knew . . ."

"Yes? What then?" she asked. He was thinking that she looked very serious. For a moment he did feel some hesitation.

"Well, I told you about that fringe element in my organization . . ."

"You called it the lunatic section."

"Right, but it's there so I'd introduce you to someone whom I'd like you to impress with your true self," he said.

"Don't tell me your mother."

He laughed.

"Hardly, but if what you're telling me had a splinter of truth to it, I would like to introduce you to someone who might have some imagination or let's say is supposed to have some."

"Really? For what?"

"Something tells me a vampire could be of inestimable value to the CIA and therefore America."

She laughed.

"Like Captain Dracula?"

He didn't change expression.

"Seriously?" he asked. "What difference would it make to a vampire who you feed upon? A steak dinner is still a steak dinner."

"You mind not using the word steak, please," she said. "Oh, so everything else made up about vampires is really dumb, but the wooden stake thing is really true?

"As I said, one of the few."

"So noted. Why is it my bullets didn't stop you but mere wood would?"

"Can't tell you exactly why. As you implied before, it has something to do with Christ on a cross." She looked away. Whatever it was, it bothered her too.

"Seriously? That's your explanation?"

"It's what we've been taught."

He rose and then sat beside her.

"I must say that I've never seen a grown woman carry a joke this far. Either you're a nutcase, a beautiful nutcase or ..."

"Or what?"

She looked at him with such intensity that he had trouble not looking away. He started to laugh.

"You're getting a little frightened, Mr. Waters. As I've seen many times in many places, laughter is often a cover up for embarrassing fear."

"All right, all right," he said getting up quickly and heading toward the ensuite bathroom. "I'll be right out. I have to pee out my fear."

He went into the bathroom, laughing.

She thought a moment and then picked up the phone and dialed Mary Plunkett's bedroom. She was positive the girl had been lying on her bed with her ear to the wall, once again living vicariously through her.

"Bring me the black box, Mary."

"What?" Mary asked.

"Just do it and quickly," Opal snapped. She hung up and went to the window. She didn't turn when she heard Sean come out of the bathroom, but she heard him getting his things together. "Wait," she said. "I don't want you to leave just yet."

"I wasn't going anywhere," he said. "I've got to make a phone call, however. It's that phone call I was supposed to make earlier."

"Don't explain. Go on," she told him. "I'll give you some privacy."

She went into the bathroom.

Seconds later there as a knock on the door. She was still in the bathroom.

"Someone's here," he called.

"It's my assistant. She has something for me. Please get it."

"Your assistant?"

He opened the door. Mary stared at him. She was in a ruby red robe that looked a good two sizes too big for her. Her face was pale with fear. She had hastily tied a bandana around her messy hair.

"Hi," he said. "She's in the bathroom but told me to tell you to give me whatever it is you have for her."

"It's all right, Mary," she heard from inside the bathroom. Mary handed the black metal box to Sean. He looked at it and smiled with confusion.

"What's this?"

"Hawthorn," Mary whispered and fled before she could say or reveal anything in her face, the primary expression being how she would look at a man about to die.

"Hawthorn?" He closed the door. "Didn't we talk about hawthorn?" He looked toward the bathroom. "What do you want me to do with this?"

"Give it to me," Opal said opening the door. "In a minute I'm going to open this door again. When you see me, do not come in or come too close. I doubt that you would anyway, but I want to be sure."

"Then what?"

"Then I'll close it again and open it in few minutes. Hawthorn takes a little longer to overcome. If you're still here, you'll have quite a pleasant surprise."

He held his smile, but it was more like a mask now. "Your assistant told me there's hawthorn in here. Didn't you tell me about that?"

"Exactly."

She took the black box and closed the door.

He stepped back.

The moment of decision had come. She remembered standing there and battling with herself not to open the box.

"Let it go," she whispered to herself. "There's no real danger. He thinks it's all been a game. The worst thing is he will remain suspicious of her presence in that room and he'll either keep track of her or have someone else to be sure there was and is no connection to the terrorist."

She wasn't worried about that. She had the extraordinary instinct to be aware when someone was following her.

Something else was driving her to open the box and consume the hawthorne. She wanted him to accept her; she had never wanted that of any man. What did this mean? Had she reached the final chapter of her dual existence? Revelation for her kind usually meant some form of death. It was truly defiance, the violation of the most sacred oath.

Who did she think she was, Juliet defying the wishes of her family? Look at that result.

And how could she be in the deepest and most intense love of her life so quickly anyway? Was that another sign to suggest the final chapter was here?

She remembered hearing the raging cries of those who passed on to oblivion. Warnings were coming into every pore of her body, but this was a thrill coming from a risk far more dangerous than any she had experienced. She had dreamed about this; it had come both as nightmares and as romantic visions and now, in a few seconds, it would be real.

She opened the box and plucked out the herb. Without hesitation she swallowed what she had.

After about a minute or so later, she opened the door. She could see it in his face. He felt as if he had just been lowered in the Arctic sea.

5.

It would take some time for Sean Waters to realize why he didn't simply run out of her apartment that night. It wasn't easy to visually digest her. She looked inches taller. Her face had elongated to provide rooms for the fangs which looked like two petrified teeth, sharp and razor thin at the ends. They had a grayish-purple color. Her complexion had faded into the pallor of a corpse. Her shoulders bulged, her neck widening and thickening. There was nothing feminine about her body, in fact. The sinews in her arms and legs were prominent, impressive.

Yes, it was difficult for him to take it in, but he could easily visualize the incredulity when and if he went to his superiors with this story and description. After all, field agents, perhaps more than in any other profession, suffered breakdowns. Living under so much pressure and life threatening situations took its toll. For him, because he had no wife and children, accepting assignment after assignment was never a problem, but, his superiors would surely think that everyone has a breaking point and he had reached his. He could almost write the dialogue of the conversation he was to have between himself and Dave Crowman, his immediate supervisor, before he had it. But have it he would. He couldn't just let this all go.

After she had come out of the bathroom metamorphosing into the human form he had known, she told him more about the process. The big test of his courage was whether or not he would remain, sleep with her and make love again in the morning with the image of what he had seen in the bathroom still quite vivid. He did it wondering if he was trying to impress her as much as he wanted to impress himself.

They had breakfast and then he told her he was leaving to fly to see Dave Crowman in Langley.

"To do what?" she asked.

"I was thinking of suggesting to him that we get you to work for us."

"You really want me to be a CIA agent?"

"I know a good thing when I see it," he said.

She held her smile.

"I would like to be a fly on the wall in that office. My guess is they'll have you committed."

"I'll take the chance," he said. "Will you wait for me to call?"

She shrugged.

"Maybe. Except for my work commitments, I go where the urge takes me. You might say I suffer from a little ADHD. You can imagine how easily I'm bored and distracted now. I'm always looking for something unique, something new. Right now, you're something new. I can't promise you how long that will last."

"Just give me forty-eight hours."

"I have no sense of time the way you do. For me, it's become . . . liquid. Minutes flow along into hours when I'm not doing something specific. That's why I'm not sure I can do what you want, Sean. I'll admit that it sounds like something original for me. No one's ever offered me such a thing. Usually, my men didn't want to share a moment of me with anyone and none had the chance to explain me."

"So you're like a black widow spider, destroying her male counterpart?"

"Something like that."

"I'll take the chance," he said finishing his coffee. "I mean it. I'll be calling you."

"You might have to call your attorney first. Aren't you restricted to one phone call?" she asked smiling.

He nodded.

"I think you're going to be surprised."

"I do love surprises. Most everything about humanity is so predictable."

He left her with that smug smile. She broke only to kiss him goodbye.

Hours later, he was on the first military flight he could get. When he arrived at Langley, Crowman immediately wanted to know how he had managed to give a target a heart attack. He saw this as a perfect lead-in to what he was going to tell him.

"Was it merely the sight of you that brought on cardiac arrest? You're one helluva lucky guy," Crowman said, "walking in on him just at that moment."

"It had nothing to do with luck. Nothing to do with me," Sean replied.

He sat in front of Crowman's desk. On his flight over, he had rehearsed what he was going to say. He had told himself how important his demeanor would be when he revealed it all. He wanted somehow to look casual about it. Of course, that could work both ways. Casual about something like this might make him look crazier. On the other hand, he was never histrionic, excitable or in any way over the top. It was this level-headed, even tone demeanor that made him so successful and appreciated. Why change over a small thing like verification that vampires exist? He had laughed at his own musings, attracting the attention of the soldier beside him reading a thriller on the plane.

"Meaning?" Croman asked.

"Meaning that it wasn't my doing," Sean said. "It was hers."

"Hers?"

"When I entered his hotel room, she was there, standing over his body. I thought it was him standing there so I pumped two shots into her, but they went through her."

"Through who?"

No beating around the bush, he had decided. Some facts are more acceptable when stated outright, especially fantastic ones.

"A vampire."

"Vampire? Did you say, vampire?"

"Yes, sir."

"You mean like a real vampire or just some blood sucking whore he picked up somewhere?"

"No sir. This was a real vampire, but she was quite different from what has been written about them."

"And you say you found her standing over the target, shot her but didn't shoot her, and I imagine you're going to say she bled him to death, fangs and all?"

"Yes sir."

Crowman stared at him, smirked and looked at the report he had been given early in the morning. He tapped the paper for emphasis.

"But the man had no wounds, no evidence of being punctured by fangs, fangs you claim you saw on her. You realize that, correct?"

"I didn't actually see her fangs then. But you're right. There were wounds, not visible when I entered the room."

"So when did you see these fangs?" he asked with no real expression of interest.

"Actually, she didn't show me her fangs until sometime later. She had to use hawthorn to bring the vampire in her out. She had her assistant bring a black metal box to her that contained some. We were in her apartment in Paris."

Crowman didn't change expression, but there was a darkness in his eyes only someone with Sean's keen awareness of what was revealed through the thoughts and feelings of an opponent would be able to sense. Crowman's patience was slipping away. Sean started to speak quickly.

"It's like an aphrodisiac. This happened after I had a drink with her and she asked me to her place. We made fantastic love. In fact, she almost killed me with sex," he added smiling.

Crowman nodded.

"Lucky you." Crowman continued to hold his blank expression, but his eyes lifted toward the ceiling.

"We were kidding a lot, or at least, I thought we were, about her being a vampire and finally, as I said, she sent out for the hawthorn to show herself to me."

Crowman sat back. He seemed to suck in his lips completely and then fold his hands over his stomach, taking a more relaxed demeanor. Then he nodded.

"Is that something a vampire normally does?"

"Oh no. I really believe there is something special between us."

Croman nodded.

"So. Is this some sort of joke you guys put together? Are you recording this conversation, Sean?"

"No sir, no joke."

"Stand up," Crowman snapped, reaching the end of his patience. He came around his desk and frisked Sean, checking for a wire. "All right, sit."

Sean did and then Crowman went to his office door and after a pause, jerked it open, expecting a few of his associates standing there and smiling. His secretary looked up surprised.

"Sir?" she asked.

"Nothing, Mrs. Loman. Carry on," he said, closed the door and returned to his chair. He stared at Sean.

"If you need a holiday, Sean, just ask."

"No holiday needed, sir. I am of healthy mind and body."

"Even after sleeping with a vampire? This is what you want me to believe?"

"Yes sir."

Crowman nodded, but didn't smile.

"Does she have a reflection in a mirror, sleep in a coffin in special dirt, flee from the sign of the cross, and keep away from garlic? Which are true? Or are all of the above true? Don't wait for the translation, Waters, just answer."

"I know this is hard to believe. I expected you to have this reaction, of course, but . . ."

"Oh no. It's a little difficult maybe, but I wouldn't go so far as to say it's hard to believe. Let's continue," Crowman said putting the report aside and folding his hands as he leaned over his desk, obviously humoring Sean. "You say you went with her to her apartment in Paris and made love to her and it was pretty damn good."

"Beyond belief."

"So, you didn't have to sleep in a coffin with her?"

"You're toying with me now."

"No, no, no, just trying to understand one of my best agents coming to me with this story. Tell me. Why didn't she drink your blood if she had you alone in her place and she was really a vampire?"

"She was satiated."

"So if you see her again and she's hungry, she'll drink your blood?"

"I don't think so."

"And the reason?"

"I think . . . she likes me."

"Likes you? But not as a meal but as a lover?"

"Something like that, yes."

"So take me through this one more time. You confront her in the attaché's hotel room, pump two shots into her because in the darkness, you thought it was the attaché. The bullets went through her, but left no mark, no bleeding and he was dead on the floor without any trauma at all? Is that a correct summary of what you saw and did?"

"That's it. She explained that she excretes a balm in her saliva that heals the puncture wounds instantly so all the medical examiner can find in her victims is evidence of severe anemia and resulting heart failure. This is happening all over the world when and where others of her kind strike. The medical examiners can't find any reason for loss of blood, leaking aneurism, nothing, but without any trauma, they settle for heart failure and close the books."

"So there's more of them out there, maybe a whole army?"

"I don't know how many there are and neither does she apparently."

"But you're sure there are more?"

"Oh yes. They don't communicate with each other much, but they know where each other is basically. I think it's something instinctive, like a sixth sense they possess. I haven't really gotten into it that deeply yet."

Crowman stared at him. He was beginning to look angry now. "I assure you this is all true, sir."

"A-huh. And this isn't some planned joke?"

"No sir."

"What about seeing our therapist?"

"I don't blame you for recommending that."

"Then you'll do it?"

"I don't want to share this with anyone but you. That's

a promise I made and one we have to keep. I mean, obviously, you'll speak with the director about it, but other than him . . ."

"Speak to the director about it? What do you want me to do with this vampire? Put her on some wanted list, tell the FBI?"

"Oh no, sir. Just the opposite. I want to put her to work for us. I think I can convinced her to do it."

"You want a vampire to work for us?"

"Of course, if she does agree, I know I'll have to have her convince you of what she is and what powers she has."

"By doing what? Not drinking my blood, I hope."

"Doing what she did for me, revealing herself. I need a little more time, but I feel confident I can get her to do it."

"Oh. Well, there's a solution then. When and if you get her to do it, we'll talk about it again. For now, I wouldn't mention it to anyone else."

"That's what I'm asking of you."

"Oh, don't worry about that. My lips are sealed and my teeth clenched. Take it easy. We'll be in touch. In fact, I suggest you take a short vacation, Sean. You need some R and R. I've been looking at your work so far this year and you've gone from one thing to another without much of a break."

"Good. This will give me an opportunity to work on her."

"As long as she doesn't work on you," Dave Crowman said smiling.

"You're going to eat that smile someday soon, sir." Crowman nodded.

"Sounds like a good snack. Okay, take two weeks, Sean. I'll be in touch."

"If it takes that long, I'll take it. If she agrees before two weeks . . ."

"Call me. I'll clear my calendar to make time for vampire viewing," Crowman said.

Bastard, Sean thought as he walked out. His anger motivated him even more to convince Opal, but when he called the number at her apartment, there was no answer. He called a contact on the Paris police department who had the address checked and called him back to say there was no one there. "I found some poparazzi who said they followed her to the airport."

"Airport?"

"Private jet. You'll have to see if you can have hers identified and get the route."

"Right. Merci, Charles."

He ended the call, feeling a cold sense of disappointment. It put him into a small panic. He had to find her quickly so he returned to the Company and put in a search.

He realized immediately it wasn't going to be a simple as he had hoped. Opal currently had ten homes, four in the United States, an apartment near Harrods in London, another home in Paris, as she had said, a house on Lake Como in Switzerland, a house on Mykonos, an apartment in Hong Kong, and a villa in Capri. Who knew how many other residences she possessed, perhaps under a different identity?

Checking the flight plans and passengers for the private jets that left Paris yesterday didn't help either. None of them listed Opal and her assistant. How could she accomplish that? He was dealing with someone who obviously had methods and tools to effectuate a clean escape when she wanted it.

He wondered how she own so much property and live so long without drawing attention to herself?

He checked the names of the previous owners of some of the properties. All of them were women. Fictitious names, he thought, new identities, even with all the proper documentation. This vampire thing was quite sophisticated. But where should he search for her? He couldn't rush around all over the planet. Every phone number he discovered and tried went into a pre-recorded message advising the caller to phone her manager.

He tried her agency and even with his credentials, they were as tight-lipped as a day-old corpse. Without a subpoena he wasn't going to pry anything out of Opal's manager. Running her credit cards didn't seem to help either. There were no records of any purchases recent enough to help so he couldn't tell in which direction she had gone.

She's good, he thought. When she wants to disappear, she can disappear. Frustrated he went home to rest and think. He had a very comfortable town house in Annapolis. As far as his neighbors were concerned, he was a traveling insurance investigator. His closest neighbor was seventy-one-year-old Patsy Morgan, who had been a congresswoman for forty years, representing a Virginia district.

After Patsy's husband Byron had died and her children had moved off in various directions, she retired in Annapolis, telling him she just felt she should be spitting distance from D.C. so she could let the Congress know immediately what she thought of some of their actions and inactions. She was feisty, funny and determined to be independent. He had the sense she knew what he really did, but kept it to herself. She was practically the only neighbor he spoke to on any regular basis. She told him he was the kind of man who needed mothering from time to time. Maybe she was right, he thought. She had the right instincts. That was certain.

She was at his door minutes after he had arrived home. She was still wearing her gardening gloves and had a smudge of dirt on her right cheek. Thin and tall, with her gray hair invading every patch of her natural dark-brown, she never stooped or lost any of her firm demeanor. Tiny brown freckles peppered her face under her eyes and over the bridge of her nose. She was one of those women who would always look ten years younger than she was, too spirited to give in to age.

"Hey, Patsy," he said. "What's up?"

"You tell me," she said entering without any invitation to do so. "I watched you drive up and the way you walked in. Something wrong?"

He laughed and didn't move from the doorway.

"And here I am proud of my ability to win at poker."

"Don't play with me," she warned. "I bet you haven't got anything to eat for dinner."

"Well, I just . . ."

"I made Bryon's favorite meatloaf. You've had it before," she said.

"Well, that's . . ."

"Very kind of me. I know. Change, shower, do what you do and come over. Don't take forever," she warned and started out. The door was still open. "You can tell me your sad story then. I need someone to feel sorry for. My kids don't think I sympathize enough so they don't tell me anything."

"Can't imagine why," he said. "I'll be over in twenty or so. Thanks."

"Make it a ten or so. I'm hungry, both for my food and a good story," she said and left.

He laughed to himself, showered and dressed with his mind still solely focused on finding Opal. What he feared the most was his meeting her again and she acting as though she had never met him.

At dinner with Patsy, the conversation began as innocuously as usual with the day's headlines encouraging her to describe some of her most memorable congressional experiences, ranging from utter stupidity to blatant graft. She went on a rant for a while and then stopped abruptly and smiled.

"What was it Will Rogers said? 'If I studied all my life, I couldn't think up half the number of funny things passed in one session of congress.'"

"Yet you stayed with it, Patsy."

"Just stubborn or stupid, I guess."

"Or dedicated."

"Whatever. Choose your poison," she said and he laughed. Then she gave him those Mother's narrow, scrutinizing eyes. "What's really eatin' you, Sean Waters? And don't give me that, 'I'm just tired stuff.' I went through it for forty-five years with my husband and he always gave up the ghost and told me the truth in the end. So don't waste either of our time. I don't have that much more to waste."

Sean shook his head and smiled. Of course, there was a limit to what he could tell her.

"Oh, I met this girl, woman, really hit it off and then she just disappeared on me."

"You can't track her down?" she asked with skepticism. She did know more about him than she suggested.

"Not yet."

"No forwarding address, telephone number?"

"None that she responds to at the moment."

"Maybe she doesn't want you to track her down, Sean. You might have to face that fact. Facing facts is something men in particular are not keen to do."

"Men? Who gets more plastic surgery?" She shrugged.

"I'm still probably right. A woman might not be as obvious about it, but she'll still leave a trail to follow. Like dropping bread crumbs."

"She didn't, but. . . ." He thought a moment and smiled to himself.

"But what?"

"I suddenly thought this might be a test."

"Test? Why would she have to do that? Test of what?"

"She's quite special. She wants to see how determined I am to find her again, how much I want to find her."

"I see. You didn't make that clear enough. Fear of commitment? I don't know why men even have that fear seeing how easy it is to get divorces these days. They're practically in coin operated machines. So what's your plan? I assume you've gone through the usual ways. Maybe," she added with a wry smile, "you have a friend in high places that can do something for you."

"No. He couldn't locate her easily either."

"Well, what does she do? She work?"

"She's a world class fashion model."

"World class and you can't find her?" she asked skeptically.

"Not yet. I haven't read about any new fashion shows featuring her and I did skim the Internet."

"She has a manager or agent, right?"

"Tight-lipped."

"Doesn't your sister work for someone in that business?"

"Yes, but I would rather not involve her in this. I'd rather not involve her in my romances," he said. There were tons of paragraphs between those lines.

"I see. Well, if she's a world class model, she'll turn up somewhere soon, won't she?"

"I suppose," he said.

"But it could be anywhere in the world and you can't wait, right?"

He looked up and nodded.

"Something like that."

"Well, far be it I give someone advice to do something illegal, but maybe you can talk your friend into an illegal wiretap of her agency or manager. They're bound to talk about some new job."

"Why Patsy Morgan," he said feigning shock and surprise, "a former Congresswoman proposing something unconstitutional?"

"Just trying to stay in shape in case I ever run again," she replied and he laughed.

Then he remembered.

All is fair in love and war and God help him, he was definitely in love.

Opal left quickly that night not out of fear of what Sean would do, but out of fear at what she had done. After all these years and lovers for her to take not only so great a risk, but betray her own creed, her own kind shocked her. Really, did this mean she was nearing the end of her so-called immortality? Some talked about that. Things happened more slowly and eventually, one was locked into human mortality.

It wasn't often she felt an inner, deep fear, a fear that vibrated in her very bones. The experience was so rare that when it came, she felt more threatened than mere mortals felt at the sight of her. She was sure of that because she truly believed that everything she felt, she felt stronger or more than they did. It was part of her blessing and curse, depending on how she felt that day.

Actually, Sean's reaction, although sufficiently full of shock, was far less severe than she had anticipated. He didn't know it, but she might have had to protect herself and others, no matter how she felt about him. He passed a test, one that carried more than just embarrassment in failure. It was a test of life itself.

But he didn't run right out of the room or reach for his weapon. He stood there struggling to take it all in, to absorb and digest what his eyes were bringing to him. It made her wonder just what fantastic things he had witnessed and how well the CIA kept their secrets. Some even thought they were aware of extra-terrestrials, especially because of the revelations of some experienced navy pilots. The days of skepticism when it came to the fantastic were shrinking.

"OMG," he had muttered, desperately trying to keep a sense of humor.

She remained before him as long as she thought necessary for him to take it all in completely, and then she closed the door, taking pains to make the sound of her locking it distinct enough. She sat on the toilet seat and waited for her body to recede, wondering what she would find when she opened that door again. Perhaps he would have his gun drawn. It would be useless as she had explained to him, but nevertheless, that would certainly end it. Or perhaps he ran. If he did, she would probably go after him. Why take the chance of someone important believing him?

To her delight he was still there, fully dressed now, standing by the window with his back to the door. When she opened it, he turned around instantly. The sight of her restored brought immediate relief into his face. She could see the muscles relax, hear his breathing and feel his heartbeat slow. She even felt his whole body soften, slip out of the defensive mode.

"What kept you from attacking me?" was his first and quite expected question. It was, after all, the most logical thing to ask.

"I'm satiated, although I do have some control even if I'm not."

"That's a relief," he said.

She smiled.

"I know exactly what you mean."

"And all those things you told me, things I thought you were kidding about, they're all true? I mean, the wooden stake? The hawthorn is obviously true, I guess."

"Yes, what I told you so far is true. You see how much trust I've put into you. I'm like Samson telling Delilah about his hair."

"Yeah, well, I don't exactly walk around with a wooden stake in my pocket."

"Maybe you will now."

"Maybe. So really, there are more of you out there?"

"There are."

"How many?"

"I told you. I don't know exact numbers, Sean. We're international. I never met one, but I heard there are even Eskimos. We're a race just like any other and we've existed and evolved like any other. We've infiltrated every people, every nationality, and every race. And like you we have our mythology. One day we'll compare notes, maybe and see how closely we do resemble each other."

He shook his head and then sat, now looking more stunned. "I've got to keep telling myself I'm not dreaming." He looked up at her quickly. "I have told myself that, but I didn't have to emphasize it as much as I am now."

"Still want to get to know me more?" she asked. "Or are you looking for a graceful exit?"

He stared at her a moment.

"Yes, I want to know you more."

"You don't sound convincing and I see the way you shift your eyes at that door. Why didn't you run out when you had the opportunity?"

"I don't know." He smiled. "Maybe it's because I feel like someone who has made a major discovery. And lived to tell about it," he quickly added.

"You have. Besides not ever getting sick, I should add we never suffer from modesty. Yes, I truly am a major discovery. The question is what are you going to do about it?"

"Well, as I said I'm not exactly going to rush out here to the nearest rag newspaper to sell *I made love to a vampire and lived to tell about it*."

"Now that's a real relief, although I think I might have read that in the *National Enquirer*."

"Right. But right now I don't know how I'd convince anyone that I'm not out of my mind . . . totally."

"I'll have to rely on that. Actually, we always have. You know that line about the devil, how the more fantastically he is described, the safer he is?"

"The greatest trick he pulled on the human race was convincing them he didn't exist?"

"Exactly."

He nodded and thought for a moment.

"There has to be a way to make sense of all this, find some logic and remain rational." His eyes widened with a thought. "How do you choose your victims?"

She laughed.

"Go to any supermarket and watch how someone studies the steak in the refrigerated case. We're not much different."

"So the one consolation for the poor jerk is he or she is choice meat?"

"Not necessarily organically raised and I do have some preferences when it comes to nationalities, but any ship in a storm. I am not a bigot when it comes to feasting on humanity," she added.

He laughed and then his eyes brightened.

"What?" she asked, suspiciously. "I can almost hear the wheels turning."

"I thought I was joking about it before, but what would you say to coming to work for the good old USA?"

"What makes you think I believe it's the good old USA?" He thought a moment.

"You said you were a citizen of the U.S.?"

"I'm a citizen of the world, although currently, I do have an American passport in my collection. How would I work for the good old U.S. of A.?"

"Work with me."

"Seriously. You want me in the CIA?"

"Why not? You have all the skills any field agent might require; actually you have more than most have, and you're brighter than everyone I know in the company, including my superiors. To top it off, you have this great cover, a world class fashion model. No one would question you going any-where, flirting with anyone. You could easily get into places we have to spend time and money figuring out, and you can reach the nearly unreachable."

She studied him a moment, a half smile on her face.

"You're serious, aren't you?"

"Yes, absolutely."

She shook her head.

"I told you. Democracy is boring. One government is like the next to me. I've seen enough of them come and go, heard the promises and the lies. Mere mortals don't have the staying power for anything eternal, except maybe their stupidity. That seems eternal."

"Mere mortals?"

"Mere mortals. What better adjective can you find than 'mere'? You're list of weaknesses stretches from the South to the North Pole. Human being are unfortunately the same everywhere."

"Okay, but you would have to admit that American de-mocracy is the most decent form of government, the form that could do the most for its citizens."

She smirked and raised her right eyebrow.

"What?"

"Excuse me. American democracy? Don't you have millions of your population who can't get a decent education? Don't you have millions in poverty? Don't you have one of the worst records for voting in an industrialized democracy? Didn't you waste billions of dollars and thousands of lives in an unnecessary war while your own infrastructure crumbles? Should I continue?"

"So you do keep up with the news?"

"I don't sleep in a coffin all day, if that's what you mean."

"What do you do?"

"You already know. Lately, I happen to be the world's top fashion model. If I wanted, I could be working every day and probably every night. Contrary to folklore, the truth is I don't much sleep. I do a lot of reading. I've read some books forty times. They're worth it. I have properties to look after, and a small empire of my own to run. Contrary to what you might think, I'm rarely bored. My aide says I keep her up too late and too long."

"Mary . . . the one who brought the hawthorn?"

"Mary Plunkett. She's something of a personal assistant. Not the best I've had over the centuries, but for now, she'll do. She's in the adjoining room."

He looked at the door.

"Is she . . ."

"No, quite the opposite. The sight of blood drains her of blood."

"Where did you meet her?"

"Like you, she accidentally came upon me right after a feed. I knew immediately she would work for me."

"How?"

"Her reaction was a combination of heartfelt terror and fascination. I've given her ten times the life she could otherwise enjoy. She dreams of becoming me. I crave adoring and needy servants, but alas, I can't vouch for her longevity in this position. In her heart she knows that, but it's testimony to my charisma that she is devoted to me nevertheless. I doubt you have a more loyal field agent in your club." He nodded and thought a moment.

"Let's get back to my suggestion. I'm really serious. In fact, the idea is getting me very excited."

"I have never worked for anyone but myself, Sean," she said.

"Look, accidentally, you already did carry out a mission for the United States by knocking off that terrorist. Why not continue, working with me? We'll make a great team and have more excuses to be together. This way I'll be confident that you'll be satiated for a good cause."

She shook her head and laughed.

"You mean it, don't you?"

"Yes."

"I was right about you," she said.

"In what sense?"

"I had a feeling you were different from most men I've enjoyed over the decades and you are. Anyone else would have run out of the room when I gave him the opportunity. I'm sure some might have jumped out the window, but you stand there calmly now and think to yourself, how can I exploit this phenomenon? Right?"

"I suppose, yes. Call me an opportunist but that's just built-in to who I am and what I have to be. A field agent especially who is not and exploiter is not a field agent for long, if you get my drift."

"You're an extraordinary man, Sean Waters. I guess I really can pick them when I set my mind to it."

"I suppose I should feel flattered even though you're flattering yourself."

"Feel flattered that you're still alive," she added, but not with any threat. It was uttered as a simple matter of fact.

"Believe me. I'm not stupid. I do. So you'll give some thought to my idea?"

"I didn't say that."

"Will you?"

She smiled.

"I doubt it, Sean."

"Why not? Having specifically assigned prey might be of some interest to you. It would certainly be different and I'm sure you like to find something different to do no matter how good you are at filling time, especially if I'm to believe you've lived as long as you say you have."

"I don't know," she said, but weakly enough for him to continue pursuit.

"Why not?" he asked. He almost whined.

He's like every other man in this way, a spoiled little boy, she thought. Wants what he wants.

"For one thing, a major thing, it requires too much trust on my part."

"Hey . . . this is the CIA. We're experts in keeping things secret."

"Tell that to Valerie Plame."

"Believe me, this is going to be different."

"Of course, you know, in order to prove my existence, I'll have to devour someone in front of your boss."

He held his smile.

And then he lost it. Was she serious? "Finally," she said, "I've gotten to you."

"Believe me, Opal, you got to me quite a bit just a little while ago."

"Why don't we just leave things as they are for now, Sean? Let's see how hard you work on coming back to me after you walk safely out of here, first," she said.

He nodded.

"Okay. That's a deal." He stood up. "I'll get back to you and if I do, you'll give it serious consideration. Deal?"

"Have your people contact my people," she joked. "We'll do lunch. Oh, wait, that's Hollywood speak. You guys don't do lunch; you do alleyways."

He stood there staring at her.

"What?" she asked.

"You look so . . . perfect; it's hard to believe now that what I saw, I saw."

"I am perfect, even when I'm not who you see now. I wouldn't metamorphose if I thought I was going to be imperfect. Too much ego. Which, by the way, is what makes me so successful on the runway modeling the world's most sought after designers. A perfect work of art for a perfect work of art." She smiled. "Can you live with someone so conceited? It would turn my stomach, I think."

"Not a problem for me. Modesty is weakness from where I stand. It makes you hesitate and hesitation is deadly in my business."

She smiled.

"Maybe we are made for each other. Where were you two hundred years ago when I needed you?"

"I'm here now," he said.

"That fascinates me actually. I admire you for it in a way."

"What?"

"Living with the constant reminder that you're dying. I don't know as I could do it."

"So you do have a weakness," he said smiling. "Okay. We made a deal."

He started for the door, paused and looked at her intently again. She held her smile.

"Yes?"

"I mean it. I'll be back," he said.

She didn't reply. She watched him leave. He thinks I'm a find, she thought. He should know how much of a diamond he is and how lucky he is to have survived the revelation.

But then the realization of what she had done and fear of the consequences set her packing. She called Mary and told her they were leaving in ten minutes, and actually in only seconds more than ten, they were on their way out. She looked for him or other men when they exited the building, half expecting he had called someone and had the place under surveillance, but her instincts told her otherwise. He was off trying to make sense of what he had seen and done. She had no doubt he would have trouble sleeping whenever he tried to sleep, and tomorrow perhaps he would question his own memory.

And I won't see him again in this way, she concluded. No mere mortal could take this sort of a confrontation with his most vivid and worst nightmares and return anyway. Nevertheless, she decided to take some precautions and go into one of her incognito modes for a while. Then, she thought, it will all pass, and she would go on.

Little did she know however, how exceptional a mere mortal Sean Waters was.

For her that was just as bad as it was good. And she knew that who and what she was would permit a contradiction just as long before a choice had to be made. There was no way to avoid it and keep what she had, hold onto what she was. It saddened her to think about it. Maybe she was feeling from that most of all.

6.

Opal had continued to reminisce about Sean as she and Mary rode away from the aborted fashion show at the St. Regis. How many times had she thought back to that night, the night she had betrayed her identity? It was practically the only thing that haunted her. She would never deny that a part of her had hoped he would run and never confront her again, and another part of her, a larger part, had hoped he would.

She had wanted to give him every opportunity to reject her. If it was too difficult to find her immediately, he could use that as a rationalization. Of course she had thought that if he did want to pursue her, he certainly would use the facilities of the CIA to locate her quickly, but she also had confidence in her ability to disappear. No one had ever found her when she didn't want to be found.

So it came as both a shock and in some ways a delightful surprise to see him sitting quietly in the lobby of her Virginia Beach resort two days later. She had just come down from her room to have some breakfast and a walk on the beach. Throughout the centuries, she had always found quiet walks on the beach to be the most conducive to her deeper, more philosophical thinking. There was scarcely a beach left in the world upon which she hadn't walked at one time or another, whether it be the rocky shores of Ireland or the soft sands in the Canary Islands. To her it was truly as if the ocean held onto time and events, a great vault of history that could be brought in with the tide. In its depth and stillness remained the whispers of all intelligent life and the mystery of the eternal.

She paused when she saw him. Contradictory feelings were wrestling in and around her heart. She was sorry he was there because of the terrible end she had envisioned, and yet, she was elated that he wasn't deterred. Yin and Yang, good and evil, every contradiction in the universe was struggling to survive the battle. For the first time in centuries, she was looking forward to the future. She was that curious about it all and curiosity was the fuel on which her life force ran.

He was wearing a sky blue linen suit with a chocolate brown belt, suede shoes, a striped shirt, and a panama hat. He wore no tie, but he looked debonair and aristocratic sitting in that brown rattan King armchair with a red cushion. He was reading the local paper as if he didn't know she was in the same hotel.

Sean looked up when she stepped over to him. He slowly put the paper down. Would he ever look at her and not feel his heart race? She wore a floral lace sheath dress and had her hair pinned back tightly, but flowing in the rear of her head and down to her wing bones. Two teardrop diamond earrings dangled on a sliver thread. She wasn't wearing any makeup, but no one looking at her would realize that. Her lips were ruby and her eyes were so sharp, one would swear she had put on eyeliner and false eyelashes.

"I thought you people avoid standing out in a crowd," she said.

"Oh, good morning," he said as casually as he could. "Do I really stand out?"

"*And every day of his life he put on a clean shirt and full suit from head to toe made out of linen so white it hurt your eyes to look at it,*" she recited. "Huckleberry Finn's comment about Colonel Grangerford," she said.

"Your world of knowledge is bound to make me look like a cultural Pygmy," he said. "Besides, I took a long time deciding what to wear for you. This hotel is a bit on the snobby side. I want to look like a pure blue blood Southerner."

She laughed.

"You are good, Mr. Waters. Care to tell me how you managed this?"

Trade secret. Besides, suppose you attempt to run away again? If you know how I do it, you'll cover up where I need you exposed and really make it hard for me. Of course, if we learn to really trust each other and you give up some secrets, I'll be more inclined to give up mine."

"Okay. I'll give up first. I'm going to breakfast," she said. "Really food or. . . ?"

She laughed.

"I like my coffee and croissant with jelly."

"May I join you?"

"I don't see how it's possible to stop you," she said, but then smiled.

He rose and walked into the dining room with her. They took a table by the window that gave them a good view of the beach and the Atlantic. The morning overcast had been swept away. Waves glistened.

"Is your assistant here, too?"

"Of course, only I don't socialize with her. She's taking care of some errands."

They both ordered coffee, but he ordered eggs and bacon as well as the basket of croissants.

"I built up quite an appetite waiting for you."

"Sorry it took so long. Why didn't you just ring my room?"

"Didn't want to take the chance of your running out on me."

"Very wise. Although," she said looking out the window,

"I probably would have been just as impressed and not fled. So we're here. You've proven persistence. Why don't you start with your questions?"

"Secrets?"

She nodded.

"How long have you been here?"

"America?"

"Yes."

"On and off, about one hundred seventy years or so. I spent most of my youth in Europe, Eastern Europe in fact, a good deal of time in Asia and some time in North Africa, Algiers in particular."

"What about the Arctic Circle?"

"You're being factitious, but I toyed with Alaska for a while and I've been to the Nordkapp in Norway, however, the blood of the residents in both places was too thick for my taste. I do have a figure to protect."

He laughed so loud, a couple in an adjoining table stopped talking and turned toward them.

"Sorry," he said. "I guess you weren't kidding about Eskimos."

"You're going to have a hard time deciding when I'm kidding and when I'm not," she said.

"Have you always had a mere mortal lover?"

She smiled and looked out the window. He thought she wasn't going to respond, but she started to talk.

"I had once tried to be celibate, to prove to whomever created us that I could control my lust. It was never absolutely necessary to have any sort of relationship, especially with prey."

"What happened?"

"Celibacy had a short life . . . boring," she said and he laughed. "So? My turn. How did you find me?"

"It wasn't easy, even for me and the CIA. You have an

agent/manager ready to go to the Supreme Court rather than give up anything. She's not one of you by chance, is she?"

"Hardly. However, she's a lawyer as well as an agent and I have heard some call their lawyers blood suckers."

He laughed.

"So? Let's hear it. Tit for tat."

"I almost gave up. I noticed how all your properties were owned by women previously and concentrated on the variety of identities. I was able to pinpoint one that had no death certificate and ran it back through our contacts in Italy. That provided a credit card number from a card issued at an Italian bank and then I tracked the activity and voila."

"Are all spy agencies as good as yours?"

"Mossad is pretty good. The Brits are as good. The Russians have slipped into the Internet to distort and persuade, and the Chinese are breathing down their necks and ours. Both of them have become more cyber spies. That's spreading rapidly to every country in fact. Some day they might put guys like me out of work, damn technology. How are you when it comes to the Internet?"

"I can hack as well as anyone in your company," she said. "I lived with a hacker in Russia for quite a while before he began to bore me. I should tell you that some of us believe once you ingest a victim's blood, you inherit some of him or her. They literally become a part of you. It's like instincts being passed along in animals. Fantastic enough idea for you?"

"I am all that I eat sort of thing?" She laughed.

"Something like that. I'm not saying I buy into it. We have our own fantasies too."

"So really, how often do you see another one of you?"

"Here and there, but neither of us usually acknowledge it very much."

"You have this instant recognition thing, I suppose."

"Yes. I suppose we do have instincts you don't have."

"How fast do you recognize one?"

"Instantly. We don't have to talk to each other either, but it's not mental telepathy. It's just a deeper understanding. A lift of an eyebrow, and slight twist in lips or a nod and everything is said."

"Like what?"

"This is my territory, for one. I make it clear I'm just passing through and that's that."

"And if you weren't?"

"We don't complicate each other's lives. There's enough for everyone. There's something to note about us. We're not greedy," she said.

"Greedy? What about these homes you have all over the place . . . any special reason for so many?"

"I'm not as comfortable in hotels all the time, especially if I'm going to be somewhere for a while, and they're all good investments."

"Real estate or . . ."

"Real estate," she said smiling. "Blood is not a rare form of metal or something. It's in abundance. But there's more to life than feeding, even though some of your species seems to think otherwise. Like that plump woman over there gouging on bacon and eggs," she said nodding.

He turned, looked at her and turned back.

"You came here instead of going to one of your many homes that are located in some of the world's most beautiful places to vacation. Why? Some special feast about to happen?"

"No. I figured you'd somehow trace my properties and thought I'd make your challenge harder."

"So you really wanted to get away from me?"

"Maybe. Maybe you're not a clever as you might think when it comes to locating someone. Maybe you had more help than you're revealing. We haven't reached that point where we trust each other completely. Maybe we never will."

He smiled.

"You are a mystery and mysteries are my business. I don't mind there being no end game."

"Sounds like dialogue right out of a film noire."

"I do watch a lot of movies. Waiting can be quite boring for a man of action. That's my own line," he added quickly. "Just in case you use it in a hundred years."

The waitress brought their coffee and basket of croissants. "No one makes these like the French do," she said smearing some jam on one. "Most of their cuisine is actually too rich for my taste these days."

"What do you favor?"

"Scandinavian, simple fish dishes. I have a thing for Hungarian goulash, however, when it's really Hungarian goulash."

"Is this Transylvania thing truthful . . . the whole Dracula thing?"

"Not a bit, but how we enjoy it," she added. "As I implied, all that does provide some good cover."

The waitress brought his bacon and eggs.

"So, are there many more of you in the United States right now?"

"You keep asking and I keep telling you I don't know numbers. Stop hoping I'll slip up."

"You can't blame me," he said.

"We don't keep track of each other's travels. No central office to go through, but I'm sure there are more here. Perhaps, I will help you help your so-called Homeland Security agency improve, show you how easy it is to establish an identity here and co-mingle."

"I bet you can."

"Oh, I know I can."

"Don't you at least meet in some central location periodically, compare notes, good blood, bad blood, etc.?"

"We don't need to meet, Sean. As I told you, we sense each other without confronting each other. The essence of who we are rests in our independence. And yet, there are things that link us so tightly, we cannot escape totally from each other. It's a comfort actually."

He stopped eating and sat back.

"Don't tell me that part is also true."

She shrugged and then went back to her coffee.

"Okay, I won't tell you. It might be too much for a mere mortal to absorb."

"Funny thing to say, considering what I've already had to absorb."

"No, I'm not trying to be funny. When I said the incredulity is protective, I meant it. Crosses, silver bullets, mirrors not reflecting them, etc. are all incorrect, but as I said, not I nor any of my kind are going to correct any misconceptions. We do believe it helps to keep our existence unbelievable and our identities secret enough for us to function, thus . . . protective. Incredulity is our shield, but that doesn't mean we shouldn't take great care. We could easily become the most hunted creatures on the face of the earth, a cooperative international pursuit."

"I doubt it would be that cooperative. Everyone wants to be in charge."

"You're right but there aren't many things that human beings cooperate with one another over. You're still trying to get climate control cooperation even though it's like church bells ringing to warn the inhabitants that hordes of savages are bearing down. However, you do cooperate occasionally when it comes to the spread of diseases. You recognize your common vulnerability with that; you might just recognize it with us. We don't favor one nationality over another, one race over another. Blood is blood, contrary to the stupid prejudices you seem to engender."

"I understand. I really should be flattered then that you revealed yourself to me."

"Either that or I should feel I've made a major mistake."

"Having second thoughts?"

"Always."

"Why did you do it?"

"I don't know. I'm still trying to figure that one out myself."

He thought a moment.

"So, if you conclude that you did make a mistake, I'm in big trouble?"

"Yes and no. I still have confidence in most, if not all you tell believing you've gone over the edge. I'm sure that was your recent experience."

He nodded.

"From the way you say it, I'll be thankful I can't convince anyone ever."

"And eventually, you'll stop trying to. So, I'm not concerned about you."

"Tender mercies."

She took another bite of her croissant and shook her head. "I think I need to get back to France for a while after all."

"I don't think I've paid enough attention to the great food I've had on assignments."

"Pity. But then again, you don't have my capacity to enjoy all the senses, especially taste."

He laughed, ate and then paused.

"What's it really like for you? I mean when you . . . get that way?"

"I honestly couldn't tell you in terms you'd appreciate or

understand. First, because I don't recall the details. I guess I'm closer to that story, Jekyll and Hyde. It happens so fast and completely, I don't have time to evaluate anything."

He nodded.

"Oh, you understand?" she asked, smiling.

"A little. Well . . . no, but how do you know when it's time to feed?"

"So you really can't get pregnant, even with another vampire and make little vampires?"

"No."

"And obviously not with a mere mortal like me."

"Imagine how many children I would have had if I could over all these years."

He laughed and then asked, "Are there any signs, warnings before you get that way?"

"You sound worried."

"Might not be a bad idea for me to know that."

She shrugged. "There are subtle changes in my size, but not terribly dramatic. My complexion begins to fade. Mary says it's a yellow pallor."

He nodded.

"I'll know before you do. Don't worry about it," she said. "Unless you're afraid I won't warn you."

"No, no. Well, maybe."

She laughed and looked away. He ate silently and then put down his fork and finished his coffee, "That was delicious. Didn't realize how hungry I really was."

"I never do until I take my first bite."

"First bite? You're a bag of laughs." He signaled the waitress. "What's next?"

"I go for a walk on the beach."

"May I join you?"

"It's a public beach."

He took the check and handed the waitress his card.

"This qualifies as a business expense," he said. "You're not giving up this recruiting?"

"As you see."

She smiled at him.

"You remind me of someone. He was determined, too. He was a Union officer during the Civil War. I was here for a while then. It made for some easy pickens . . . all that blood wasted on farm fields. It was like your Native Americans watching the slaughter of the buffalo for their hides, all that meat left to rot. Mere mortals. Their capacity to inflict harm on their own species never ceases to amaze me," she muttered and stood up.

He signed the bill quickly and followed her out.

"What about this Union officer?"

"He wanted me to marry him. He actually went AWOL to pursue me. In the end I had to end his misery."

"Huh? You don't mean . . ."

"Sometimes, there is no room for compromise," she said and walked toward the path to the beach. He paused and then caught up.

"Is that some kind of veiled threat?"

"Was it veiled? I must be slipping." She smiled and walked slower.

"All right. I hereby promise not to be uncompromising and obstinate, but at least hear me out. Fair?"

"Hurry. Soon I'll hear nothing but the sea," she said. "You're not really going to be an agent. You'll be a freelancer. You have no obligation to take on any mission or obey any order. I just envision times, situations, where you could be very effective.

"Of course, if it doesn't coordinate with your own nutritional need, it's moot anyway."

"Not always. When I said I have control; I have control."

"Well, that's even better."

"What's the reason I should I do this again? To please you?"

"And yourself. They'll always be something of a challenge and it might be more interesting than some random victim. Do you have any standards, rules about that?"

"I personally like to take an arrogant one. Vanity is very accommodating."

"Perfect."

"You love that word."

"When I'm with you, it just keeps popping up." She laughed.

"Who would know about this?"

"My immediate supervisor and the director, I imagine. There's no reason for anyone else to know and it would be far too much to convince any others anyway. I see it this way," he added. "You'd be sharing my life's work. Connecting, bonding."

"What makes you think I want to do that?"

"You took a risk with me back in Paris at your apartment. I have the feeling you haven't done that often, if at all. Am I right?" He paused. "You can't see it, but my fingers are crossed."

She paused and looked out at the sea. Then she turned to him, her beautiful eyes reaching so deeply inside him, he felt she had seized his heart and held it in her hand, permitting every beat.

"You're right," she said. "That's astute. Comforting, actually. All right. I'll explore the idea with you, but at any point, I can back out, stop, whatever?"

"That's what freelance means."

"Let's not talk about it anymore," she said taking his hand. "Let's not talk at all."

They walked on. She could feel his excitement through in his fingers and she smiled to herself, amazed at her own powers and sensitivities.

We are truly the chosen, she thought. We have such power.

They spent over an hour on the beach. Later, he took her for a ride in the BMW 435I convertible he had rented, and they stopped for lunch at a sweet little restaurant with a tiled patio that looked out on the ocean. Candy cotton clouds seemed pasted in the sky despite the wind. It was as if the whole world was holding its breath to see what would happen between her and him.

She got him talking about his youth in ways he had never spoken with anyone, bringing up anecdotes and incidents that he had never described. What he had always considered very personal suddenly became something he wanted to share, at least with her. The most important thing about it was he enjoyed being open, naked and vulnerable, which was something he feared being, especially at this point in his life and what he did.

Perhaps she did have some sort of magic. Her smile was mesmerizing. He thought she could have gotten him to reveal state secrets. It was as if his very soul had opened to her exploration. How could it be any different to be in love?

Surely, this was what he felt, where he was at moment, in love. Why hadn't her forbidding form smothered all feeling for her? Who would or could understand that not happening? He himself was fascinated with that question.

Was the answer simply that when she was Opal, she had the power to make him forget, cause him to lose any fear and be trusting? How do you fall in love with someone who might have you literally hypnotized? Shouldn't he be more cautious, more skeptical about his own feelings? Or was he like someone intoxicated who didn't mind it, who in fact enjoyed it?

Wasn't it really his chronic skepticism that made him so successful in his work? He was proud of that, but deep down was he unhappy about it? Did he want so much to believe in something or someone that he would deliberately risk his life to have faith? Maybe he was so afraid of changing because of her that he wanted her to change because of him. Get her to commit and he would feel safe, feel stronger because he had convinced her and in that way, proved he was powerful too. Was it a natural competition between two strong minded people, or did he really want her at his side?

As she talked about herself, he thought she could describe the places she had been with such poetry. He had been to many of the same places, but she was getting him to see them in a new light, taking him from some dark place that depressed the beauty. After all, most of them had been more like battlegrounds. She made him feel like he should return to each and every one of them, not as an agent, but simply as a human being, a man. It was impossible not to listen to her. She was beautiful in so many ways, especially in the way her eyes lit up when she was describing something she had enjoyed. Truthfully, she made him feel that he had been more like a blind man. It was as if had sleepwalked through most of this life. She was that enchanting. Perhaps the Greeks literally had seen her when they had formed their vision of Venus.

Afterward, on the ride back, they were both silent. It was as if they realized words would be inferior to the way they now sensed each other in a smile and a touch. She had let down her hair to ride in the convertible and just watching those strands dance in the breeze brought a deep pleasure.

He thought he would check into a room when they returned, but she insisted he stay with her.

"I'm here only tonight," she told him. "I have a commercial to shoot in Richmond, Virginia."

"That's perfect. Excuse the use of the word," he added quickly, "but I can introduce you to my immediate supervisor."

"You really mean it, don't you? You are not kidding."

"Absolutely, I mean it. It's one of my homerun ideas." He held his breath while she thought about it. Then she nodded.

"Okay, but I don't want to meet him in any office. He has to come to the location I decide would work."

"No problem."

"By himself."

"Of course."

"Let me think about it a little more," she said after a moment. He was disappointed that there was still some hesitation, but he said nothing.

After dinner, they walked the beach again.

"I really didn't realize how beautiful it is by the ocean. I can see why you're drawn to it," he said.

"All life comes from it, even ours."

"Will you ever tell me how you became what you are? Or is that part of the fiction true . . . vampires feeding on mortals and turning them into vampires?"

"That's not true, but I won't tell you. Not yet, maybe never. Don't pursue that," she added with a warning. "Too much knowledge is a dangerous thing."

"Fine," he said holding up his hand. "I know when to back off and when not to."

"I know you do. You have many exceptional qualities otherwise I wouldn't be here with you or you wouldn't be here with me."

"That I believe," he said.

The breeze lifted her hair, whipped some strands over her face. He pushed them aside and they kissed.

"Is it ever different, different enough?" he asked in a whisper.

"Searching for a compliment?"

"Hoping for one," he said and they kissed again, only she was the aggressor this time.

"It's special enough," she said. "To build upon," she added and he laughed.

"Talk about being cautious," he said.

They walked on and then returned to the hotel. She remembered that the love they made that night was different from the frenzied, hot sex they had at her apartment in Paris. Their foreplay took longer. It was as if she, especially, was taking her time to study him as if she was intrigued with the possibility of him being something far more than even she was. It made him nervous at first and then it seemed to light him up even more. He wished it could go on all night, but in the end, he finally confessed to being exhausted and she let him sleep. He slept late into the morning and when he awoke, she was gone.

But this time she wasn't trying to disappear. She left a note telling him when and where to contact her the following day. She explained she was doing a commercial for a skin lotion company and told him exactly where to go. He visited her on the set and during the break for lunch, she told him where to arrange the meet with David Crowman that night. It was to be held at a cheap roadside motel north of Richmond.

"He's going to be pretty frightened, Sean, so I hope you're doing a good job of preparation."

What surprised him was the underlying note of threat. It was clear she was telling him it might move out of her control if he didn't handle his end correctly. It gave him some hesitation.

But he made the call and asked Croman to appear. "You want me to fly down there to meet your vampire?"

"Exactly. There's no other way to convince you," Sean said. "This might go hard on you if it's a joke or there is no one like the woman you're describing."

"I'll risk my career on it."

Crowman was silent.

"I must be crazy," he said.

He agreed to the meet, but Sean had the sense he was doing it more to humor a well-respected agent than anything. Sean even had the feeling Crowman continued to harbor the belief this was all part of some inner office practical joke. Crowman probably half-expected a group of agents waiting to pop out of the darkness and shout, "Trick or Treat."

Nothing Sean could say would wipe that smirk off David Crowman's face. The proof, as has been said for decades, if not centuries, was in the pudding. When he was on his way to the motel with Crowman, she called his cell phone and gave him the room number. They arrived just after ten p.m., pulling up in front of the room she had designated. Mary Plunkett was waiting outside.

"Is that her?" David Crowman asked immediately. "No, no. It's her personal assistant."

"Vampires need personal assistants?"

"She's a world class fashion model, David. I explained all that. Mary Plunkett handles her personal needs and lives with her, travels with her."

"So she's a vampire, too?"

"No. She's a devoted mortal servant." Crowman shook his head.

"Okay, Sean, let's get this over with," he said and got out.

Sean joined him and Mary stepped up as they approached the room. She held something wrapped in a silk scarf.

"Evening, Mary," Sean said.

"My mistress wanted you both to see and verify this first," she said and opened the black metal box to reveal the hawthorn.

Sean nodded at it. Crowman smirked and then picked it up and smelled it.

"So this is hawthorn, right?"

"Correct. As I explained, it has the effect of . . ."

"Turning her into a vampire. I know," Crowman finished, now showing impatience. "Can we get on with it?" he asked Mary. She looked at Sean as if to warn him too and then she opened the motel door.

Opal was standing by the bathroom door. She was dressed in a robe and had her hair down. They entered quickly and Sean closed the door.

"This is David Crowman, my immediate supervisor," Sean said.

"Let me make it perfectly clear, Mr. Crowman. Once you see what you see here, you will promise your life on keeping it secret. No one, not even someone as high up in the CIA as you are can protect himself from us."

"Scout's honor," Crowman said dryly, lifting his right hand. He looked like he was fighting back laughter now.

Opal smiled.

"Sean?"

"Go for it," Sean said.

"Mr. Crowman," Opal said approaching him. "Look at me very carefully. Touch me wherever you wish."

David Crowman's shirt collar suddenly became too tight as Opal opened her robe. His breathing slowed and then deepened. His eyes looked like they had lost motor control.

"You're very beautiful," was all he could utter. She took his hand into hers and brought it to her neck and then over her breasts.

"Jesus," he said to Sean.

"Relax," Sean said.

She released his hand and nodded at Mary who stepped forward.

"Sean will explain. Normally, I wouldn't let you see me for more than a few moments, but I understand you will believe we've pulled some sort of magic trick or costume trick on you, so I will ask you to touch me again, to approach, and to look carefully. You will know in your heart, in your very blood, what is true," she added.

Then she plucked out the hawthorn tablet and took a bite of it.

Mary gasped and stepped back as if she thought Opal would literally explode. Crowman caught the action and his slight smile faded quickly.

Right before their eyes, Opal began her ascension. Her body began to swell, her hands thicken and then her fangs began to emerge. Her pallor changed and the softness in her body hardened everywhere. Crowman couldn't swallow, couldn't move. Opal reached for his hand, but he tried to pull back. Her speed was incredible and she grabbed it and held it so tightly, he nearly cried out in pain. She drew him to her and when she lifted him off the ground, he finally cried out like a little girl, pleading for Sean to stop it.

Opal looked at Sean who nodded and then she lowered Crowman to the floor, turned and went into the bathroom.

"Holy shit," Crowman managed. He sounded like someone was squeezing his throat.

"We'll wait for a few minutes" Sean said and went to the television set to turn it on. "Say, Mary, anything to drink?"

He sounded casual, unaffected, but inside he was dying to laugh, especially at the shocked expression still frozen on Crowman's face.

Mary went to the minibar and opened the door. She stepped back so he could see the choices.

"Soda, booze, what, Dave?" Sean asked.

"Give me the scotch straight," Crowman said and sat on the bed. Mary brought it to him. He opened it quickly and downed the small bottle in one gulp.

Sean opened a can of ginger ale. He turned up the television set and sat beside Crowman who looked as pale as a corpse and seemed unable to get his vocal cords vibrating. Finally, he turned to Sean.

"What happens now?"

"She restores. The hawthorn complicates it a little so it takes a little longer than usual. She explained it to me. Right, Mary?"

"Yes sir," Mary said.

"What if she doesn't . . . I mean . . . could she come out of there the way she went in?"

"Mary?" Sean asked.

"No. She'll restore. She always has."

"I can't believe this," Crowman said.

"It does make you question your own sanity."

"She was so strong. She literally picked me up as if I were a baby. What else can she do?"

"I haven't seen it, but when necessary, she can morph into a bat. Unless, that's a joke she's pulling on me. Mary?"

"She can do that, Mr. Waters."

Sean looked at Crowman.

"How did you . . . get her to cooperate like this?"

"I made her an offer she couldn't refuse."

"What?"

"I told her I'd love her forever," Sean said.

Crowman's eyes truly bulged. He rose to get himself another small bottle of scotch. A little over ten minutes later when Opal opened the bathroom door and stepped out, he almost jumped out of his skin, but he sat there mesmerized.

She was as beautiful as she had been.

"Well?" Sean asked him.

He looked at Opal again.

"Welcome to the CIA," he told her.

7.

Opal's smile deepened as she recalled all this, especially the way David Crowman fumbled his words, agreed instantly to her demands and eyed the door that night. She felt confident he wouldn't go out to broadcast this story. He was still in a state of disbelief himself, even when he finally left with Sean.

"I hope he won't be a problem in the morning," she told Sean.

"Not after it all settles in," he replied. "The man's ambitious. He sees an opportunity and won't squander it on gossiping, believe me."

"I have no choice now. And neither do you," she added. "We've just linked our destinies. Are you sure you're comfortable with that?"

"Wouldn't be here if I weren't," he replied.

"What else would you have done, Sean?"

"Probably taken a few aspirins and gone to sleep."

She laughed.

"Nowadays, people believe what they want to believe and not what's true," he added. "It's the old Nazi propaganda plan, the bigger the lie, the easier it is to get people to believe. You simplify and repeat."

"That's not just nowadays," she said. "It's always been the M.O. for mere mortals, and the Nazis, no matter how much credit they want to take, didn't invent it."

"I guess you would know," he said.

And that was how it had all begun.

She stopped smiling and remembering and focused her gaze on the cringing Mary Plunkett as they continued away from Opal's aborted fashion show.

"When we get home, Mary, I want you to go your room and contemplate today's nearly fatal blunder. You need to give it deep thought and review what you could have done differently."

"Yes, Ma'am," Mary said. She was grateful for whatever it was that had put Opal in a merciful mood.

Mary sat back and tried to keep her gaze down. It was still very difficult not to stare at Opal. She knew, however, that she was watching her, even if she had her eyes closed and looked asleep. Those eyes would suddenly pop open, the pupils large, blazing.

"I've told you constantly, Mary. Do not stare at me like that. You draw attention. I can feel your envy, besides, and that's annoying."

"I'm sorry," she said. She had probably apologized over a thousand times this year alone for something she had done or said.

She gazed out the window. They were drawing close to Opal's Connecticut home. It was a two-story folk Victorian with nearly an acre of ground. Opal didn't tell her that many stories about her past, but when they moved into this house, she described how she had taken a lover who owned a similar house outside of Bath, England, close to two hundred years ago.

Mary was always grateful for any anecdotes or information Opal voluntarily provided. She knew from the start that Opal didn't need an adoring mortal so she tried to contain her excitement and admiration and simply show interest. Sometimes Opal really enjoyed telling one of her stories. She could see her reliving it.

"How can you remember so much?" she once asked.

"Even you can remember more than you think you can," Opal told her. "It's scientifically true that mortals have the brain capacity to do far more than they accomplish. We're simply given the capacity to do it all immediately. We don't waste what we've been given."

"Oh," Mary said. She had no idea what the hell Opal meant, but she nodded and looked impressed.

Opal didn't speak again in the limousine until they arrived and both had started toward the entrance.

"I'll come up to see you shortly," she said.

The tone in Opal's voice told Mary she wasn't quite finished with her. This was going to be more than a verbal chastisement. Mary started to offer her excuses again, but stopped instantly when she saw the look in Opal's eyes. It was no use. Forgiveness didn't exist. To Opal the concept was blasphemy because it opened one up to vulnerability. Mary merely nodded and went through the entry way, up the stairs and to her room. The size of it, the beautiful furnishings, her big screen television, her wardrobe, shoes, and her own cosmetics were far beyond anything Mary had imagined she would have. She often reminded herself of the insignificant small world from which she had come. she had and what she was able to do.

And she had accomplished all in a moment, a lucky moment that could have been quite unlucky.

She had been on her first ever vacation out of the United States. She had scrimped and saved, denying herself a better cut of meat, wearing shoes until holes appeared in the soles, never buying any new clothes, and never going to the movies. She had the cheapest possible television service and didn't have a telephone. Who would call her anyway?

She had traveled coach, catching an airline sale to

London. When she had arrived, she had forgotten that she needed to exchange dollars for pounds. The rate confused her. Another American tourists, a nicely dressed elderly man with richly thick white hair and a soft, fatherly smile explained it to her before she got her luggage so she didn't make a fool of herself. Still, it was quite a bit more than she had anticipated. In fact, she found she had to scrimp even more than she had to get here. Going to a really nice restaurant was out of the question. She lived on fast foods and avoided expensive tickets to exhibitions, but at least took in most of the sights she had wanted to see.

One night on her way back to her inexpensive hotel, she heard a single, sharp scream in an alleyway. Why she stepped into it, she would be unable to explain to anyone, even herself. She was certainly not an exceptionally brave person. Something drew her curiosity.

There, under the weak glow of a fixture just above a doorway, she saw what at first looked like a shadow of a pair of huge wings hovering over something. It stepped back and a man in a suit and tie seemed to float to the ground. She stepped forward and the wings shrunk, but whatever it was turned to her and she saw Opal Stone in her vampiric form, huge, neither feminine or masculine, but something in between.

She didn't move. She watched as Opal gradually metamorphosed back to her beautiful self. She was shocked, of course, but she didn't turn to flee. It wasn't only that she was too frightened to move. She surprised herself with her fascination in what she was witnessing.

"Out for a stroll?" Opal had asked stepping toward her. She threw her hair back over her shoulders.

"Just returning to my hotel," she had replied. Her voice didn't even tremble. Opal smiled.

"American?"

"Yes."

"Vacationing?"

She just nodded. Opal was upon her now and in the better light Mary could see how beautiful she was. She looked past her at the body sprawled on the pebble walk.

"He had a little too much sex," Opal said still smiling. Apparently, she had immediately decided Mary had some qualities she could utilize. She asked her detailed, prying questions, neither of them moving much toward the street.

"Doesn't sound like you have much of a life," Opal said.

"I don't," Mary had admitted without hesitation. She looked again at the folded male body. It looked like it was twisted in a way that couldn't be comfortable, maybe not even possible. He'd have to have a broken spine to twist like that, she had thought.

"Is he going to be all right?" she asked.

"Not in this life," Opal had replied. "You're not afraid?"

"Oh, I'm afraid," Mary had admitted and Opal had laughed, really amused.

"Come with me and help me be a fisher of men," Opal had said putting her around her shoulders to turn her back to the street. "I'm at the Ritz this time. I have a suite. I'm hungry. We'll order some filet mignon," she said, "and I have some clothes that will fit you. I'm looking for a new assistant."

"Really?"

Opal had just begun her rise to fame, but Mary wouldn't have known anyway. Woman's designer fashions were as much in her interest as becoming an astronaut. But she would learn quickly. It was still a mystery to Mary what Opal had seen in her, but that was one gift she didn't want to question. Surely she would not base her decision to take her in if she had thought she was simply stunned, but why question it?

Just like what had happened now, there were at least a half dozen times when she had made mistakes and suffered Opal's wrath. None of them were as serious as this one, however. This one had truly put Opal, and, she was right, herself into danger.

I'm such a fool, she thought. I'm careless, stupid, mindless, sloppy, and negligent, she recited, whipping herself with each word. It was her way of fortifying herself for whatever was to come. I deserve whatever happens to me, she concluded and took a deep breath.

Would she fire her, kill her and dispose of her? No one would know and no one would care. What sadder thing was there for a mere mortal, as Opal called them, than to realize your death would have absolutely no impact on anyone or anything, except of course, some hungry worms?

She sat on her bed and stared at the door. She was so frightened that she had to close her eyes. She didn't hear the door open. When she opened her eyes, Opal was standing there before her. She often did that . . . appear so quickly and silently that it seemed she could just materialize.

"Did you understand what I told you in the car? You should realize that if something happens to me, something happens to you, Mary, you will lose everything and more. You won't be spared. You're too involved, too much of a witness. You'd be considered an accomplice to whatever they fantasized."

"I do realize it," Mary said. She kept her arms folded protectively over her small, but perky breasts. She was a little wider than she would like to be in her hips, had thighs that were too big for her size and unfortunately had her excess weight on her waist with a little pouch of a stomach that made her look four months pregnant, maybe five when she was being honest with herself.

She couldn't help it. There were too many delectable temptations. It drove her mad that Opal could eat and drink anything, no matter how rich and fattening, and never gain an ounce. It was foolish of her to try to compete, but she had little will power. Opal found that amusing. Lately however, she occasionally had been helping her with her hair and makeup. Mary had a comely face, childlike but nevertheless as Opal liked to say, "A face with potential." Everyone had some potential hidden so well that most times, he or she didn't know it.

She shivered. In a moment she would know whether she would live or die.

Opal flicked open the small, razor sharp blade in her gold bracelet. An Italian prince in Genoa had given it to her over two hundred years ago. The blade was no more than an inch or so long, but, according to the prince, had been used to slice at least a dozen or so arteries over the years. He claimed he had taken it from a famous femme fatale.

Opal said she knew that it was all fabrication. He was creating the fantastic tale to impress her. She pretended to be impressed and grateful. Mere mortal men were so easy to fool, but she did like the bracelet. However, she soon tired of the prince and killed him in his own bed after he had made mediocre love. To her the punishment for failure to produce orgasms was always a capital crime.

Mary gasped. She knew the small blade's history and its purpose.

Opal handed it to her.

"One way to remember, to drive home your mistake would be for you to give yourself a scar."

"Give myself a scar?"

"Something always there, Mary. This thing about accepting responsibility is not enough. So what? You accept responsibility and then go on as if nothing had happened. Accept it and pay for it and remember it for as long as you're in that body."

Mary took the small blade.

"Where should I . . . I mean . . ."

"I would advise you to put it somewhere you will see every time you undress, Mary."

Mary tried to swallow, but couldn't and gagged for a moment. She looked at the knife. This would hurt.

"I don't want you to forget this mistake. It's too serious. We almost lost it all. You understand, don't you?" Opal emphasized. "I need to know you realize it all."

"Yes, Madame."

"Decide and do it. I haven't got all day."

Mary took a deep breath. A place where she would see it every time she undressed? Mary had her own fantasies and hopes for romance. Eventually, Opal would miraculously turn her into an attractive enough woman to capture a good looking man's attention. Someday, she, too, would find the perfect man, the man who would save her perhaps, take her away safely to live comfortably. It was difficult enough with the figure she had, but to add an ugly scar somewhere he would see it, maybe just when they were to make love . . . it might turn him off.

"I look at my feet almost always," she offered meekly and lifted her foot.

Opal smiled coldly.

"Your feet? Don't be ridiculous, Mary. Get up. Get up!" she ordered.

Mary jumped to her feet.

"Take off your clothes. Go on. Get undressed."

Mary hurried to strip. When she was standing naked, Opal stepped beside her. They both looked at Mary in the full-length mirror.

"Well? I see places you will always see, don't you?"

Not on my breasts, my perky little breasts, Mary thought. She can't mean that.

"Yes, but . . ."

"Do it above your right knee," Opal suggested.

"My knee?" This was better than she had feared.

"That's what I suggested, Mary, unless you have another, more suitable location, something even more visible."

"On no, no."

She looked at her knee and then brought the sharp blade to her skin. Her blood leaped to the surface. Opal sighed at the sight.

"So red, so true. Don't worry. That won't heal without a slight scar," she said taking the blade back. "It's the nature of this metal.

"Close your eyes and concentrate on what you did wrong today," Opal said.

Mary nodded. It hurt like hell, but she didn't cry.

"Don't think of this as nothing much, Mary. The worst death I saw was the death by a thousand cuts. Remember that," Opal said.

Mary nodded. Opal turned and left her. The moment she was gone, Mary hurried into the bathroom to wash and bandage her wound and then looked into the mirror and finally permitted herself a smile of relief.

She could go on. It wasn't over yet, this great ride, this living in a fantasy. She stopped smiling when she envisioned Opal standing behind her looking at her through the mirror.

She didn't have to say it. She thought it and loudly, too. *God help me if I make another serious mistake.*

Opal changed clothes. She liked the tight, thin leather black turtleneck blouse and slacks when she metamorphosed into a bat and back again, and tonight she would do just that. The clothes still fitting and undisturbed was part of the magic, particularly this outfit. It simply felt like the proper outfit for a kill and besides, she looked damn sexy in it. *I'm ever the model*, she thought, *worried about my appearance, even in my classic form.*

She called Crowman.

As soon as he answered, she said, "And?"

It was as if their earlier conversation had simply been put on hold. He was used to her by now. There would be no small talk.

"Ugarte comes out of Morocco by way of a company out of Madrid supposedly producing a new line of cosmetics. It's a cover," he said.

"No kidding? I didn't need the CIA to arrive at that conclusion, Mr. Crowman."

"Yes, of course. Four of our men over there are taking it out as we speak."

"And Ugarte?"

"Apparently, he left the show soon after he was told you weren't going to appear on the catwalk. Was it possible he was testing to find out if you were more vulnerable than you were in the past?"

"You grasp things fast," she said.

She was dripping with sarcasm, but he responded with, "That's my training."

"His limousine driver didn't know where he was," he added. "We're sure he was telling the truth."

"Of course he was telling the truth. Ugarte no longer needed a limousine. You know what he is if you referred to the material Sean Waters and I gave you," she said.

She had provided him with very rare and unique pictures of her enemies, including some photographs and drawings. Of course, someone who didn't know the truth about her would probably think of them as pictures from a Hollywood B film.

"Oh yes. I have that all in my personal safe here."

"Did you ever refer to it? Don't you believe any of it?" She shook her head, remembering how both she and Sean had little faith in Crowman's ability to digest and understand all he was being told and shown. Despite what she had demonstrated for him, he always had this look of incredulity, the look of a man who had hoped what he saw was a dream.

"Yes, yes, of course, and based on that, I was thinking that maybe he figured we'd be on the Madrid location by now and returned to prevent it. He could get there that quickly, couldn't he? I mean, I'm not really that clear about . . ."

"No, he couldn't. That's too far. Besides, he doesn't care about them. He wouldn't waste his time protecting anyone. Of course he's still here. He's tracked me down. I can't say I never expected it, and I'm even a bit surprised at how long it has taken him. However, if I don't take care of this, I may very well have to change my identity again and I'm quite comfortable in my present identity."

"Oh, I see. I'm sorry. Well, what are you going to do about tonight, I mean our . . . your assignment?"

"If you don't hear from me in two hours, consider the mission uncompleted."

"And the reason?"

"I'll be dead."

"Well, shouldn't I send some people out there to provide protection?"

"To protect me? What would you tell them without exposing me?"

"I could . . . they would know nothing more about you than anyone else knows."

"Mr. Crowman, really? What could they possibly do for me that I couldn't do for myself? Besides, you'd be sending them to a certain death if you put them up against Ugarte. Use them for more sensible assignments," she said and hung up.

I have to tell him this? She thought. What an idiot.

Oh, Sean, why did I make such a promise to you? More important, why do I feel I have to keep such a promise to a mere mortal?

She went to the window and looked out at the night. She heard nothing. Of course, he's probably here already, she thought. I had to come by limousine, but he didn't.

She realized he was probably waiting for her to metamorphose into her bat form. It would be easier for him to take her when she was a bat. She had heard many stories of their kind being trapped as bats, despite their speed and ability to maneuver on a dime.

She sniffed the air. He was nearby. He could be just outside, waiting with his crossbow. In fact, she had been both surprised and grateful he had decided to come at her with a spear in Eze. He was an excellent archer and could easily drive a wooden arrow right through her heart when she was in her bat form or otherwise. She'd come tumbling down to earth and return to her human form in seconds before decomposing. That much of the folklore was correct.

This was going to be a very tricky maneuver. She opened the window, deliberately making as much noise as she could. Then she stepped back and reached under her bed to pull out the bat she kept in a cage for just such an occasion. It comforted her to have them around in all her homes. There was an explainable affinity between them. The moment she grabbed the cage, the bat came to life and charged at the thin bars.

"Patience, my pet," she told it. "Don't be in such a rush to die."

She brought it to the window, studied the grounds a moment and then opened the cage. Instantly, it flew out and just as quickly as it appeared, the arrow, seeming to be alive itself, shot up like a rocket and pierced the creature. It tumbled downward exactly as she had envisioned herself doing. Ugarte came out from behind the oak tree and ran eagerly toward the falling bat. She saw he had popped his stark white wings out of his wing bones. He wanted to be in full regalia for his historic kill. His kind would treat him like a king for taking out one as accomplished as Opal Stone.

His kind, she thought with the traditional vampire curse attached: *may his ashes reformulate in hell and burn again and again.* Ugarte was one of the deformed vampires, parasitic, who dug up fresh graves to feed on the dead and then cover the graves to hide their disgusting feasting. They were an abomination, direct descendants of Cain, distortions, the Supernatural's cruel joke, ugly beyond words, Ghoul Birds as they were known throughout time because of their wings and their frequenting of graveyards.

For as long as she knew, she and her kind were mortal enemies of Ghoul Birds. Whatever the reason, there it was, this eternal hatred of each other, this eternal pursuit and battle. Maybe it was another Celestial joke.

Ugarte stood over the dead bat, waiting for the anticipated metamorphosis and the subsequent decomposition. Then he would feed on a real vampire corpse. They believed it insured their immortality.

He's practically drooling, she thought. Only the hunger for a kill and the instinct of self-defense could trigger so quickly a metamorphosis in her. It took only moments. Then she leaped from her four story high bedroom window, soaring down and onto him before he realized she was falling from the same sky as the bat. He looked up as she sliced her right palm through his neck at the Adams Apple. His head rolled off, his eyes bulging with surprise. She scooped up his torso before it collapsed and carried it to the front entrance.

She heard him screaming, screaming at his loss of torso. Without delay, she charged into the house, the torso under her right arm, and cast it, wings and all, into the gas fireplace. It crackled and spit in the flames.

Upstairs, recuperating in her bed, Mary Plunkett heard the unearthly scream and gasped. She got out of bed and looked down to see what looked like a human head burst into flames and roll about the lawn.

Madame has defeated someone else, she thought, another one of them. There was a definite note of pride sounding inside her despite how she had been treated and threatened. It also gave her a sense of power and security. She was with the right person, if she could call her a person, after all.

Without any further thought, she returned to her bed and turned on the television set, hopefully to catch a romantic movie. There was really nothing else for her to do tonight.

And she was as safe and snug as could be.

Why even the pain above her knee had gone away.

8.

"All's well that ends well," Opal told David Crowman. Normally, she wouldn't have bothered to call, but she felt especially proud of herself tonight and she wanted to reinforce her power and expertise so Crowman better would understand how inferior he was; they all were.

"Meaning?" Crowman asked.

Where does Sean get the patience to deal with such bureaucrats? She gave thanks that there was nothing in the form of an organization for her and her kind. All that bound them was instinctive. No rules had to be adjusted or new ones created. There was no voting, no dictating. They were all leaders and they were all equal citizens of their own kind.

What other form of life beside mortals needed laws passed and evaluated. Do bees have a supreme court? Do they change their behavior after a raucous political argument?

In a way her disdain for humanity was helpful. She never suffered from a single pang of conscience. She was as free of guilt as a human being enjoying a succulent piece of Chateaubriand.

"Ugarte's no longer a threat. I'll be on my way to carry out the mission tomorrow."

"Oh. Good. Thank you. Is there anything . . ."

"If you have the opportunity, you can tell Sean all is well. There's nothing more for you to do or say," she said in the tone of someone giving him permission to die and then she hung up.

The following morning she was off on her private jet to Washington, D.C. Although she wouldn't sleep overnight, she had arranged a suite at the Watergate. As soon as they arrived, she took a nap while Mary arranged her things.

Her target was supposed to be at this dance club frequented by Middle Eastern diplomats, although the music and the food were certainly not Middle Eastern, and the women who were brought there or went there on their own were nowhere as inhibited or intimidated as they were in the countries from which many of the diplomats came. They were like communists or anti-Americans who secretly enjoyed American products, movies, books and foods. Their positions enabled them to get away from the restrictions they imposed on their fellow citizens. What hypocrites, Opal thought, but then again, when and where had she not experienced hypocrisy? It was as natural to mere mortals as was drinking water, she thought.

When she prepared herself later in the day, she chose one of her sexiest dresses, a curve-sculpting bandage fabric and bustier design. The hem flounces created a sexy mermaid look. She wore her hair down with only a pair of diamond drip earrings. No necklace brought more attention to her bare shoulders and low top with almost half of her breasts exposed.

Of course, her fame gave her entry to any place anytime, even the most restricted clubs. These days because of her television work and the magazine spreads and covers, someone in authority almost always recognized her. Most were surprised and delighted she had decided to go to their places. It usually helped her get the attention of whomever had been designated the target. Like any full time agent even though she wasn't one, she didn't know precisely why he or she was a target. Sean told her it was to be assumed and accepted on face value that the agency wouldn't unleash their people unless it was for good cause, for national security, no matter how tenuous the relationship. Someone somewhere had decided it was a necessary kill and that was it. In one way or another, Opal thought, they all can't get away from, *Ours is not to reason why. Ours is but to do or die. Why am I a part of this?*

She knew the answer . . . love, but she still couldn't believe she had agreed to the arrangement and carried out the assignments. To rationalize, she did tell herself it made the hunt a little more interesting and more fun. Tonight was no exception. None of her kind had any other purpose for a kill other than to feed and stay healthy and alive. However, the concept of a greater good was not only alien; it was ridiculous.

She knew what her target looked like, of course. The moment she approached the bar, he turned from the woman and the man he was with and looked her way. He wasn't thin; but he was slim with black eyes too big for his narrow, boney face in which a mouth looked more like a gash just below his long, narrow nose. If he wasn't a man of some power, he would never be able to be with the good looking women he prayed upon, she thought. How typical. The feminine pride in her raised her disgust. This would be easier than she had imagined and she was primed for a good feed. She had actually held back for this even though she had come across many delicious possibilities, especially today, which was a carryover from the hawthorn in the lipstick crisis.

She caught his gaze the way a baseball pitcher might catch a line drive and threw hers back at him. It was like casting a fish line and hook, seeing his mouth open, the hook slip in, and his mouth close. He rose, excused himself and sauntered over to her with his awkward gait. With each step, his torso looked like it might topple. He was a bit tipsy.

"Good evening. We have met before, I hope?"

"I don't think so, but that doesn't mean I don't want to meet you now," she said.

She could actually see the connections in his brain and feel the heat as his libido activated. How obvious they were, these so-called sophisticated men, theses suave, educated world travelers who thought so highly of themselves. They didn't realize that with the expensive covering aside, they all had the same wiring, rich and poor, educated and un-educated, powerful and weak. What was it Sean always says? "They all put on their pants one leg at a time."

She smiled at the memory of when they had made love at her swimming pool at her Palm Springs house, but the am-bassador mistook it for his pleasing her. How arrogant, she thought. He believes his mere presence is enough to amuse me.

"I was joking with you, of course," he said. "I know who you are. Just recently, I saw you on the cover of Runway Magazine."

"You read such magazines?"

"No, no, I don't, but my wife does."

"You don't object?"

"Me? No. I'm enlightened. My wife can read what she wants. I don't treat her the way the West sees Muslim men treat their women."

"That's very democratic of you."

"Pakistan is a democracy."

It didn't surprise her that he thought she should know who he was too.

"Of sorts," she said and he laughed.

"There isn't a democracy in the world to which you couldn't apply that comment."

He looked back at the table he had been at and then at her. "I'm with some boring people out of necessity."

She pretended to look about the bar and the tables. "Someone was supposed to meet me here, but he's not here and I despise being made to wait."

"As should a woman like you. He must be a complete idiot."

"His wife thinks so," she said and the ambassador laughed. "Might I offer you a drink?"

"I didn't think you drank alcoholic beverages, especially a high government Muslim official like yourself who has to live by example."

"Ah, so you really do know who I am?"

"I think my housekeeper had a magazine with your picture in it. I encourage her to keep up with world events. I'm enlightened, too."

He roared and then leaned closer to whisper. "I'm not drinking. I'm offering you a drink."

She could easily smell the alcohol in his breath. Irish whiskey, she thought.

"That's still encouraging sin, is it not?"

"Like good Christians and Jews, I sometimes indulge in the forbidden."

"Again, how democratic of you." She nodded at the table behind the one he was at. "Those your bodyguards?"

"A necessary annoyance. What would you like?"

"Champagne. I see they carry my favorite one, Moet and Chandon," she said and turned to the bar. He sat beside her and ordered her drink and a plain soda water for himself.

How obviously phony, she thought. What they'll do to impress.

"So, you have been to Pakistan?"

"Not for some time," she said. She had been there one

hundred and twelve years ago, but she certainly wouldn't tell him that.

"It's a much maligned country. There is much to recommend it. We have landscapes that rival any in the world, stretching from the Arabian Sea. There are sites that go back as far as any in ancient Egypt and Mesopotamia."

"I like your enthusiasm about your own country. Maybe you will be kind enough to show me some of it someday."

"It would be my pleasure. It's not such a farfetched thought. Our women have become more and more Westernized and I'm sure many, like my wife, follow the fashion market. Perhaps you will come there to do a fashion show."

"And you approve of this increasingly westernizing of your women?"

Their drinks were served. He shrugged.

"I'm just a poor government official, more like what you call here a career diplomat. I take orders. My opinions have all been formed, organized and delivered. Why? Do you keep up with world events, too?"

"Politics bores me," she said.

"What doesn't bore you? What fascinates a woman like you who most likely has seen so much and enjoyed so much?"

"Men, but refined, interesting men."

"I'm sure you don't lack for any."

"No, but I'm very particular."

"As you should be."

"Actually, some things about politics intrigue me. I've been to many embassies, but never yours."

"That's an oversight. Perhaps I can correct it." She looked around.

"Well, my friend is rather rude not showing up on time, or even close."

"You would go there now?"

"I certainly won't sit around waiting for him," she said taking a long sip of her drink to indicate she would leave immediately.

He brightened with expectation.

"My limousine is right outside."

"How convenient. I sent mine away, expecting a long, exciting and satisfying evening," she said, not hiding what that would entail.

"Well don't give up on the hope," he said.

"I never do," she replied. "Cynicism is such a drag. Pessimist get older faster," she added and he laughed.

"I'll keep that in mind every time I get a dark thought."

"You don't have any now?"

"Hardly," he said. He actually licked his lips.

This was so easy that she almost got too bored to continue, but an assignment was an assignment. Sean would shake his head and tell her, we close our eyes and swallow when we have to. It comes with the territory. This isn't my territory, however, she thought but never said.

She took another long sip of her champagne and glanced at him. He looked stunned by his luck. She touched his left hand and the ring he wore.

"Very beautiful. I saw one very much like it once . . . on an Arabian prince."

"Maybe it's the same ring."

"Maybe."

She finished her drink.

"Ready?"

"Always," she said offering him her hand. When he took it, she could feel the heat and even sensed the movement of the blood in his veins.

He offered her his arm and escorted her out, taking pleasure in the envious eyes that followed their progress toward the door. He couldn't resist turning back and smiling at the hungry wolves, a little bit of swaggering.

One of the bodyguards rode up front with driver. Another sat across from them and two others followed in a second vehicle. Ironically, it annoyed and even angered her that he wasn't nervous. It didn't surprise her, however. Throughout the centuries, she found that men of power were always this arrogant, believing themselves to be invulnerable. They lived in protective bubbles and could destroy or radically change another person's life with the flick of a pen or a nod of the head. Such men traipsed over places reserved for the gods or God, depending on what century she was in. They muddied these deific places. When she took out one of these men, she not only satisfied her blood thirst, but felt justified and imagined she had deific approval. She didn't exactly tell him, but it was precisely this feeling that helped Sean get her to serve his beloved country.

She was certain if anything differentiated her from the others of her kind, it was this. Perhaps she thought too highly of herself. So what? What was the danger now?

She didn't like the way the ambassador's bodyguard stared at her. She could feel his disdain. In his eyes she was just going to be another sexual conquest, used and discarded like just so much garbage to be recycled perhaps and enjoyed by another powerful or rich man. She thought she would like to cut off the bodyguard's head, but of course realized she couldn't physically harm anyone else without bringing all sorts of trouble, investigations, and political crisis. This was the main disadvantage to doing this so-called good work. She wasn't sure how much longer she could keep it up out of her love for Sean Waters. Actually, she wasn't sure how much longer the love affair would go. It already had lasted longer than any she had ever had. She had no doubt that someday, it would be over and he would diminish and get filed in her library of lovers. It was, after all, as inevitable as death was for mortals.

When they arrived, guards stepped aside, servants rushed to do the ambassador's bidding. Aside from the standard devices to detect weapons, there was nothing else to prevent her from having full entry and access to any place in the embassy. How powerful sex is, she thought and for a moment was philosophical about it and its historical use. Except for the femme fatales she had met over the centuries, who else used sex as a weapon as well as her own kind had and would? It made her proud, but also continued to diminish any sense of guilt she could possibly experience. If we weren't meant to be this way, we wouldn't be, she thought? That was as far as she would go with any moral considerations.

She was taken with the ambassador's patience when it came to this assignation he had envisioned for himself, but then she thought that men with his power and authority had no reason to rush anything. Everything waited on them and nothing was ever too late. He paraded her before the paintings they had in exhibition, the artifacts, and the large photographs of world leaders who had visited and signed important documents at the embassy. He particularly wanted her to see him with these people. There was an exhibition of historical Pakistani dress and jewelry. She remembered and recognized some things, but didn't reveal it.

Finally, he worked his way into his private quarters. They went into the living room first.

"I'm afraid I can't offer you an alcoholic beverage," he said. "Would you like a Rooh Afza. It's a grenadine style syrup and . . ."

"I know what it is. Not necessary. You're alone?"

"My wife is back in Islamabad for some family events. We are often separated."

She checked the windows and looked down at International Court. The street was moderately busy for this time of the evening.

"Doesn't it get a little lonely?" she asked with her back to him.

"I'm too busy to be lonely," he said.

She could feel the heat of his body from across the room. The scent of his blood permeated her nostrils and stirred her appetite. She felt her ascension starting.

"You are a very, very beautiful woman, Opal," he continued. He was coming closer now, moving in for the seduction he surely had fantasized from the moment he set eyes on her.

In fact, he was so involved in this fantasy, he didn't seem the incremental changes in her body, but by the time he put his hand on her shoulder, he realized she was taller than she first had seemed. How could that be? And the shoulder . . . it was actually growing under his palm.

He gasped when she turned around and for a moment, he lost his voice and nearly lost control of his bladder. Before he could turn to run, she thrust her hand and seized his neck, squeezing it so hard, he couldn't breathe. His eyes bulged as she brought her mouth and those fangs down on his neck. His inability to push away or stop her was terrifying enough, but the feel of her teeth penetrating an artery threw him into a panic. His whole body shook.

Her left hand went under his right arm pit and she lifted him as she usually did so she would be more comfortable feeding. He wiggled and squirmed like a fish out of water, but nothing he did had any effect on her. Finally, mercifully, he passed out. She drew her last drops and then secreted the balm that instantly closed the two gaping holes. That done, she dropped him gently to the floor.

It took a good ten minutes for her to return to form this time. She vaguely noticed that it was taking longer these days. She could recall it happening in less than five minutes, eight or nine at the most, when it wasn't caused by hawthorn, that is. I guess this is what old age means to a vampire, she thought with some amusement. When she was ready, she fixed her hair, straightened her dress and then screamed.

The bodyguard who had ridden in the rear of the limousine with them burst in first, followed by the one who had ridden up front. She flopped in a chair and waved her fingers at the ambassador, acting as if she couldn't speak.

"What happened?" the first bodyguard demanded.

"Get an ambulance," she finally cried. "He gasped and collapsed in front of me."

He immediately started CPR.

Other servants came rushing up. More guards appeared. Not having any success with the CPR, the first bodyguard signaled his companion and they lifted the ambassador off the floor and set him gently on the sofa. Someone went for a cold wash cloth to put on his forehead, which was a pathetic gesture. The ambassador's personal secretary arrived and immediately after looking at the ambassador went to Opal to question her.

She described how they were having a nice time together, implying he was perhaps more aroused than anything, and then suddenly, he gasped, clutched his chest and collapsed. She put on an Academy Award performance, sobbing, gasping. She was given a cold glass of water and taken aside to be comforted. A while later, the paramedics arrived and began their own attempt at CPR. They were as unsuccessful, of course, and quickly carried the ambassador out and to the ambulance.

After they left, the ambassador's personal secretary asked Opal if she wanted to be taken anywhere. She said she had called for taxi. It was there minutes later. The personal secretary followed her out.

"Maybe it would be for the best if you weren't mentioned in the reports," he suggested.

"Very wise," she said. "For all involved." He nodded.

"However, do give the ambassador's wife my sympathies," she said, sounding as though she actually meant it.

The look on his face almost made her laugh. She got into the taxi quickly and called Crowman.

"It's done," she said.

"A grateful nation thanks you," he replied, almost in a whisper.

I didn't do it for a grateful nation, she thought. *I was hungry and it pleases Sean.* She almost voiced her thoughts, but swallowed them back, hung up and sat back.

She laughed thinking about the autopsy soon to be performed. One thing they would learn quickly was that this Muslim had alcohol in his blood. They had a whole laundry list of things to cover up.

The dirty sinner, she thought and continued to laugh about all the little ironies until she arrived at the Watergate, her favorite Washington D.C. hotel ever since the day she had met Sean.

How she missed him.

She would call and describe the events of the evening. He so enjoyed the details of her seduction and set up. She smiled thinking about his appreciation of her.

They were far apart this evening, but at least they could share a good kill. How many couples could do that?

9.

Since their wonderful reunion in Virginia Beach, whenever Sean and she could, they celebrated her successful completion of an assignment with a trip to the sea. The resort they chose depended on where they were at the time. A little more than a year after they had met, they had to go to Bayeux in Normandy and this time decided to combine work and pleasure. She had quickly rented a beachside villa. It was very close to where the target was staying.

The Company had tracked an American mole in the state department who was working for the Chinese. He was in Normandy for a meet. It was important he not die a violent death because they didn't want the Chinese to know he had been discover.

By now Sean and Crowman believed Opal was their best and fastest dispenser of such surreptitious lethal punishment. With her, no secret chemicals, no convoluted action was necessary to make it look like an accident. In fact, hardly any planning was necessary to bring down a target. However, Sean thought the mole was going to be a challenge for Opal because he was gay.

"Why is that a challenge?" she asked.

"No feminine seduction powers will work on this guy."

"I hate to ruin your fantasy, but I don't necessarily bother with seduction all the time, Sean. I do it because it amuses me and builds up my anticipation the same way you get excited on the way to a lobster dinner," she told him.

"True, but your feminine guile gets you easier access normally. I'm sure you'd agree, right?"

"Got me you," she said and he laughed.

There was a real lightness to their relationship now that he loved. It was as if as long as they were in that zone together, he was safe. Once in a while, he would have that far-off, deeply thoughtful look, however. She knew what he was thinking, but usually she didn't pursue it. This one time, on their way to the beaches to look at the war memorials and the cemeteries, she asked him.

"One cc of type A positive for your thoughts," she said. "I was just thinking that I'm like someone going with someone with multiple personality syndrome. I'm not sure who you'll be in an hour."

"I've provided you with enough symptoms to be warned," she said smiling.

How crazy to find that amusing, he realized.

"Yes, but besides that, it's not that reassuring having an affair with someone you know will outlive you by a few centuries."

He was right. After all, he was the first mere mortal with whom she had a love affair who knew her second and truer identity, without her feeding on him, that is. Her original concerns returned, the concerns that at first convinced her to run from him. Was this eventually going to prove to be a serious mistake? And if so, what did it mean for her own longevity to have such deep trust in any mere mortal? When had they ever proven trustworthy in the past?

"You're thinking too much. Remember your Shakespeare, 'Yon Cassius thinks too much. Such men are dangerous.' I saw an original production of Julius Caesar in London. When I say original, I mean it and it was very impressive."

He looked at her with surprise.

"How do you remember all this?"

"My personal assistant often asks the same question. She's become quite annoying about it, actually. I hesitate to tell her anything about my past these days."

"So? What did you tell her in the beginning when she realized your incredible memory?"

"It's who we are. Some things are best left unexplained with scientific or factual answers."

"Maintain the mystery?"

"Always."

"We both have to be like tight-rope walkers now, Sean. We don't look down. We just move forward. No one lives in the immediate present as firmly as a tight-rope walker. If he or she starts thinking about the past or the future beyond the next step taken, it's disaster. Besides, what's better than the here and now?"

"Maybe us poor mortals aren't built for that as well as you and yours are. Besides, there's no drama if there's no past or future at the moment. We have to compare. Right?"

"Speak for yourself."

"Always do. I'm not oblivious to the fact that you and I are almost from different planets. In fact, maybe we are. That might explain you and yours."

"So stop the car and I'll be out and be gone," she said. Even she was surprised at her burst of anger. She could count on the fingers of one hand how many times she had been emotionally disturbed in a relationship with a mere mortal, how often one of them actually had gotten to her. Damn, she thought. I did make a mistake.

"Hey, calm down. Aren't you suddenly the more sensitive one," he said smiling. "Don't you know stress can kill even you? Maybe not today or tomorrow, but sometime within the next hundred years."

She stared at him and then she broke into a laugh.

"It is ludicrous to think one of you mere mortals could have so dramatic an effect on me."

"Oh really. How about this? Could it be that you are having real feelings for me, feelings that will meet the test of time? I mean beyond my hot blood and sex?" he asked. He wasn't kidding. He was genuinely interested.

She lowered her chin and raised her eyes.

"Now you want to analyze a vampire? Next you'll set me up with a therapist."

He shrugged.

"Why not? I've had some good psychological warfare training. Let's start. When did you first realize you were a vampire?"

"When I found my teeth in someone's neck." Sean shook his head.

"You're never going to be serious about this stuff, are you?"

"Seek not to know. I just told you. Forget the past. Today is everything," she said very firmly. "Don't keep challenging me on this."

He nodded, still holding his smile, but perhaps not as firmly. Later, when they were walking hand in hand on Omaha Beach, she paused to look out at the sea and it was his turn to wonder about her thoughts.

"What has you so pensive?" he asked.

For a moment she didn't respond. All of his previous questions had put her in a philosophical mood. She was afraid of it. Too many questions were raised and stirring up philosophical discussions always led to sadness. Experience had taught her that tragedy, after all, came only to those who could think, envision, and ponder their own existence against so vast a universe. It was almost better to live and think like a lower form of life with no memory of the past and no vision of the future. Why couldn't she get him to understand or was that truly beyond mere mortals?

Nevertheless, this place, this great battle in Normandy during the Second World War which reminded her of so many she had seen and heard about, kept her thoughtful.

"C'mon. Tit for tat. What are you thinking?" he pursued.

"That day of the Allies Normandy invasion, death came in like some great storm out of the sea," she said. "I can hear it roaring in with the tide."

"No, it was waiting on shore. Sitting in bunkers."

"Whatever. All I have known in human history is brutality. I have met very few mortals that I can say truly emulated Jesus or any of the wonderful prophets. Men and women have to isolate themselves from this everyday world in order to find that kind of peace and contentment."

"And? I know you have a point here. What is it?"

"It brings no surprise to me that I exist, that my kind are out there. I suppose that's what I'm saying."

Sean nodded.

"What?" she said seeing the way his gaze moved over and over her face.

"You're so beautiful it hurts. I ache for you as if I had sword in my chest."

"See? Even expressing your love, you have to refer to something violent. It's in your nature so I'm not so abhorrent, not so far from you and your kind. It's all right," she said quickly, kissing him when his smile faded. "You see my beauty in the lap of the danger and it excites you to come nearer. You're like a bullfighter facing the bull. In that moment before the bull actually charges, the bullfighter must approximate the highest sense of life. He comes very close to what I can feel and you can feel this moment. A slight movement here or there and he is in the arms of death."

"And you're saying I am in that sort of danger when I'm with you?"

"Always," she said. "And that should enhance the experience for you."

"I thought you told me you have control of yourself."

"Oh, I've lost it a few times here and there over the last few centuries."

"Thanks. There's a nice way for you to build my confidence in this relationship."

"Too frightened to go on or too curious and excited?"

"I'll let you know when I know. That is, if I'm still alive."

She laughed and kissed him.

"I really do love you, Sean Waters. Being with you makes it all feel . . ."

"Like?"

"Like nothing else has happened; nothing else matters. Why am I so blessed, considering who and what I am?"

"Yours is not to question why," he said. "Remember?"

"When you stop questioning, you're ready to fertilize flowers or weeds."

She held him closer. They walked on silently. She remembered thinking that the sound of the ocean, the roar of the waves, had not changed for hundreds of years. Perhaps there was something yet eternal about this existence, she thought, something more than my alliance with death, my service to the Grim Reaper.

That night she wanted to make the best love she had ever made. He knew it and for a moment looked terrified that he would not live up to her expectations, actually her needs. She put her forefinger on his lips when he hesitated.

"Don't worry, my love. You cannot disappoint me."

"Nor can you me," he whispered.

She didn't say it, but she thought, I hope not.

However, she didn't have to hope. Every time Sean made love to her, he was amazed at the softness of her skin, the sweet test of her lips, the lushness of her breasts and magic in her eyes. Since the first time he had met her and the time he introduced David Crowman to her, he had never seen her in her vampire form, but those previous two times were more than enough to embed itself in his mind forever. Those times her skin looked scaly, more like a reptile's skin with a yellowish tint. He imagined every part of her body was hard, her muscles like steel, her nails truly tiny knives.

Now, when he made love to her, it was as if he were sinking into a soft, mushroom cloud. Her lips were delightfully demanding and her breath perfumed with a scent that could have made him hard and hungry by itself. Her touch was so exciting that he felt as if he had developed dozens of new erroneous zones.

But it wasn't only the feel of her body, the scent of her skin and breath that brought him to new heights. It was the way she moved, turning their love making into an erotic symphony, using his body as she would a finely tuned instrument. He found himself reaching back deeply into his manhood to find a little more sexual energy, a little more endurance. His cry at the end was really a cry of disappointment, the sort of disappointment a long distance runner might have if he collapsed before he had reached the finishing line. Only, every time they made love, that finishing line went farther out, just a little beyond his reach. She kept raising the bar.

He turned over in disgust.

"What's your problem?" she asked.

"My peter has petered out before I so desired."

"But not before I so desired," she said.

He turned back.

"Seriously?"

"Scout's honor." She raised her palm. He smiled and pressed his against it.

"You know, I had this dream about you and me."

"Here it goes. You are determined to be an amateur psychiatrist when it comes to us."

"No, really. It was quite nice, not analytical. Not a Freudian dream. In this dream, because we made love, I began to . . ."

"Become like me, one of us?"

"Yes. You've heard that before?"

"Never."

How could she emphasize that he was the only one with whom she had developed a relationship and revealed herself without taking her lover's life? It would either make him too confidant or too paranoid to continue. She wanted to see neither. She desired only the status quo, but in her heart, she knew he would want more and that could certainly bring tragedy.

"Funny," she continued. "I had the same dream only for me it was quite the opposite. I could no longer ascend and therefore, became a mere mortal with a limited life span."

"Did it make you unhappy? I imagine to you it would be like a bird falling in love with a man and having to give up flight."

She laughed.

"Very good. You read my thoughts. The truth is, I'm undecided. We have a so-called curse, I'm told. If one of us should truly fall head over heels in love with a mere mortal, we could lose our powers. It's sort of what happens in the Biblical tale of Samson and Delilah."

"You've referred to that one before."

"It teaches a good lesson. He lost his strength; I could lose immortality."

"Yeah, but yours isn't in your hair? Is it?"

"No. I imagine however, that there are some mere mortal woman so into their hairdo, that it would be more important."

He laughed.

"So we know this vampire myth is not true then."

"Oh, and how, pray tell?"

"Well, you're head over heels in love with me and nothing's changed."

She smiled and looked away.

"Aren't you?" he asked, sounding a small note of fear and disappointment.

She turned back to him and smiled.

"I'm as much in love with you as I've ever been with any mere mortal man, maybe a little more."

"Doesn't sound promising," he said. He leaned back again and looked up at the ceiling.

"Now you see? You've gone and made yourself depressed. I warned you about thinking too much."

"No, no. On the contrary. It's a challenge and I love a challenge."

"You could have fooled me," she said and put her forefinger on his heart, "and that would have been a first."

She leaned over him, her breasts grazing his chest and then they kissed. He closed his eyes. Was he ever more content? Was this an evil thing he was doing? Where did it rank in order with the many unconventional and certainly unchristian-like acts he had performed in service to his country?

"It's getting late," she said. "I should be off to his hotel."

"Silly question, but you don't need any help, do you?"

"I love questions that answer themselves," she said.

"I'm glad you're doing this. Are you happy about it? You're knocking off an evil guy."

"Honest?"

"Whenever anyone says that, I'm sorry I asked."

"For us there is no evil guy, Sean. Good and evil are fantasies invented by your religions. When we're not who we really are, we play by your rules or I should say, the rules governing where we are at the time. What's evil to some of you is good to others. Not every one of you believes for example, that the ends justify the means. Wasn't it your poet Walt Whitman who said, *Do I contradict myself? Very well, then I contradict myself, I am large, I contain multitudes.*"

"A philosophic vampire," Sean said smiling. "I'm getting a real Liberal Arts education hanging around with you."

"Just another perk. Anyway, why don't you get something to drink. Relax. I'll be back in an hour or so," she told him.

He watched her get up and slip into her black blouse and slacks. She returned to kiss him and then she left.

She knew her target was up in his hotel room and hoped this would be quick with no distractions or complications. She felt impatience swelling inside her. She had an appetite for new blood. Of course, she needed it to sustain herself, to keep her youth and beauty, but this was more like eating for the sake of eating and not dining. This was nothing to savor. She hadn't told him the whole truth. She had no desire for this pursuit. It was more like swooping down like a bat on some unaware victim. For centuries she never thought much about the victims. They were merely a source of energy, life. She gave them as much thought as mere mortals gave cows and chickens.

She felt no guilt ever, so she had to conclude that her kind had no conscience. She did avoid praying upon children. Her logic for that, however, was the same logic a fisherman used when he threw a small size fish back in the water. Let it grow to provide a more substantial meal. She doubted fisherman thought, oh, the poor little thing. I can't kill this. No, it was simply more practical to let the crop develop, and that's what her victims had been to her most of the time, her crop.

Although she didn't feel she had any sense of conscience, she found she really did have strong enough emotion to care deeply for Sean. She didn't think it was purely and only sexual. She genuinely enjoyed his company, his sense of humor, and his manly focus. Of course, as she had told him, she had no allegiance to any country or cause. If he had viewed human history as closely as she had and been involved in so many versions of what they called governments, he might have the same cynical opinions. No, there was no doubt. Her desire to carry out the assignments was purely to please Sean. She wanted to be important to him, to win his respect and so his enemies became hers.

And that feeling, that need was real. It impressed her. Maybe he had affected a major change in her after all, something she never believed a mere mortal could do. Or as she thought many times when she was with him as well as afterward, maybe she was becoming more and more like the crop. That could be very dangerous.

She entered the boutique French hotel as quietly as possible. She was in luck because the desk clerk was busy with some German tourists who were lodging a complaint. The clerk didn't see her slip through the lobby to the small stairway. She could be as silent as a snake anyway, slithering on air, maneuvering as discreetly as a shadow over the wall. At the top of the stairway, she turned right to go down the short corridor to the victim's room.

Pausing in a corner, she scooped out the piece of Hawthorn from the plastic bag and consumed it. It took a little longer than she had anticipated, but when it finally kicked in, it felt like she had wandered into a hurricane.

Moments later, it was easy to pick up his voice through the walls. He was on the phone. She waited, still impatient, hovering in the shadows, and the moment he hung up, she knocked on his door. She could have easily torn it off its hinges, but this had to be as silent and quick as possible with absolutely no evidence of any confrontation.

"Yes?" he said without opening the door. His suspicion was justified, of course. He had not been expecting anyone.

She spoke quickly in Chinese telling him she must see him and give him an important document. Hearing the dialect was convincing enough for him. He opened the door. He was a short, stocky man, balding with beady brown eyes and thick orange lips. Before he could utter a cry or even attempt to close the door, she swept in and over him, pressing her lips to his to suck out his breath. He gasped and folded in her arms like soft putty and she kicked the door closed.

As she continued to ascend, his eyes registered his terror. When she pierced his neck, she lifted him and held him up as if he were an ear of corn. Gulping, instead of sipping continuously, she drove him quickly into unconsciousness. All resistance died and his arms fell to his sides. It wasn't a good kill in her terms, far too quick, making her feel like a glutton.

When she had fed enough to do the damage and satisfy her need, she lowered him to his bed and watched the bloody holes in his neck close. She stood by his side until he gasped his last breath. Then, after she metamorphosed, she left his room quietly. As softly as she had gone up the stairs, she descended. The desk clerk had his back to her and was on the phone complaining to someone about the German tourists.

Some travel agent apparently had given them incorrect information about their accommodations. How inconsequential all their worries and concerns are, she thought, smiled to herself and practically floated across the lobby again like some shadow and left the hotel.

She thought the stars were particularly bright and plentiful tonight. There was an explosion of joy in the universe. She could feel the energy that had traveled light years to reach this planet. Having fed and now content, she was at the peak of her very being, every sense heightened to its fullest. She could hear people talking, understood exactly what they were saying as they crossed a small foot bridge a good three thousand yards away and she could hear laughter from an open window in a building nearly a half mile away. She picked up the aroma of fresh bread and the sweet smell of homemade candies and gelato from the small shop on the corner. Every aroma, every sound was accessible to her by merely focusing on it. It was as if she owned the world, as if it were all here solely for her.

Isn't it great to be me? She thought, laughing to herself.

Then she thought about Sean waiting for her at their seaside resort, probably sitting on the patio, having a cocktail and looking out at the white caps as the tide shifted and waved. He was enjoying the moment, not thinking about the past or the future. Nothing was more important than the here and now, she thought. I told him the right things. Focusing on tomorrow is always accompanied with anxiety. The sea is magical this way. It washes away anything and everything that might compromise the pleasure of being alive at that moment.

She had other similar memories of such moments, but this night it all seemed so much stronger. As she strolled, she reviewed some of her more satisfying lovers. Because she could bring up an image of an event or a face she had seen hundreds of years ago just as vividly as she could bring up Sean's now, it was sometimes hard to put it in the right prospective. However, she was always haunted by the realization that time would take him from her. He would fade back and maybe he would soon lose that special note she heard whenever she thought about him.

Death for the mere mortals really was best described the way the Mexicans described it, three deaths. The first death occurred when the body stopped functioning and the soul departed. The second occurred when they were interred in the earth. And the third death occurred if and when they were no longer remembered by anyone.

I promise I will always try to keep you alive, my love, she thought, perhaps by occasionally continuing to do the work you were so proud to see me do.

It suddenly occurred to her that she was doing precisely what she had warned him against . . . thinking too much. I really am becoming more like mere mortals. This was the danger of a serious relationship with one, the reason why her kind, her family warned her against it. Danger loomed ahead if she didn't heed the warnings. They insisted on being heard, considered and obeyed.

I don't want to care about the future, she defiantly thought. Drive all this away, she told herself. You have the power to do that. Think here and now. Practice what you preach. She paused below the patio where he was sitting and watched him for a while. He sipped his drink and looked out at the sea. Once in a while, he glanced at his watch.

He's worried about me, she thought. What a strange new feeling it was to have someone worry about her specifically and not as just another one of her kind doing the worrying. They really weren't worrying about her anyway. They were really worrying about themselves and considering what a mistake by her or any one of them could do to them. What Sean was doing for her was making her feel special in ways she hadn't felt for centuries.

She smiled when she saw how happy he was to see her when she stepped out on that patio. He hadn't heard her coming. It was as if she walked on air. His face exploded with relief . . . and joy.

"You look like you were afraid I wouldn't return," she said. He nodded.

"I was."

"Did you think your government mole would stake me?"

"No, I wasn't worried about that."

"Then what?"

"I thought you might have tired of me and pretended to be carrying out the assignment."

"Why did you think that?"

"Something I heard in your voice when we were walking on the beach."

"Now, really . . ."

"After all," he quickly continued, "a woman who has lived as long as you have lived, had as many lovers, as many as a sultan, might just feel it was time to move on."

She shook her head and leaned back against the railing. "You're such a fool. Can't you see how much I've committed to this relationship? I'm violating rules set down for centuries and taking risks no other of my kind even would think to take. You're special to me."

"I want to believe that. I really do."

"Then believe it. When and if I want to leave, you'll know. Don't worry. They'll be no doubt."

"That sounds a little frightening, maybe more than a little."

"I thought you were beyond fear," she said sitting on his lap and playing with his hair.

"Hey, give me a break. I'm not sure how to play it. You're my first vampire lover," he said. "All the other women I've been with stopped at giving hickies."

"What?"

"Little blood traumas under the skin as a result of intense sucking on one's neck," he recited.

"How boring. Just go with the flow. I told you."

"Flow? Did you say, 'Flow'?"

Her smile quickly evaporated.

"Stop."

"Okay, okay. Don't get mad. I'm just having some fun with you."

"I'm not mad. I'm simply a little impatient. You should be able to tell by now when I'm really mad."

"I'd rather plead ignorance and hope for forgiveness."

She laughed and kissed him. It was a long kiss. She brought her lips to his neck and teased him.

"Don't worry," she said. "I know if Crowman saw you had a hickey, he might get very worried."

He laughed and then lifted her in his arms as he stood. "How strong we become when aroused," she whispered. "It's the way we flirt with being Superman."

He carried her into the bedroom and put her gently on the bed. Then he dropped his robe. She lay back and enjoyed the way he peeled off her clothes, pausing to kiss her as he revealed another area of her magnificent body. When he lowered her panties, he pressed his face into the warmth between her thighs and then moved up and over the small of her stomach, to her breasts and then her lips. She was so sweet, so fragrant.

"I'm warning you," she whispered. "I'm insatiable tonight."

"That makes two of us," he said and brought himself comfortably between her legs, beginning his thrusts slowly, gently. He was determined to play her like a sexual symphony. In his mind, he could hear and see the notes to follow as if there was a conductor standing beside them. He recalled the way they used Ravel's Bolero in the movie *10*.

Am I Mozart or Beethoven? he wondered.

She smiled as if she could hear his thoughts, closed her eyes and pulled him deeper into her by grasping his buttocks. It felt as if she would never let him retreat. She had orgasm after orgasm. At one point he was actually afraid he would disappoint her. He didn't think she tolerated frustration well. He couldn't help worrying about it. If his heart beat any faster, it would surely explode. He was having trouble breathing.

"Mercy," he cried when he came. He felt her fingers grip him tighter. He was feeling a little pain in her grip, but he didn't complain. He waited until he felt her slowly relax and then he rolled over on his back.

"I thought the term was 'Uncle,'" she said and he laughed. He was glad to laugh. "Don't worry," she said. "I've had no better."

They both closed their eyes and slept for a while. When he woke, she was standing by the patio door looking out at the sea. The moonlight gave her beautiful skin a delightfully soft gleam. He rose, put on his robe and brought her hers. She put it on, took his hand and led him out on the patio.

"Let's cuddle," she said lying on the cushioned chaise. He lay beside her.

They just held each other for hours that night, the two of them on the patio watching the sea and listening to the song it played since the planet had begun. She was so moved by the moment, she almost told him how she had begun, who she really was. But she didn't.

She kissed him and hours later, she let him carry her back to bed where they made love again, but softer, calmer until he was exhausted and fell asleep, the moonlight shining on his neck. She propped up on her elbow and looked down at him, running her fingers over his hair and his lips. He was so exhausted, he didn't wake. She could smell his blood and hear it moving through his veins. He was sweeter than most men she had known, a delicacy.

It took all her power to keep her fangs inside. She would never say it, but when it came to their relationship, that was her only fear. It was her only nightmare, but one that was coming more and more often, waking her in a sweat when she reached the point when his life slipped away like a deep sigh.

And she was the reason why.

10.

She and Sean parted in the morning. He was off on another assignment and she had returned to her Westport house. She had gone to sleep late, hoping to sleep until noon and pamper herself all day.

The ringing of the phone had woken Opal out of another troubling Sean Waters dream. Of course, she always feared he would be killed on an assignment, especially if she weren't with him. That's what happened in her dream this time, only he had come back from the dead, resurrected by her god because in his infinite, all-knowing wisdom, he had decided she needed him to continue. He was her Lazarus, and she had accepted him with open arms. After crawling out of his grave, he could only recall falling asleep. He had no horrid memories or thoughts, but just before the phone began ringing to wake her, in her dream he had said he feared he had the blood lust.

She heard herself cry, "NOOOOOO," and that cry merged with the piercing ring of the phone.

She had nearly ripped it off the cradle.

It was Crowman.

"What?" she said instead of hello.

"For the first time since you agreed to work for us, we have a small complication," Crowman said.

It was two days since she had taken out the Pakistani ambassador for them. As they had anticipated, the news reported he died of heart failure. Since he was on a mission their government wasn't eager to reveal, not much more was said about him. What Crowman liked about it all was that an autopsy would show no poison, nothing but a serious iron deficiency. He did get a call from Nikki Korniloff, a top KGB man.

"We don't know how you're doing it," Nikki said. "But we know you are."

Denials meant nothing, so Crowman just laughed and called him a paranoid.

"A requirement for our profession," Nikki said.

Crowman was enjoying himself for the first time in a long time. But he knew things couldn't run this well forever. Nothing did, even something like this.

"What small complication?" she demanded. She had barely an iota of patience for the man.

"I have trouble understanding it all myself," Crowman said, "so I'm not the best one to explain the problem. I would like to arrange a clandestine meeting between you and Dr. Stuart Weiss. He heads our lethal substance division."

"The agreement we made was that only two people beside Sean would know about me, you and your director. Are you now telling me others know?"

"No, no," Crowman said quickly. "Not to the extent we know."

"What does that mean? To the extent? You're equivocating, Mr. Crowman. Have you betrayed me?" she asked, her question laden with threat.

"Absolutely not. I merely meant some know we have an undercover agent, a subcontractor, who can manage unusual deliveries, but nothing more. I swear."

"Swear on what? Which Bible?"

He was silent a moment.

"I made a promise to Sean Waters," he said after the pause. "That's sacred to me."

"You made a promise to me as well. Isn't that one sacred as well?"

"Of course. I merely meant . . ."

"I don't understand how I can meet with this Dr. Weiss then."

"He doesn't know . . . what you are. He's only been told you're a subcontracted field agent who is on a need to know basis concerning his information and the findings reported to us."

"Which are?"

"Something about some substance discovered in the Pakistani ambassador's blood. I just learned this myself five minutes ago. It's been kept out of the press, of course. The KGB, not even the Mossad know anything about this assignment you completed. There are suspicions, of course."

"Substance? What substance?"

"His sources told him it was a form of coagulator, but nothing like they've ever seen. It's stirred up a great deal of interest, especially in Weiss's division. They're thinking it could prove very valuable for the military . . . treating otherwise lethal wounds. Maybe it's a side benefit to all of this."

She was speechless. No one had ever discovered that. It was too disguised and well beyond the reach of even the most powerful microscopes to find the characteristic cells. There were grave implications here. Someone had made significant forensic strides or maybe . . . there was another explanation, one involving the supernatural. It wasn't unusual for her to be paranoid about such things. The Ghoul Birds were a clever, sneaky bunch.

"Are you crazy?" she said. "We . . . I can't share anything like that with anyone."

"There's more," Crowman continued. "They did something different in the autopsy. They measured the volume of blood in the body and the loss of blood has them puzzled because they were unable to find any reason for blood loss, no aneurism, trauma, anything. They're conjecturing, of course, but they think that it has something to do with this substance. But they don't know what. "That's not something usually pursued in an autopsy that has otherwise shown no reason for blood loss. They do analysis of bone marrow, for example," he quickly added.

Except the Ghoul Birds, there wasn't anything in this world that caused her any fear. She didn't like this nervousness and trepidation, especially because it originated with a mere mortal.

"You have to understand," Crowman continued, "that these people are particularly suspicious, paranoid. In their world everyone is a potential enemy, villain. Everyone is looking for ways to eliminate someone else. So they did a far more vigorous autopsy. Added to that. . . ."

She didn't need the explanation. She knew this was happening because she was taking out high priority targets. The effort to analyze them would naturally be greater, but she had never confronted the possibility of any mere mortal making the discovery.

"What, added to that?"

"Unfortunately, the ambassador had recently had a thorough physical."

"How recently?"

"Ten days. Considering his schedule of events, dinners, etc., the possibility of severe anemia is at issue. People have it for other reasons, of course, so in and of itself, that isn't as important, but this other problem, other substance. As I said, I don't fully understand it, but I think it will become clearer after you talk with Dr. Weiss. Then we can talk. Some changes obviously have to be made."

"I don't like it," she said. It occurred to her that maybe this was the time to resign. Sean would understand.

"I'll be there at the meeting with you," Crowman said, trying to sound reassuring.

She nearly laughed. Did he really think she would need someone like him to hold her hand?

"I'm not afraid to meet with him. I'm not afraid of any mere mortal man or woman, Mr. Crowman."

"I know. I didn't mean that. I meant . . . I'd be there to be sure you're not compromised in any way."

"The consequences of that are far worse for you than they are for me if I'm compromised," she said sharply.

She could hear him choke up.

Of course, the CIA's alliance with such a frightening, evil creature as a vampire would trump the United States and other countries' alliances with former Nazis. There were times when the ends did NOT justify the means.

"That's precisely why we need to take this meeting. I should add that the director insisted."

"He did, did he?"

"Yes. I want to be there with you and why I thought we should get on this right away and see what we can do to prevent any problems. I should tell you that we've heard nothing from our sources to indicate the Pakistanis are thinking about anything other than a very sophisticated poison. So you can put your mind to rest about that."

"As can you, but since I was the last to see him alive, they'll be investigating me then," she said.

"I was getting to that."

"Then any meeting between us is very dangerous, isn't it?"

"Give me some credit. I think we can arrange for a very safe rendezvous, Opal. However, until we meet, you should be alert to and sensitive to anyone calling on you, following you, spying on you."

Alert to? she thought. He's telling me to be alert? If there was ever a time she needed Sean, this was it, she thought. He had a way of translating their stupidity into meaningful action and words.

"This incident you recently had at the St. Regis fashion show," Crowman added when she didn't reply.

"What about it?"

"It tells us you're not completely invulnerable, Opal," he said. He said it timidly.

"That was a Ghoul Bird!" she practically shouted. "I told you about that, warned you. Despite how much I . . . we hate them, despise their existence, I would not even think to compare human intelligence with theirs. Your kind are no match for either of us."

"I understand. I'm just trained to be careful," he said weakly. "We keep your phone lines clear, but with what can be done concerning satellites and cell phones, the tracking that can be done . . . I'm afraid now that you're possible on their radar, we're not going to be able to communicate that way any longer."

"Maybe we should stop communicating altogether then," she said.

"This is just a little glitch. We'll figure out how to deal with it. Please don't think that way," he said, now whining. "Opal?"

"Call me with your arrangements. I'll meet with the poison doctor or whatever you call him," she said and hung up.

She threw off her blanket. Her sleep was ruined.

"Mary!" she screamed.

Downstairs, Mary had just put up some coffee. Opal's voice seemed to penetrate through the ceiling. She nearly dropped the pot, put it down quickly, and hurried up the stairs.

"Yes?" she said stepping into Opal's bedroom. Was she going to blame her somehow for the early morning phone call? She knew she had gone to sleep only hours ago, and even though she appeared to be able to live on three or four hours of sleep, any interruption could make her very irritable.

"Draw my bath."

"Yes, Miss," Mary said, nearly curtsying. Sometimes she felt as if she were back in the eighteenth century with her. Often, Opal used expressions that were archaic, residue from centuries past that would seep into her twenty-first century dialogue. To be sure, that wasn't any annoyance. In fact, it was fascinating, and whenever she could get Opal to talk about the past, especially her past, she was grateful. It beat any history lesson she could have had in school.

"Don't forget two drops of each of my bath oils," Opal added as Mary headed for the bathroom.

Opal fell back against her pillow and pouted for a few moments. She hated complications and disappointments. Of course, she recognized that she was as spoiled as any living creature could be. Rarely did she fail to get what she wanted or get what she wanted out of someone, mortal or not. Life wasn't as complicated before she became part of Sean's team.

The phone rang again and once again it jolted her out of her deep thoughts. She didn't like the trepidation she was feeling now either. Would every stranger looking her way, every call, and every passing car give her grave concern?

"Pronto," she said. Something made her think in Italian. "Opal, it's Judith. I have a wonderful new offer on the table and the shoot is at one of your favorite locations, Capri. Not only that, but I've moved your fee up twenty-five percent." Opal smiled. That's why I was thinking Italian. I can still anticipate events.

"Very nice, Judith."

She had chosen Judith Klein to be her manager because

she owned and managed a boutique agency that handled only two dozen or so high priced fashion models. It wasn't only the personal attention that attracted her to Judith Klein Management; it was the fact that she had to contend with only a limited number of people. Right from the beginning, she had made it crystal clear that her privacy was paramount. Nothing was more important. As a result no one, no assistant, no secretary, no one else but Judith ever called her from the agency.

"Then you'll go?"

"When?"

"Tomorrow. I have you and Mary booked first class to Napoli and a helicopter will take you to Capri. Do you want me to have a car waiting to take you to your home there?"

"No. My driver is on call."

"Fine. The shoot is on a boat. They want to capture the grotto, of course, and some of the magnificent scenery as backdrop."

"To complete what? Don't tell me their shooting a shampoo."

"Hardly," Judith said laughing. "It's Faniti's new swimsuit line, including the wraps and robes and hats."

"Anyone else modeling on the boat?"

"You're it. You've worked with the photographer before, too, Pete Sawyer."

"Perfect. I'll have Mary call your assistant for the travel details," she said.

"Everything okay since that fiasco at the St. Regis? I still don't understand what happened."

"Neither do I. Forget it."

"Oh, I will, but I have the check, by the way, with a bouquet of roses for the office from Beaute. He's called three times to see how you are."

"I don't want to work for him again," Opal said.

"That's harsh, isn't it?"

"No."

"Whatever," Judith said with that tone suggesting Opal would probably change her mind. Talent agents, whether they be movie, theatrical, fashion or what always wore rose colored glasses. They dealt so much and so often with promises, grand possibilities described over lunches and dinners at the most upscale restaurants, they were simply inundated with someone's dreams. They took baths in hope. However, Judith herself would admit when pressed that one out of a hundred proposals, no matter how rife with guarantees and so-called power brokers, usually came to fruition.

Where did all the failed proposals and sure things go when they died?

What a burial ground that must be, Opal thought. She was grateful that this one characteristic of mere mortals was never one of hers—Pollyanna, infectious optimism. How many times had she sat with Judith and some producer and associate and listened while they fed each other's sure things? It was truly as if they all lived on top of a bubble. When it burst, they came tumbling down and into a well of disappointment. But the survivors, like Sisyphus kept pushing that boulder in vain up the hill and were right back at the restaurant table listening to new wonderful proposals that couldn't miss.

"It's ready, Opal," Mary said stepping out of the bathroom. "Get on the phone and call Judith's secretary. We're going to Capri tomorrow. She'll give you the travel details. Tell her I want four extra days after the shoot so we can enjoy the house. You need new clothes. We'll do some shopping for you in Capri," she added.

Mary's pale, meek face blossomed so quickly and brightly, Opal smiled.

Maybe, she thought, I should try to do something more, something substantial with Mary. I'd risk losing her, but it might be fun.

"I want you to go on a diet now, Mary, a strict diet. You need to lose fifteen pounds at least, and you'll start doing some training. This sitting around reading romance novels and eating the wrong food is over. I need you to look outstanding. You have the potential, as I have suggested."

Mary couldn't speak.

"Don't stand there gape mouthed, Mary; it's unbecoming. In fact, there are things about femininity that I want you to learn. I don't think I've ever asked you, but you are still a virgin, are you not?"

Opal started to get out of bed to go to her bath, already assuming the answer.

Mary shook her head.

"What?" Opal paused and smiled. "You had sex?" Mary nodded.

"With a man?"

"Yes."

"When?"

"It was at the orphanage."

"Really? Well then, come into the bathroom, Mary. You can wash my back and shoulders and tell me your tale. I need some amusement this morning. I feel old and ugly."

Old and ugly? When, Mary thought as she followed Opal, did I ever see her not looking beautiful? Even when she rises, she looks like she could go directly to a magazine cover. What, she wondered, was the price she paid to be what she is and live forever? Mary had no doubt she would pay the same price.

Only, from the little she garnered from Opal, she understood it wasn't the way it was depicted in novels and films. Opal didn't succumb to any seductive male vampire and willing give over her soul to join him in eternal life. Even if she willing accepted Opal's fate, she couldn't achieve it. That remained an obviously well-guarded secret.

Still, she couldn't take her eyes off her when she was naked. It wasn't a gay thing; it was truly a deep, breathtakingly deep, appreciation of the beauty of the human form. Opal did tell her that for a time, she was a model for a famous artist. She wouldn't reveal who that artist was, but Opal assured her that her body was depicted well and was hanging on the walls in famous museums and in the homes of very, very wealthy people.

"What if someone recognized your face?" she asked Opal. It was rare that she had the nerve to ask any questions, but on this particular occasion when Opal was willingly telling her about her nude modeling and some details of her past, she thought she could risk it.

"People look like other people the world over and through time. Haven't you ever heard that everyone has a twin somewhere?" She smiled. "Believe me, Mary, I don't harbor any of the same fears you do or any mere mortal does."

There were so many other questions she wanted to ask, but felt lucky to have gotten one in before Opal's eyes told her the door was shut.

Opal lowered herself into the marble tub. The special bath oils she had come from some Middle Eastern place. There were no labels on them, nothing to describe their origins or their ingredients. They gave the bath water a soft blue tint and when she felt it with her fingers, she saw immediately that it softened her skin and made her fingers look almost childlike. Did the oil come from some ancient fountain of youth? Can it be drunk like water? She was tempted many times to bathe in it as well, but knew that if Opal discovered she had, it would be the end, and a horrible end at that. Opal was so good at seeing things, knowing when she was being lied to or when there was an attempted deceit. Mary was confident that she would notice even a drop missing. Maybe someday, she would offer it to her, especially, after what she had just said.

She began to wash her shoulders and neck with the soft sponge. Opal closed her eyes and smiled.

"Okay," she said, "tell me every nitty-gritty detail about your loss of your virginity."

Do I try to elaborate and make it sound better than it was? Mary wondered. Even to her it seemed so ordinary, so nothing. She rarely thought about it herself. Opal would certainly be bored. She might even laugh at her.

"It was with another orphan, a fourteen-year-old boy, Bobby Robinson. Unlike me, he had known his parents. Both were killed in an automobile crash and neither had a brother or sister. Both sets of grandparents were dead. Without any close relatives, or at least any who wanted him, he was placed in a foster home, but his foster parents were abusing him and two other wards in their home, an older girl and an older boy. Bobby was only five at the time."

"So he used what they taught him on you, is that it?" Opal asked.

"Oh no. He was more afraid of sex after all that had happened to him than I was. I was the one who initiated it."

"Really? I'm starting to have a more positive image of you, Mary. Go on," Opal said.

Mary hoped she wasn't humoring her. She did look very interested and to have Opal really interested in her, she thought, was quite exciting. Now, she couldn't disappoint her.

"We went into the basement of the orphanage because I told him I was going to let him see me naked."

"How old were you?"

"Fourteen. He was fifteen. He watched me undress and then I let him touch me . . . everywhere and he got excited so I touched him and then I showed him how to do it with me. I had just read a good novel with lots of sex in it. No one knew I had the novel. He was very timid and almost stopped a few times, but I was insistent and made him stay."

"Remarkable, Mary. You do surprise me."

"It was remarkable. I thought for sure I would be pregnant, but nothing happened."

"What about Bobby?"

"Shortly afterward, he started to be with a prettier girl."

"Sure. Now that you had launched him, he dumped you."

"That's right," Mary said.

"From that time forward, you've never been terribly fond of men?"

"Oh, I have . . . in my dreams," she said.

"Well, we'll have to see if we can bring those dreams into reality," Opal said.

Mary brightened again. Did she really mean it?

Maybe, just maybe, she would let me become like her, be one of them.

Then, every sacrifice she had made would certainly be worth it.

"Rub a little harder, Mary. I'm not that fragile," Opal said.

Mary put all she could into it. Opal closed her eyes and stretched out her beautiful legs, and just for a moment, only a moment, Mary wondered if she were more interested in women. The thought frightened her.

But not because she was afraid of being gay.

She was afraid it might disqualify her and end any possibility of becoming one of Opal's kind.

11.

Sean risked a phone call. He was in the Czech Republic, following a target to Prague. The Russians were up to no good again. It wasn't an officially sanctioned Russian project and not the work of some oligarch. Some members of the government had contracted with elements of the Russian Mafia to sell dirty bombs to a fringe terrorist group determined to drive American influence out of Eastern Europe. He had to intercept the delivery.

Usually, when he was on assignment, he was as focused as a cobra. He walked, ate, thought and slept the assignment. Little or nothing else crossed his mind. He was convinced he had inherited this power, as he liked to call it, from his father, who could vacuum his mind before, during and right after performing any surgery. The famous story that illustrated this was his father getting a phone call from his uncle to tell him his mother had died just minutes before he was going to wash up to operate on someone's liver to cut out a malignant tumor. He thanked his uncle, hung up and washed up. He told no one, even after he had finished the operation. It was truly as if he could freeze his thoughts and then defrost them when he was home.

Normally, Sean could do that. There was no doubt in his mind that it was the reason for his success as a Navy Seal and as an agent in the CIA and why up until now he had escaped any real harm. He didn't make mistakes, not even small ones, and he was fairly certain that the other side, no matter who they were, knew who he was, respected and feared him.

When he was growing up, he thought his father was too unemotional, too detached from him and his sister. Most of the responsibility for raising them fell on their mother's shoulders. She was the one who visited the school, spoke to the guidance counselors, attended whatever events, sports, in which they participated.

His parents had a limited number of friends. His father always tried to avoid family events. Sean could count on the fingers of one hand how many weddings, funerals, anniversaries and even birthdays his father had attended, even when his calendar was clear and he could have easily attended. It made him wonder if his father saw the people upon whom he operated as individuals or just material, supplies. He once asked him if he remembered the first patient upon whom he had operated. He looked at Sean and said, "I remember his kidney stones. There were so many and they were so large."

He blamed his father then for his own limited personal relationships. He had been with many women, but throughout his high school, college and Navy Seal days, never had one that had lasted any significant length of time. Commitment frightened him because he didn't think he had the emotional stamina to love someone as intently as was necessary for a lasting relationship, nor had he met anyone whom he thought would be understanding enough to tolerate his work.

His sister didn't suffer these self-doubts and was married almost hours after graduating from college. She had been with her prospective husband for years and liked to describe the two of them as pieces of life's puzzle that fit perfectly. He wasn't jealous of her as much as he was curious as to why she had escaped the emotional deficiency syndrome he felt he had suffered. Weren't daughters supposed to be closer to their fathers? She should have been the one to be more like their father and not him.

All of this helped him to explain to himself why he had developed so close a relationship with a supernatural creature. Opal and he had certainly had more intensity that any normal, hot blooded human couple would enjoy, but in the back of his mind, and as he suspected, Opal's, hovered the awareness that this could not and would not last. It was like the courage one had when he or she stepped onto a roller coaster ride. No matter how dangerous, heart stopping it was going to be, there was the realization it would end. That was at first disappointing, but then again, who would get onto one if he or she wasn't sure it would end?

"Crowman just called to tell me I shouldn't be taking calls on my cell phone," Opal said as soon as he called.

"This phone can't be tracked," he said. "The signal is convoluted through different relays."

"He wasn't worrying about those who call me as much as he was about me."

"Huh?"

"Call my land line. It's been insulated," she told him and hung up. He did and she continued the conversation, telling him why Crowman was setting up a meeting with a specialist in poison.

"I don't like this," Sean said after a moment. "He shouldn't be bringing you into another contact at the Company."

"No kidding. Those were my exact thoughts."

She told him about Ugarte again and Crowman's comment about how the episode at the fashion show proved her vulnerability.

"I don't like this," he repeated. "Don't do anything until I call you. I'm calling Crowman."

"Isn't it a no-no to call him now?" she asked.

"I don't care."

"Wait. Don't do it. I know what you're thinking. Look, if Crowman is arranging to take me out, I'll know pretty quickly. I'll handle it. I did suggest to him that it would be worse for him than for me if I were treated like Valerie Plame. Obviously, he knows I'm not going to pursue lawsuits. However, there would be hell to pay in a different court of law and I mean that literally, not just for him, but perhaps for your whole organization."

"You're probably right. I can't believe he'd risk that, that the director would permit it or he would do anything without clearance."

"Are you telling me there are no rogue actions in the CIA? Please, Sean. This whole arrangement is quite rogue."

"I still don't think this sounds good. I don't want to stand by and . . ."

"Sean, please, don't concern yourself with this right now. I'm sorry I told you anything. You'll miss something there and that could cost you your life. I promise, I'll be all right. Or . . ." she added after a little pause, "are you thinking that if something happens to me, something has to happen to you, too?" She smiled to herself. "Whom do you worry about more?"

"I think you already know the answer to that."

"Very political reply."

"It's not meant to be."

She laughed and then grew serious again.

"What if your Mr. Crowman has become convinced you're one of my kind? That I've turned you into one of us. I'm sure he spends many an hour trying to understand our relationship, your relationship, I should say. He can't imagine himself in my bed with my lips on his neck. Although, he has looked at me with unbridled lust, from time to time, I still terrify him. I'm sure. It's in his and the DNA of everyone involved with him and you to be super paranoid. I don't imagine a day passes when he doesn't question his decision to have started this or continue it."

Sean never thought of that.

She could feel his concern flowing through the phone signal. She laughed again to ease his mind.

"Just watch out for wooden stakes, arrows, and wooden daggers and check out any pills before you swallow in case someone has slipped you some hawthorn supplement," he advised, half-kidding.

"Very funny."

"I have another few days here. Maybe you should come here."

"No, no. I'm off to Capri tomorrow for a lucrative shoot.

Take some time off and meet me there after you've completed your mission. They owe you downtime. We'll have a glorious experience. The famous artist John Singer Sargent did a portrait of me there in the eighteen seventies. It hangs in my living room. I'll be interested in your opinion."

"I've never been to Capri."

"More reason to come. I'll be waiting for you. The island will dazzle you as much as I will."

She hung up.

Neither of them ever ended a conversation with the words, I love you. Either they were untrue or they simply didn't need to be said.

He wondered when he would know for sure which it was. He put his phone in his pocket and went off to meet his Czech contact. Maybe, just maybe, he could speed things up a bit and get back there to meet her in Capri earlier than she had anticipated. As he walked along through the Old Town Square and past the tourists looking up at the medieval astronomical clock waiting for the hour and the Walk of the Apostles when the figures would move around, he thought about Opal's joking about Crowman's fears about him. He wondered if it was possible Opal was somehow, someway turning him into one of her kind after all. Maybe there was some slow process underway through their lovemaking and he was completely unaware of it. Would he resist when he found out?

He realized he was actually arguing with himself. Was he getting neurotic?

Wasn't it true he slept less? Didn't he have a bigger appetite and yet he hadn't gained any weight. Was he being conceited when he looked in the mirror and thought he was more handsome than ever, that there was a light in his eyes he hadn't been so aware of?

He saw the way some young women looked at him, especially now as he walked past the tourists. He couldn't help but smile back at them and enjoy the effect his smile had on them. He wasn't like this before he had met and been with Opal, was he? Would he develop a blood lust soon? If he had these fantastic ideas, why wouldn't Crowman have them? Or more important, Opal's and her kind's eternal enemies, the Ghoul Birds?

He hurried along, walking at a brisk pace, actually looking more like a man being pursued. This wasn't smart, he thought, and slowed down. The trick was to never stand out, but instead to meld with the crowd, to be as unobtrusive as possible and never do anything that drew attention to yourself. I'm making another mistake, he thought as he walked past the Jewish cemeteries and made another turn down another side street.

There was one thing he liked about the side streets in Prague. Like most Eastern European cities he visited, they were quiet, often empty. It was as if they were frozen in time because the buildings were often so old. There were no tourist attractions on these side streets. He could hear his footsteps echoing.

This time of day, the shadows on the eastern side were darkening and expanding. He checked his watch. He would meet his contact in ten minutes and would get the update on the exchange between the Russian Mafia and the terrorist group. He obviously wanted to intercept the dirty bomb before they met. Intel had told him it would be coming into the country between twenty-four and forty-eight hours. He needed more accurate detail and their informant was supposed to have it today. If it was twenty-four hours or even less, maybe there was a way that he could speed up this assignment.

Despite the emptiness of the street, he couldn't help feeling watched, even followed. It simply came over him like a chill. He believed in instinct, but this was different. It didn't seem to come from within. It was more like a brief cold breeze had washed over him. He turned and looked back. The shadows on the buildings hovered like shadows caused by candle light, by the flickering flame. One of those shadows separated and moved toward him. He stood there watching it slink along walls, over the sidewalk, slipping on the windows and converging until it took the form of a man. He spun to his left and saw him standing there. He was tall, maybe six five with a brassy complexion that reminded him of imitation gold.

Where the hell did he come from? Sean wondered. The movement of that shadow resembled a large bird or was it more like a bat?

For a moment they just stared at each other; then, the man smiled and slipped into an alleyway. Sean walked to it quickly and looked, but the long alleyway was empty. How could anyone move that fast?

"What the hell was that?" Sean mumbled to himself and continued to stare at the alleyway. Did he imagine it? He had been having strange dreams lately, sometimes waking in a sweat. Was this part of it, some residual effect of being with Opal? He shook off the troubling thoughts and continued on to meet his contact, but he knew deep inside himself that if he continued to lose his focus, he would soon be in the cross hairs of some enemy. It was only a matter of time.

And whom could he blame for that but himself?

Opal watched Crowman's sleek black limousine crawl up the drive. It seemed to inch up like a reluctant rodent, inching its way close to something to eat, but ever so cautious. She waited and watched, but no one got out.

What do they think, she wondered, that I've been sitting here by a window anxiously awaiting their arrival and now I'll come running out like some grateful underling?

As a fashion model and a woman of the world, she knew the signals and indices of power. She would never forget how people behaved in Henry the Eight's court. Nothing had changed. If you wanted people to respect and desire you, you waited for them to come to you. Never, never give the impression you were desperate and needy. A look of indifference, an aura of self-confidence could easily compensate for or cover up weaknesses and deficiencies, not that she had any. It was a practice of the mere mortals, the arrogant ones.

Crowman and his superior struck her as prime examples. It probably came from their power. With a phone call, a literal flick of the finger, they made life and death decisions. No mortal man or woman could withstand the overwhelming deific self-image. This was one of their major flaws. She never understood why their god created them with such holes, cracks and potential rot. She had known great Cardinals, even Popes, Archbishops, philosophers, great artists and great writers, and none, as far as she was concerned, ever came up with a good enough answer to that question, an answer that satisfied her.

Finally, Dave Crowman's driver got out and went to the front door. He was obviously more than a driver. He was burly, heavy shouldered, and quite conscious of every move he made. His eyes went everywhere and the pistol he carried made a bulge under his jacket at his waist.

If this is their idea of undercover, she thought, God help the CIA.

She heard the doorbell and grabbed her fox fur collared black leather jacket. She had decided to pin her hair back and let it flow down her neck to the center of her wing bones. Thin slivers of diamonds looked liquid as they spilled from her lobes. She had put on a pair of distressed blue denim, high waist skinny jeans, a pair of zoom pumps and a light blue turtle neck top. Her makeup was a little more subdued than usual, but nothing could ever take away from her eyes.

Mary stepped back from the door but turned immediately to look up the stairway as Opal descended. Sometimes, she just enjoyed watching her walk, make an entrance. She was even fascinated with the way she sat. There was a feminine grace that made her every move look like poetry. Just as a perfect poem would have nothing unbalanced in it, so too was Opal's body as it floated along.

"I don't expect to be gone more than two to three hours at most, Mary," Opal said eyeing the driver. Now that she saw him close up, he looked pretty uncomfortable in the chauffeur's uniform. It was a good size too small in the jacket.

"Is this the best you people can manage?" she asked nodding at him.

Crowman's driver had no idea what she meant at first and then it occurred to him that she was a top fashion model and was probably criticizing his clothes. What the hell difference did that make? In fact, he had no idea why Crowman wanted to pick her up in the first place. What business did the CIA have with a fashion model? Especially one so famous? Could someone like this be a covert agent?

"It was last minute," he said smiling. "The regular driver has the flu."

"I never permit myself to do anything last minute," she said walking past him. "I'm surprised you people do."

Mary watched them approach the limousine. The driver looked awkward in his move to get around Opal and open the rear door. In fact, he almost tripped and fell on his face. She turned and looked back at Mary, shaking her head. Mary smiled and then closed the door.

She likes me again, Mary thought. She really likes me.

Opal sat back in the limousine and looked at Dave Crowman.

She really hadn't been interested enough in him to look at him that closely before this. But suddenly, she wanted to do just that.

It was obvious he was very uncomfortable being so closed in with her. As she had told Sean, Crowman's fear was tangible. She could actually hear his quickened heartbeat. He had trouble looking at her directly and shifted uncomfortably in his seat. He wasn't that tall, but he apparently was sensitive to his height in an agency where most men were close to six feet or over, so he wore lifts. That, plus his legs being long in proportion to his torso gave the impression he was much taller than he really was.

Crowman kept a thin light brown mustache under a slightly pinched nose and above somewhat orange tinted, almost feminine lips. He had piercingly sharp dark blue eyes and good cheek bones, Opal thought, but his thinning hazel brown hair revealed too much forehead and an annoying patch of tiny freckles, annoying because they looked too much like a rash. His ordinary gray pin-stripe suit was obviously prêt a porter and did little for him. The sleeves were too long and his shoulders looked lost. Someone in so high a position should care more about his appearance, she thought.

Clothes do make the man.

"Sorry about this . . . this meeting so fast, being needed so quickly," he began. He even stumbled over his apologies. Was he that unaware of his revelations of weakness? "Would you like something to drink?" He nodded at the bar.

"No. Tell me everything you know about what's happening," she said, impatient with any small talk.

He shrugged.

"I told you just about all of it over the phone. I'll leave the technical descriptions to Dr. Weiss, but our sources tell us that the substance discovered in the chemical analysis is a compound never before seen. The only, what should I call it, ingredient? I guess that's a good word. The only ingredient that bore any resemblance to anything was something akin to Vitamin K."

Opal stared silently. Her silence unnerved him even more.

He had to keep talking.

"He's going to want to know if you came up with a formula for this on your own, a new poison or where you got it. He knows everything approved for us to use. I think he's a little annoyed something went past him, something was used without his approval, more than anything. Anyway, you can tell him whatever you want, of course, but my suggestion is to simply say you don't know what he's talking about. Or, you can tell him you would rather not divulge the source of your material.

"In other words," he continued, "it's not important that Dr. Weiss get any information from us. It's what we get from him. As I tried to say on the phone, I want this meeting for you so you can figure out how to deal with the findings. Maybe it's important to you for other reasons," he added. That almost made her laugh.

"And the director asked us to have this meeting with Dr. Weiss?"

"Yes."

"Sometimes, I wonder if you really ever told him about me."

"Oh, of course I did."

"He's never asked to meet me."

"That's not unusual even in this case."

She smiled, skeptical. He shifted uncomfortably in his seat.

"So then what does the director specifically want? What does he expect will come from this interrogation?"

Crowman shrugged.

"I'm sure it's his way of stroking Weiss. He told me to handle it however we saw fit and that's what I'm doing." He paused, gathered some courage and added, "I wouldn't be in this position if I didn't have his full confidence."

"I'm happy for you. So then, he assured you that Weiss does not know about me?"

"We're always on a need-to-know basis, even among the high level personnel. Why make it sound like something ominous?" He almost whined.

She smiled at him which only made him feel more uncomfortable.

"Really?"

"Why be so suspicious?"

"It's not rocket science, Mr. Crowman. You feel somewhat exposed and want to know how to close up anything that might lead to your exposure in all this. He didn't politely express that to you?"

"Well . . . yes, not in so many words, but . . ."

"So if there is a gaping hole, he'd like you to make it all go away, right?"

He just stared at her. He started to shake his head, but stopped when she moved just a little closer and put her hand on his arm.

"If you're not honest with me, we can fall into bigger problems here," she said, her voice dripping with threat.

Crowman's eyes widened. He crossed and then uncrossed his legs. It was as if he thought she just might ascend in the limousine and suck the life out of him here and now.

"I'm being honest," he whined. "This is just so . . . unexpected. I mean, all your other deliveries and the aftermaths to date were perfect. No one suspected anything unusual. It was all clean, neat and now . . ."

"Don't lose your lunch over it just yet, Mr. Crowman." She turned to look out the window.

A small cloud seemed ominous as it fell below the trees lining the highway. It immediately made her think of Sean. She didn't like that. If Ugarte had found her, another Ghoul Bird probably knew something. Perhaps she and Sean had been followed. It would be easier for them to go after Sean as a way of drawing her out. This was another consequence of developing a serious relationship with a mere mortal. She had always known there was that danger and in the past, she had brought any relationship to an end before it could present such difficulties, but this time . . . this time she was having trouble doing so.

Am I getting more and more like them? she wondered again. What was it Kurt Vonnegut had written? Beware of whom you pretend to be. You might be whom you pretend to be? Something like that. It was proving true, perhaps.

It was always clear to her why this would be a great danger, not only for herself, but for the others wherever they might be. Whenever one of her kind endangered the rest, there was an unwritten rule that she or he must be eliminated. Was she on the verge of that? She might be soon hunted by more than just the Ghoul Birds. Who could she now trust and was this relationship really worth all this risk?

She couldn't help wanting to do what she wanted when she wanted to do it. None of the others in the family were that different. They were all spoiled. They had the power and the immortality. Why should they ever deny themselves anything? That was a dangerous contradiction, however. Just like any species crawling, flying, walking on this earth, there was a universal sense of self-preservation, except maybe, and this suddenly intrigued her . . . except maybe human beings. They were blindly on a course of total self-destruction. Look what they were doing to their environment, not to mention their own kind. They were capable of such great cruelty to each other. At least we don't harm or destroy our own kind unless one becomes dangerous to the rest. They do it for other reasons, power and greed at the top. We're never greedy. Maybe this was why we were the chosen, she thought. Yes, she thought, that must be the reason.

The silence during Opal's musing unnerved Crowman. He shifted in his seat and mumbled, "It's all going to be just fine."

She looked at him again, holding back laughter. The higher up a mere mortal rose in his company or government, the more paranoid he became. Kings had food tasters, didn't they? She knew government leaders who had reasonably similar men serve as stand-in's, especially when and where there was a possibility of an assassination.

"How is Sean doing?" she asked, more like demanded.

Crowman blanched at her tone.

"You spoke to him. You tell me," Crowman said, finally acting like the man of power and authority he was, at least to the other mortals.

"You know how Sean is. He wouldn't tell me if he was having difficulties."

"That's good," Crowman said. "He's one of my best."

"Let's not play word games here. Is he really all right?

It's important for me to know for other reasons. For both of us to know," she added sharply.

"As far as I know, he's doing fine, but you should know that every minute is different from the minute preceding when you're on an assignment."

"What is that, some CIA philosophical axiom?" Crowman shrugged.

"Just simple truth," he said. She could see how clever he felt, and how that gave him more courage.

"I don't know why anyone says that. I have never found the truth to be simple," she replied.

"Really?"

"You of all people should know this, Mr. Crowman. Lies, lies are what are simple."

He raised his eyebrows.

"Lies are simple?"

"The motivation for them is simple. The greatest lies have been very simple. If you get into an elaborate explanation, you run into difficulty. You lie, stick to it, and lie until you're believed. It's called politics."

He laughed until he realized she was really talking about him and what he does.

"How do you live with such cynicism?"

"I don't lie about it," she said. "Didn't you ever hear that the truth will set you free?"

He nodded. In his heart he knew that arguing with her would never end satisfactorily.

At least, for him.

They rode the rest of the way in silence.

12.

Despite his attempted bravado, Opal thought Crowman looked uncomfortable from the moment he emerged from his limousine after they had parked in the coffee café parking lot. He nodded at a short, balding stout man sipping a mocha coffee at a corner table.

"That's Weiss," he muttered.

Weiss had a notebook on the table and sat with his legs spread far apart as if he had to balance his rear on the seat. However, it was the look on Grady Weiss's face when he saw Opal that almost made her laugh aloud. Apparently Crowman had not told him with whom he would meet. For Opal, the choice for the meeting was an over-the-top effort to appear unconventional, a Starbucks outside patio. At this particular location, no one appeared to recognize Opal or pay her and Crowman much attention. Crowman's driver followed them up to the table and then stepped ahead to turn to her.

"Would you like any special coffee?" he asked.

"Chai tea," she said.

"Just ordinary coffee for me," Crowman told him.

"There's no such thing anymore," Grady Weiss said.

Crowman smirked and turned to his driver.

"You know what I like Brody." The driver nodded and hurried off.

"Grady, this is Opal . . ."

"I know who she is. My daughter has a pile of fashion magazines as high as the ceiling in her bedroom. If she knew I was meeting you . . ."

"She won't," Crowman said sharply. "Of course not. I merely meant . . ."

"Ashante," Opal said holding out her hand. Weiss looked at it for a moment and then rose halfway and hurriedly took it. He didn't know if he should kiss it or shake it and looked at Crowman, who gave him no clue. He shook limply and sat.

"I must say, I'm impressed, David. This is what I call top notch recruiting."

"How do you know it wasn't I who recruited him?" Opal countered.

Weiss started to smile, but Opal's glare stopped him instantly.

"Well, in any case, I had no idea," he said. He turned to Crowman. "You guys amaze me. On the other hand, I suppose we have our modern day Mata Hari."

"I'd rather not be compared to her. Mata Hari, which was her stage name, was a very poor spy, if that," Opal said. "She's was little more than an exotic dancer who bedded anyone with any name value or wealth or power."

"Well, I don't know . . ."

"I do," Opal said.

"You talk like you knew her."

Opal finally smiled.

"I know enough," she said.

Crowman shifted uncomfortably in his seat.

"Let's skip the small talk," he suggested firmly.

Weiss nodded. He opened his pad.

"It filtered down to me, as I like to put it, that you were the last person to be with the recently desist Pakistani ambassador. When the data started streaming into my office, I realized that someone was using some very sophisticated chemistry and most likely did not expect to be discovered. Since this was one of our approved operations, I contacted the director who also had concerns and ordered us all to meet."

"What is it you want? What are these concerns?" Opal asked sharply.

The director knew what was happening, according to Crowman. This mock follow up then was a way to cover his own ass, Opal thought. Typical.

Weiss looked at Crowman, who nodded for him to continued and Weiss then turned to her.

"I thought that would be pretty obvious."

He paused as if he expected her to fill in the blanks. She continued to stare blankly. There was one human personality flaw she couldn't stomach, arrogance.

"All that's obvious is your failure to express yourself simply," she said.

He reddened.

"The formula. I'm referring to whatever was used. What else? The Company is about control. We can freelance, but the freelancer has to work within our parameters. I approve the Company's use of any lethal material to be ingested. That way we avoid surprises, which is what we have here," he added, giving Crowman a look of chastisement. Crowman didn't react.

Opal looked away. She felt her patience receding and her anger rising. Crowman was right about him. This wasn't about Company policy as much as it was about bruised egos. It was clear to her that this clod was jealous and obviously threatened. The Company considered him their top expert on lethal substances and here he was in the dark about something a non-professional had utilized.

"In short," he continued when no one spoke, "protocol has been broken here."

"Protocol?" Opal said turning back. "Aren't you being a tad overly dramatic?"

"Of course not. Protocol is essential to an organization like ours. We're talking about checks and balances, efficiency. I'm usually consulted before anything unusual is employed. We have to be prepared and from another point of view, protected in the event such a substance would be turned to be used against our side, if you get my drift."

"You do drift," Opal said.

Weiss's bulky cheeks turned from red to pale gray. Crowman's driver brought their drinks and no one spoke while Opal deliberately took her time to sip and enjoy her tea. The driver returned to the limousine and stood beside it with his arms folded. He reminded her of an Egyptian palace guard. Now there's a rich well of delicious blood, she thought focusing on his thick neck.

Weiss cleared his throat.

"Am I boring you?" he asked.

"I don't know the formula," Opal said with a nonchalance that raised Weiss' eyebrows.

"Don't know?"

"It was something given to me by a confidant."

"Given to you?" He looked at Crowman who was as deadpan as ever. "How did you know it would be effective, efficient, and quick enough?"

"I saw it in use and was satisfied." Weiss shook his head.

"That's not the way we do things."

"It's the way I do things," Opal said.

"And you," he asked Crowman, "approved this operation on this basis?"

"She has never let us down," Crowman said dryly. "I had no reason to be concerned."

Weiss shook his head again and sighed.

"Do you have any more? For me to analyze that is?"

"Not at the moment," she said. She glanced at Crowman as she spoke to Weiss. "I could possibly bring some to you in the near future. Maybe deliver it myself."

Crowman's eyes widened. Her veiled threat was clear. Of course she could bring Weiss the formula. She could bring it the same way she brought it to the Pakistani ambassador.

"How did you get him to drink it? Or was there some other way to get it into his body?" Weiss pursued.

Opal smiled and leaned toward him.

"Really, Mr. Weiss, did your legendary Mata Hari reveal her secret ways? How I do what I do is my intellectual property."

"Intellectual property?"

"And so protected by unwritten copy write," she added and sipped her tea.

Weiss shook like a wet dog.

"None of this is making any sense to me, Dave. The man had a significant loss of blood with no trauma whatsoever. This is quite an unusual lethal substance, to say the least. It's important I know everything about it."

Crowman shrugged and finished his coffee in one long, annoying gulp during which his Adam's Apple looked like a loose pinball.

"We have a unique arrangement with Opal," he began. "She doesn't do anything we don't ask her to do, but how she does it is entirely her business."

"No, it's not. It's our business if she's working for us. The director specifically ordered . . ."

"As soon as it is possible, I'll provide you with what you want," Opal said firmly.

"You mean to tell me if you were given an assignment this afternoon, you would be unable to carry it out because you don't have your copy written material?" Weiss asked, now showing his back teeth with his rubbery, wide grimace.

"I take on what I can when I can. I have a life, Mr. Weiss. Do you?"

He reddened again, fumbled with his cup and shook his head.

"This is getting us nowhere, Dave. The director won't be happy."

"Happiness is at best a fleeting pleasure," Opal remarked and finished her tea. "But do tell us. How did they arrive at their conclusions so quickly? That might be helpful to me which will be helpful to you."

He stared a moment, looking like a petulant child who wasn't going to give her anything if she wouldn't give anything to him. Then he relaxed.

"Besides having had a physical recently, the ambassador had a serious wound healing."

"Wound?"

"He fancied himself something of a fencing expert, once even tried to get into the Olympics, I understand. You look like you didn't know this, Dave?"

"I didn't," Crowman said now having his turn at looking annoyed.

"Anyway, during a reckless bout he was cut on his right side, under his ribs and had to be stitched. The wound was only three days old and when his corpse was in autopsy, they found it was completely healed, gone. The stitches had fallen out. This led them to discover the extraordinary coagulation and the puzzling loss of blood. Perhaps you can do a little better at explaining now?" he asked Opal.

She shook her head.

"Maybe they had the days wrong and it had long since healed."

"No, that's not possible." He narrowed his eyes. "Are you hoping to sell your formula? Is that what's happening?"

For the first time since she had sat, Opal felt uncomfortable. She looked at Crowman and he surprised her with the answer.

"We have had some preliminary discussion about that," he said.

"Without my involvement?"

"When I say preliminary, I literally mean on the way here today."

"I see." Weiss turned back to her, this time with a deep smirk. "Then you do know the formula?"

"No, but I can get my hands around it when I need to," she replied. She was starting to enjoy the way her double entendre answers were unnerving Crowman.

"Well, any further discussion should include me. I'm sure the director would agree."

Crowman nodded and then looked at Opal.

"You have any objections to that?" he asked her.

"Not at that moment. Of course, I can't predict what might occur over time. Not even the CIA can do that."

"We're not ready to continue the talks yet, Grady. I'll call you," Crowman said quickly.

"May I ask why not?" Weiss asked Opal.

"Timing," she said. "It's not the right timing and you know that timing is nine-tenths of success."

He grimaced again.

"Timing? How could . . ."

"It's a matter of a certain need, when it arises," she said quickly. Her patience was so thinned out, she was sure it was about to break, and no telling what would happen then.

"I have no idea what she's talking about," Weiss said. "Let me handle it," Crowman said, practically begged. "I assure you that your concerns will be addressed and satisfied."

"I do have another appointment," she told Crowman and tapped her watch.

"Of course." He rose and pulled out Opal's chair when she stood.

"It's been a delight meeting you, Mr. Weiss. You personify my image of a perfect Company soldier," she said.

He widened his eyes, truly confused as to whether she was giving him a compliment or ridiculing him. He chose the former and smiled.

"I hope we're meeting again soon," he said.

"Sooner than later," she said, nodded and walked to the limousine.

Crowman remained back to say a few more words to Weiss and then quickly joined her.

When they pulled away, Opal turned to him. Her instincts had all reported and she was now quite certain of what she always suspected.

"The Director doesn't know anything about me," she said. "You lied about that to both me and Sean, correct?"

"Why, no, I . . ."

"When I say know about me, you know what I mean, so don't equivocate and tell me he knows I'm freelancing for you. He only knows me as a fashion model, correct? What did I tell you about lies?"

Crowman had no idea how Opal could sense these things, but he understood it was fruitless to continue with a lie.

"Our organization is quite complicated," he said. "What difference does it make who knows all about you and who doesn't?"

"But he's your superior."

"For now," Crowman said dryly.

"For now? Beware of ambition, Mr. Crowman. I've seen princes come and go, generals destroy themselves. It's the bastard child of Envy whom you know is a green-eyed monster that mocks the meat it feeds upon. You'll be consumed by yourself."

"I don't think you should be lecturing me," he said, indignant. "You're not exactly the paragon of virtue here."

"I am what I am. I don't deny it to myself and that," she added leaning toward him and causing him to sit farther back, "my dear Mr. Crowman, is what is truly the difference between us."

She sat back and turned away.

"Anyway," Crowman said as sharply and as strongly as he could, "you heard what he told you about how they went about making the discoveries in the autopsy. That was the bigger point for this meeting. Now you know that you have to be sure your target has no recent wound that is known. This miraculous healing process . . ." He thought a moment, his eyes brightening. She could practically hear his thoughts.

"Don't ask," she warned.

"But why not? Think of it. If there really was a way to bottle what you can do . . . imagine the value of such a substance, especially, as I had suggested, for soldiers wounded on the field of battle."

"I wasn't designed for that," she said. "I'm really not here to benefit all mankind."

"Maybe you don't know yourself as well as you think after all," he replied.

She was silent.

He could be right, she thought, but in ways he never dreamed.

They rode on in silence and she avoided looking at him until they drove through her gated entrance. As soon as they pulled up to the house, Brody got out and rushed to open the car door for her. She paused before getting out.

"How will you handle your director when Weiss gets back to him?"

"No worries," Crowman said. "I can take of it."

"Be careful," Mr. Crowman. "Ambition often exaggerates one's capabilities, which is not discovered until it's too late."

"Thanks for the advice," he said dryly.

Probably wasted, she thought and stepped out. The more commerce she had with mere mortals, the happier she was being who she was.

Je ne regrette rien, she thought and hummed Edith Piaf all the way up to her bedroom.

Sean sensed something wasn't right the moment he entered the apartment building. There was an ominous cloud of stillness over the short entry way and narrow stairs. He hesitated and listened, but heard nothing. Very slowly, he began to ascend, his fingers slipping under his jacket to reach his pistol.

As he continued up, he thought the shadows on the walls flickered the way he had seen them flicker on the buildings. It gave him pause. For a long moment, he didn't move. Why he pulled back against the wall, he would never really know, but later he would wonder if he hadn't heard Opal's voice, a warning. Just as he did, an arrow flew past him, close enough for him to feel the breeze on his face, and struck the stairway. He crouched, turned and readied to fire, but there was no one there. He waited, frozen in position.

An arrow?

He pulled it out of the step and looked at it. He had never seen anything like it. A poison dart was one thing. He had employed and knew others employed them, but an arrow? He held onto it. Was this something Opal had actually anticipated when she joked about others thinking he had become a vampire?

After a few more moments, he hurried up the steps and turned onto the second floor. Very carefully, he made his way down to 201. He looked back, watching every shadow, and then knocked. No one responded so he knocked harder and the door swung open.

There, sprawled over the sofa in a clear state of rigor mortis was his contact. His arms were out in crucifix fashion as were his legs. His head was tilted to the left, but Sean saw no trauma, no wounds, and no blood. His eyes were wide open and reflected a look of utter shock as though he was still being tormented even in death.

Sean didn't completely enter immediately. He stood in the doorway and looked around carefully, anticipating someone coming at him from the narrow hallway to the right. No one did. He entered, felt the man's neck for a pulse and realized he hadn't been dead very long. He continued to examine the body, looking for some trauma, some wound, but found none. He looked about for signs of struggle and saw none. It was almost as if the man had been killed elsewhere and brought here to be on display, but how was he killed? Poison? Or could it be another vampire, one with Opal's powers?

He went to the window and gazed down at the street. Nothing looked unusual. After perusing the rest of the small one bedroom apartment, he called in to report. Crowman got on the phone almost immediately.

"He's dead, but I can't find any wounds. I guess he was poisoned," Sean said.

"We've been updated. He wasn't giving you correct information, Sean. We think he was a plant."

"Really? Did we take him out"

"No. I don't know anything about that. In any case we're sending in your backup. We've received good Intel indicating an arrival late this afternoon on the train, five o'clock from Budapest. Stark Collins will be leading the team."

"I don't understand this. Who killed him?" Sean asked staring at the corpse. "Wouldn't they want him to keep me thinking otherwise?"

"I don't know. Maybe he did die of a heart attack."

"He doesn't look like someone who was in any chest pain and his position, the way his body is laid out . . . a Christ metaphor."

"Forget about him. It doesn't matter now."

"Well, should I get over to the railway station?"

"No. You've been compromised," Crowman said. "Just come home. We'll take care of it now."

"Compromised? This whole thing doesn't make any sense. This guy has been of service to us before, and I have never been fooled by . . ."

"There's a first for everything, as we've both been discovering."

He looked at the corpse.

"I don't know. There's something more going on here."

"There's no point in your remaining there, Sean. Just get back. I'll have something else for you soon, I'm sure."

"Okay. How did the meeting go for Opal?"

Since he was the one who brought Opal to the Company, he thought he had a right to ask.

"We learned something important, something that will be taken into consideration for any future assignment. I'm sure she'll explain when you see her again."

"Was she unhappy?"

"I would hesitate to describe her feelings about anything at any time, Sean. I'm sure you're better at that."

"There's nothing different about her when she's not . . ."

"When she's not who she really is," Crowman finished. "See you soon. Just be extra careful on your way out of there."

"Right."

He hung up, but he didn't rush right out. He studied his informant's corpse. He checked to be sure he hadn't been smothered to death and looked for signs of oxygen deprivation. Crowman might be right. Anyone would think the man had simply had a heart attack, he concluded.

"But why try to kill me then?" he asked the corpse, who was apparently a double agent. "I was no longer a danger to you guys."

And why did they come after him with an arrow? Why not use a gun? What, did someone think he was a vampire, too? Suddenly, Opal's joking about wooden stakes and arrows wasn't so funny.

He looked over the arrow again. It was machine perfect, straight and hard. Even the head was formed of a hard wood. He also saw what looked like very curious markings, elongated shapes, and carved into the stem. He had to show this to Opal. She would know more about it for sure.

Still clutching it, he made his way out and down the steps carefully and began his journey down the street. There were more people around and he didn't worry about how quickly he moved this time. He was quite annoyed, however. He hated aborting any assignment. It hadn't happened many times, and when it had, it was for other reasons, reasons that didn't have much to do with him. There was something more going on here. He felt sure of that.

At least he could get back in time to join Opal in Capri, he thought when he entered his hotel. He packed and left for the airport as quickly as he could. There was a taxi waiting just outside the hotel. Like most of the taxi drivers he encountered in foreign countries, this one was relatively quiet, probably afraid to test his limited English. Sean was in too deep a train of thought anyway. All sorts of possibilities and ideas were zigzagging through his mind as he turned the arrow over in his hands.

Suddenly, however, the driver made a sharp right turn down a side street.

"Is this some sort of shortcut?" Sean asked.

The driver nodded, but Sean didn't like it. With every turn he made, he seemed to find ways to get farther and farther away from traffic and people. One turn took them to what was clearly a dead-end. He did it so quickly, Sean had little time to get to his pistol.

When the driver turned on him, Sean was paralyzed for a moment. The driver had grown in size and he had fangs. His skin was rapidly turning reptilian and his eyes looked like they had pupils floating in blood.

He started over the seat toward him and Sean instinctively jabbed the arrow in his throat. He roared. It was deafening, but the arrow had surprised him enough and apparently had a significant enough effect to drop him back. Instantly, Sean went to his weapon and pumped two shots into his head. The driver slumped in the seat, his eyes wide, but strangely alert and alive.

Without any further hesitation, Sean opened the door, seized his small bag's handle, and leaped out of the taxi. He hurried away, looking back only once. The driver didn't come out. In fact, the taxi started away and from the glimpse Sean had of it, the driver looked normal size again and there was no arrow in his neck.

What the hell was that? he wondered as he continued to race down the street.

Another vampire?

Or was it something different? Am I completely in that-world now?

More important.

Who exactly is after me now?

And why?

13.

The cloudless sky in Capri was a Byzantine blue, light celestial. Opal recalled the frescoes of Hagia Sofia in Istanbul. Lately, this was happening more and more. An image, a color or a sound would revive memories centuries old. Nudge a ghost and it rose from the darkest and deepest layers of her mind to swirl once again right before her eyes.

"Who's that?" she heard and snapped back into the present. She saw Sean waving from a small motor boat and told Pete Sawyer, the photographer, to put it on hold.

Pete Sawyer didn't hide his annoyance, even from her. Of all the commercial photographers with whom she had worked, Pete Sawyer was the most temperamental. He hated any interruptions and often cursed a cloud changing the light. He saw himself as a world class artist with a camera and to be fair, Opal would not deny that he was. She truly appreciated the way he painted light, shadows and angles to produce the pictures that somehow made her and whatever it was she was supposed to sell integrated. Nothing looked awkward on her ever.

In fact, Pete was so good a capturing her beauty that she actually worried he would somehow see beneath her surface and discover her true inner self. She had visions of him developing a picture and being shocked by the image, for it always seemed to her that her second-self lived just under her skin, waiting to emerge. Her human self would be sucked in and made to wait for her truer self to be satiated. Then it would sleep, restful and content.

In 1950, she was in Russia and had heard about a scientist who had developed a camera that could capture a person's aura. Curious herself, she permitted this electrical engineer, Semyon Kirlian to take a picture of her. With his wife, Valentina, he had developed a style of photography that caught the electronic pulses around a person. They had no idea what they had discovered. When they saw her picture, she was in an aura of black and they thought it had failed. She mentioned it to Lucine Karayan, a faith healer who was something of a go between members of her kind at the time, and she advised her never to permit herself to be so photographed again. It was too dangerous.

"What's happening?" Pete asked stepping back and looking in the direction Opal was looking.

"My boyfriend has just arrived."

"Boyfriend? Now? You're working. Can't he wait for you to finish?"

She glared at him.

"No," she said. "You can wait or jump off the damn ship with all your equipment."

She could be just as temperamental when she had to be and the good thing was that everyone expected it and just about everyone tolerated it. A diva was a diva.

He laughed defensively and held up his hands. He knew that Opal could be more fragile and deadly than nitroglycerin. And in the end, like any other photographer, he would bear the brunt of the blame.

"Fine, fine, I need a short break. I'd like some of those clouds to pass as well," he said nodding at the sky. He could see that it didn't matter what he said. She wasn't listening.

The boatman brought Sean up to the eighteen-foot sailboat they were using for the shoot, and he climbed aboard. He had changed into a tight Italian knit turquoise short sleeve shirt and white jeans with blue boat shoes. She thought he looked quite striking with his high fashion sunglasses.

She kissed him gingerly, keeping him from doing much more, especially touching her face.

"Make up," she warned. "Took a few hours to get it right for Mr. Sawyer this morning," she added swinging her eyes toward Pete.

Sean smiled and nodded.

"Sorry it took so long for me to get here, but they held me over for the debriefing longer than I had anticipated," Sean whispered.

"Why?"

"I have a lot to tell you," he said.

She nodded.

"So do I. Did Crowman discuss our meeting with his Weiss?"

"Not in any great detail. Should he have? He did say something about your having to take something new into consideration."

"I can't understand why he didn't get into more detail. Whom else would he confide in about me?"

"Well what's it about?"

"Apparently, the autopsy done on the Pakistani revealed some unknown chemical resembling Vitamin K."

"What? Your secrete to heal the wounds?"

"Yes. This is the first time I've seen or heard anything like that. They have been able to pinpoint it, but Weiss wanted the formula, which I obviously cannot provide."

"You're right. It is odd that David didn't get into detail about it with me."

"Maybe not. Maybe he didn't want you to interfere with his dream negotiation."

"Dream negotiation?"

"He left me proposing I get the formula to him. He saw it as a tremendous battlefield advantage . . . healing soldiers on the spot."

Sean's eyes widened.

"Wow. I guess it would be."

"Can't be done, Sean."

"Yeah, I understand. How did these people make the discovery? No one has before, right?"

"Well, that was really what Crowman meant by taking something new into consideration."

"What?"

"The target had a serious wound. As a consequence of my healing balm, it was gone when they took him in for autopsy."

"Really? Well . . . that's something Crowman should have known. It's his screw up."

"Right. He was angry about that, which leads me to something else."

"Oh?"

"Why would it matter to anyone but me that a target had a wound healing?

Sean nodded thinking.

"It gives me reason to believe David Crowman has never shared information about me with your CIA director," she said. "Do you know for a fact that he has?"

"Well, just that he said he has." He thought. "I guess I don't know for a fact."

She nodded.

"He's an ambitious man, Sean. Be careful. I think he's using both of us for more than just protecting the good old United States of America."

Sean looked at her sharply.

"You think?"

"Mere mortals have a tendency to use each other until it's no longer necessary and then discard each other," she said. "My kind is not that different. Read your Bible. It's rife with it."

"Opal," Pete cried excited. "It's perfect now with the way

the clouds are and the sunlight. Please," he pleaded, holding out his hands palm up.

"He'll hemorrhage if I don't get back to it," she whispered, her lips so close to his ear, it was as good as a kiss. "And we'll have another die of acute anemia."

Sean laughed.

"Go on. Do what you have to. I'm sure I'll enjoy watching you at work," Sean said. "I mean . . ."

"Better shut up and get yourself something to drink and sit over there with Mary," she said pointing to a chair behind Pete Sawyer. Mary sat patiently in the one next to it, sunning herself. "He's right. We have a certain window for these shot because of the lighting, the shadows on the water and background he wants."

"Gotcha," Sean said and moved toward the small cold box that contained the soft drinks. "Hey, Mary, how are you doin'" he asked.

"Fine, Mr. Waters."

"I see you've done something new with your hair. Looks very nice."

She smiled at him.

"Thank you."

He thought her complexion was much better and she even looked a bit trimmer. For the first time, he noted her nice facial features, especially her eyes. He held his smile and she kept hers.

"Capri obviously agrees with you."

"Oh, it would agree with anyone, Mr. Waters. Look at the scenery, the weather and the quaint streets."

He nodded. She even sounded more confident. Opal was right when she said a woman's self-image might be more important than a man's. "Woman are simply expected to look good all the time. Men are expected to look like men, which," Opal said, "unfortunately means sloppy in America these days. It's almost a uniform," she said. "When did it all change and being comfortable mean slovenly and slapdash?"

"Things going well with this shoot?" he asked Mary as he looked back at Opal.

"Perfect," she said. "It's always perfect. Opal doesn't know imperfect."

Sean sensed that she really meant it. He took his seat. He had never seen Opal at work and was really intrigued.

Sawyer immediately came back to life and started his direction and set up. Sean watched with so pleased a look on his face, Opal couldn't help but laugh.

Which annoyed Sawyer, of course.

"If you don't mind, I'd like you back in character, seizing the demeanor we've taken great pains and time to conceive."

She nodded and obeyed. The better she cooperated, the faster the day's shoot would go. Even so, it took the better part of two more hours. When it ended, Mary Plunkett moved quickly to help Opal wash off the heavy makeup. She knew she hated it. The boat was turned around and headed toward the port.

Sean continued to wait patiently until Opal beckoned to him and then he practically leaped to obey. He joined her on the mat sprawled on the deck when she sprawled out and looked up at the sky. He lay beside her. The wind had kicked up and was whipping his hair about, but he didn't care. Looking down at her, he didn't care about anything. It was as if she could draw him out of this world with her eyes. He kissed her again, this time longer.

"Whenever I kiss you after being away, I feel like some poor slob who was stuck in the desert and has been given his first glass of water."

She laughed.

"I've had my kiss called many things, but not a glass of water."

"You know what I mean."

"Of course." She looked at Mary who was putting her things away and at Sawyer who was busy wrapping up his cherished equipment and then turned to Sean. "Okay, tell me what happened in Prague."

He braced himself on his elbow and related the events, describing his confrontation in the taxi as calmly as he could. The soft smile she wore slowly evaporated. When he was finished, she didn't say anything. She rose and walked to the aft side of the boat and looked back at where they had been.

"What's wrong?" he asked coming up beside her.

"My family is angry at me."

"Family? I never heard you mention any family."

"The rest of us," she explained.

"Is there . . . are there parents?"

"Not parents in the same sense you mean. There are those who are older and supposedly wiser."

"Well, why do you say they're angry? What did you do? What did I do?"

"I'm sure I've been with you too long in their way of thinking. From the way you describe your informant, I think it's obvious that one of us killed him. That's why you found no trauma, no bloody wounds. As to the arrow . . . it's not a Ghoul Bird. They have no interest in my loves and wouldn't follow any of them. They don't kill mere mortals. They thrive on death, but the dead need to be in a state of decomposition, except when they can kill and feed on one of us. That's because if we die, we decompose so rapidly, it's as if we were dead and buried for months, and of course, it's a big victory to them.

"No," she continued, "no one out there suspects you've become like me, but it's a message, clear and simple. They kill me through you in a sense. You're obviously easier to get to as well."

"I stabbed him in the neck with the wooden arrow. I thought that would be fatal for one of you."

"You didn't go deeply enough probably. He simply pulled it out and healed instantly."

"But how do they know about us? Are you being watched?"

"I told you. We just know about each other. You've heard of the sixth sense? Well, this is the seventh or eighth. I'm not exactly low profile anyway, Sean. You've already appeared in four gossip columns and one magazine article, even though the references were vague to most . . . *an unidentified escort?*"

"My sister's pretty excited about it. She's hoping I get you to throw something her way."

"I think this is all more serious now."

"You don't have to tell me twice. I'm the one who barely escaped being pinned to the wall and having his throat ripped out in a taxi. What's the big deal anyway? Why are they so upset?"

She thought a moment and nodded.

"This thing with the Pakistani ambassador, the discovery of the healing balm . . ."

"What about it?"

"If I didn't seek out such high profile targets, such a thorough and complete autopsy might not have been done, hadn't been done in the past. I've endangered, exposed another great secret."

"Oh." It was becoming clear to him. "Well, what do we do now?"

She shook her head and took on that silence that gave him the impression she had transported herself somewhere else and it was only the shell of her body beside him. He stood quietly, waiting.

The boat drew close to its mooring. Opal looked at the dock.

"My driver is here with my car. Where are your things?"

"The man who brought me out is holding them."

"Get them. Quickly," she said.

He nodded and stepped onto the dock, turning to help her step out of the boat.

"Hey," Sawyer said rushing over to Opal. "You did great, as great as usual."

"Thank you, Pete."

"I'll be seeing you soon again, I hope."

"Could be," she said without enough enthusiasm to please him. He glanced at Sean as if he had concluded it was Sean's fault she wasn't being as nice to him as he would like. Opal caught it.

"I mean, I hope so, Pete. You're the best in the business." He beamed.

"Thanks. So are you."

He waved to Mary who had everything bundled in two bags she carried over her shoulders, and then he continued to gather his equipment.

"Sensitive guy," Sean said.

"I haven't met a true artist who isn't and I've met quite a few. It comes with the territory." She gazed around, her eyelids narrowing with some suspicion. "Hurry."

"Right," he said and took off toward the boatman who had brought him out.

Opal's driver hurried down the dock to take everything from her and put it into the trunk. She waited, looking in the direction Sean had gone. She didn't get into the automobile until she saw him returning. The driver stood there holding the door open. She kept looking around, studying everyone and everything within a hundred yards.

"We have one more passenger, Beika," she finally told her

driver. "Put his things in the trunk, please. Get in, Mary," she ordered. Mary moved quickly.

Sean handed Beika his suitcase and slipped into the car to sit beside Opal. Her continued silence made him nervous. He could see she how intently she was studying everyone and everything outside the car.

"I'm pretty sure no one followed me here," he said. "As usual, I took a convoluted route and . . ."

"Wait," she replied.

She didn't mean wait to see; she meant wait to discuss it. Her eyes fixed on Mary, who sat looking out the window, but who was obviously still eavesdropping. He understood and sat back.

"This is one beautiful place. The hydrofoil was half empty. I was surprised."

"It's not the height of the season. You'd be lucky to get a seat then," Opal said. She smiled at a memory.

"What?"

"I came over on a luxury sailboat, once. He was a young multi-millionaire out of Milano. Inherited every penny and was just learning how to spend it. He actually got seasick and I spent most of the trip talking with the boat's captain."

"Just talking?"

"Well . . ."

He laughed.

"You're never seasick, right?"

She raised her eyebrows.

"You've never had a sick day in your life, have you?"

"The closest to feeling ill is intense hunger when it takes longer than I anticipate to feed," she whispered.

"That's it?"

"That's it."

"Maybe I should join your family."

Mary turned sharply, eager to hear Opal's response. She

said nothing. The car wound its way around the island and up to Anacapri.

"These views are spectacular," Sean said. He looked down as the limousine moved closer to the edge of the road on turns. The sea crashed rhythmically against the rocks below. Terns sounded like they were celebrating. With all the traveling he had done, Sean realized he really rarely stopped to smell the roses.

"We're really high up. It's magnificent."

"As they say, you ain't seen nothin' yet."

Sean saw she wasn't exaggerating. Opal's villa was ensconced in an acre of luxuriant, terraced gardens, and surrounded by tropical flowers. It had a large, circular pool in the front and to the right on the approach. The villa had three terraces from which one had breathtaking views of the island's western coast and the sea that wove its electric blue into sapphire along the currents. She told Sean she had bought the villa from a wealthy German aristocrat. It had enough bedrooms and bathrooms to house eight people very comfortably.

On the ride up, she had described some of the parties she had staged there and some of the wealthy and powerful guests she enjoyed over the past ten years.

"The summer retreat for the Roman Emperor Tiberius is right nearby. If you can't relax here, you can't relax period," she told him, but as soon as they had reached her villa, she became nervous again. She didn't move when Beika pulled into the driveway and got out quickly to open her door.

"Anything wrong?" Sean asked, seeing her hesitate.

"They're not here now," she said and then turned to him and added in a softer voice, "but they were."

He felt the chill move through his body like an arrow carved out of ice.

Mary rushed out to get Opal's things put away. Opal followed slowly and Beika began to carry in his suitcase.

"I can take that," Sean told him. He took the suitcase.

Beika nodded and handed it to him.

"We'll be going to dinner at eight," Opal told him. "But we'll be walking about the streets first so be ready at seven fifteen."

"Very good, Ma'am. I'll be here," he said. There were the first words he had uttered. He had a strange accent.

Opal anticipated Sean's question.

"Croatian," she said. "Besides driving and taking care of my car, he watches after the villa. He sleeps above the garage," she added nodding at it.

"Does he know . . ."

"He knows only Opal Stone, the world famous fashion model. When I fed on this island, it was only on a particular obnoxious tourist. The last two were Russian mafia, nouveau rich," she said and Sean laughed.

She put her arm through his and led him into the villa.

The entrance led to the large, beautifully decorated living room with Tuscan wall décor that included Pomeriggio arched framed wall art, a large Sarantino wall mirror, Vina Bella wall sconces and a Tuscany rooster wall plaque. All the furniture was vintage, including two Amelie aubergine slipper chairs. He felt like he had stepped into another time.

The portrait she had mentioned was quite large and over the mantle.

"You've never been anything but beautiful," Sean said. "I kinda like your hair then, too."

"I'll wear it like that for you one day."

"I wish I could paint."

"Paint with your eyes and use your brain as a canvas," she said.

"Why do I feel you've said that before, not to me, but to at least a dozen other men?"

"I've said almost everything before except maybe . . . I love you."

He brightened.

"I wish I could believe you."

"You have my permission. Believe me," she said and he laughed.

"Let me tell you about the rest of the villa. There's a bedroom behind the kitchen. Mary sleeps there," she said. "There are three other bedrooms down here, one for a single and the others for doubles with en suite bathrooms."

She nodded at the gracefully curved stairway, and they started up. There were only two rooms, a study with large windows proving sea views, and Opal's large bedroom with windows that provided additional sea views, a patio door to the terrace and a large, luxurious en suite bathroom with an area for her vanity table. The closets were so well hidden, she had to show him how to find the sliding door. The four post bed itself was custom made and one and a half times the California king. It was curtained all around.

"What's that headboard made of? I've never seen any-thing like it."

"Something I picked up in Kenya over a hundred years ago," she said. "Those are fertility symbols."

"Appropriate for a bed headboard, I suppose."

"Well, I don't have children, but it works for me," she said smiling. "Put your things away and we'll have some Cappuccinos on the terrace."

"Okay." He paused. "What made you say they were here?"

"I wouldn't call it a scent. It's more like we can see it."

"See it? See what? Tracks?"

"It's not easy to explain to a mere mortal. It's like we leave our imprint in the air, but only we can see it. It's what I was talking about before when I said seventh and maybe eighth sense."

"Listen. I've been meaning to ask you something. Could you leave out the mere when you say mortal?"

"The longer I live among you, the harder and harder that gets to do," she replied and he laughed.

Perhaps we'll have a good time here yet, he thought and went to put his clothes away.

They had a wonderful swim before they dressed for dinner and then Opal had them driven down to where the taxis and buses were waiting for tourists to take them to restaurants or down to the boat dock. The taxis all had cloth covered roofs, open on the sides to give their passengers the sense they were riding in a convertible.

"From here on, we walk," she said nodding at the center of Capri. "No cars."

"Delightful." He took her hand and they paused at the sightseeing area to look out at the sea and the mainland of Italy. "It's almost unreal," he said.

"It's always been this beautiful," she said. "Time can't put wrinkles on the face of what's eternal."

"You included?"

"Especially," she replied.

"It doesn't ever end? I mean . . . naturally?"

"I never heard any one of us say that, but I have my suspicions. C'mon. This is not the time to talk about endings of any kind."

She took his hand and they continued down the cobblestone street. Although it wasn't as crowded as it was during July and August, there were still many people strolling and pausing to look at the displays in the windows of the beautiful upscale shops. Smaller groups of tourists were herded along, their guide speaking in English and Italian. He and Opal paused when they approached the turn and saw the large patio, now filled with people having cocktails.

"This is the famous Grand Hotel Quisisana. Now it's frequented by the rich and famous. Originally, it was a Sanatorium created by a Scottish doctor in eighteen forty-five. The son of a very wealthy man I was seeing was sent here and we visited a year after it opened."

"Did he get better?"

"No. Not because of that, but eventually, it was turned into a pensione and eventually became a full-blown hotel. Shall I tell you that I've had many a rendezvous here?"

"No, don't tell me. Just because they might have occurred a century ago doesn't reduce my jealousy."

She laughed and they walked on. Despite the beautiful night, the laughter around them, the luxurious looking shops and restaurants, he sensed she was still quite nervous. Her eyes went everywhere and occasionally, she would pause and look back.

"They're still here?"

"Someone is," she revealed, almost in a whisper.

"What happens if one of you confronts another in a state of belligerence?"

"It's not pretty," she replied. "But that's not what will happen here and now. If they have decided my fate, someone will try to assassinate me."

He stopped walking.

"What? When?"

"Not in public," she said. "We kill only in private. Besides, maybe I'm leaping to conclusions."

"No you're not. Don't sugarcoat anything for me. How

can I doubt anything you suspect after what I told you happened in Prague?"

She looked away quickly. He put his hand gently on her arm.

"What is it, Opal?" he pursued.

"It is more likely perhaps that all they want to do is eliminate you," she said. "Teach me a lesson. That's why they went after you twice in Prague."

"So once I'm gone, they'll be satisfied? You won't be in any danger?"

"Very possible, but not definite."

"Maybe I should just get the hell out of here."

"Leave me now? That's not fair. Your enemies became mine, didn't they? Well let's see some reciprocation."

He shook his head and then smiled.

"You're right. What's fair is fair. You took risks for me; I take risks for you."

She smiled.

"We're so perfect for each other," she said. He wondered if she was kidding.

They turned down a side street and walked to the restaurant she had chosen.

It was a small Italian restaurant, and apparently one Opal frequented often. Everyone knew her, especially the owner, who, Opal explained, was the chef. He prepared all the food and then had a second chef who cooked, baked and fried whatever was on the menu that night.

"You will find that everything is so fresh," she said. "Most good chefs in Europe ignore the freezer."

"How many meals would you say you've eaten?" he asked, partly teasing, partly out of real curiosity.

"Don't even try to conceive of it," she warned. "Look, if I asked you to imagine ten people standing over there against the wall, you could easily do it, but if I asked you to imagine one hundred thousand, you couldn't."

"I get the point. You're never bored, tired with what you eat?"

"You forget," she said leaning toward him, "my senses are ten times what yours are. I enjoy every pleasure far more than a mere mortal. Sorry. I mean mortal. I'm in what you call ecstasy daily, whereas you'd be lucky to experience it once in a lifetime."

"You oughta be a vampire salesman."

She laughed and then in fluent Italian, ordered the wine and their appetizers. Antonio, the owner, came over to give her his recommendation, a caprese ravioli, the specialty of Capri.

"You're in for a real treat," she told Sean.

"Every moment with you is a special treat," he replied. "I know," she said and quickly added, "I'm no good at modesty. Whenever I try it, I sound insincere."

She looked up when a single man entered. He was tall, thin, and dark skinned with very clear blue eyes and looked no more than forty even though he had a head of stark white hair. Sean widened his eyes and she shook her head.

"It's no one," she said.

"I guess this thing with the Pakistani ambassador was the straw that broke the camel's back, huh? I mean," he added after the waiter served their wine and appetizers, "you've been with your mortal men for long romances. You described a few dozen to me since we met. There's nothing else that's particularly different about me, right?"

He thought she wasn't going to respond. She drank some wine, ate some of her appetizer and dipped some bread into the olive oil. She looked away and for a moment he wondered if she hadn't heard his question. When she looked at him, however, he saw she had.

"I'm with you longer than I've ever been with any one mortal man."

"So it's just the length of time? We could stop seeing each other for a while or . . ."

"No. It's more," she said.

"The healing balm? The assignments you take from Crowman from time to time? That's the whole thing?"

"That's a big part of it, but . . ."

"But what?"

She looked like she was going to cry. He thought there were actual tears in her eyes.

"Opal?"

"You're the first mortal I've been with who knows what I am and is still alive and that is more important to them. They see it as an unexpected weakness."

"Really? All those years, no one else shared the secret and lived?"

The waiter brought their entrée.

"Some water, sans gas," she ordered. "Just taste this. Enjoy the meal. We'll talk about all this later."

"You make it sound like someone's last meal before execution."

"The condemned should be this lucky," she said savoring the first bite. "It's just as good as anything else to die for," she added and he laughed and began to eat.

"Wow," he said. "You might be right."

Afterward, she took him for a walk along the Via Tragara, past the Casa Morgano and on to the end of the walkway where there was a wonderful place to look out at the sea. He was struck by the silence, the delicious quiet, and the way others spoke in low voices as if the scenery, the sea and the stars intimidated everyone. Loud laughter or chatter was almost sinful. She had her arm through his, but she didn't speak and he felt as if his words would break a magical spell. Finally, she turned to him. In the moonlight her face looked more silver than brown and her eyes seemed to absorb the moon's yellow tint.

"None of us who has betrayed the secret of our identities has survived long after. We think of it as the beginning of the end, what you might consider the onset of age. Something essential has broken down inside us, this great need to preserve ourselves. It's almost suicidal to make such a revelation to a mere mortal. Sorry. I have to use mere in this case."

"Then why did you do it?"

She shook her head.

"Don't think I haven't asked myself that often. I've even been tempted to . . ."

"Eliminate me? Crowman?"

"It wouldn't satisfy them," she said. "Once one of us has done this, what's to prevent him or her from doing it again? We have no room in our essence for forgiveness."

"So, when you said before that they might only be after me, you were not telling the whole truth?"

"Probably not. See, what happens? I'm starting to behave like one of you, burying my head in the sand, rationalizing, equivocating, and avoiding the truth. I don't do that. At least, I haven't over the last few hundred years."

"So I'm rubbing off on you?" he asked, smiling.

"In a sense, yes. There is another theory. I have no tangible proof but . . ."

"What?"

"Eventually, we . . . how shall I put it . . . degenerate into the state of mere mortality and then die just as any of you might, from a disease, old age, a fatal accident, whatever."

"Degenerate?" He shook his head. "I suppose I could be called a degenerate."

"It's just a myth probably."

"Well, what are you going to do in the meantime? I hate to be responsible for destroying your endless ecstasy."

She laughed and then grew serious again.

"I was depressed about it, even frightened for the first time in my life, which is quite a long time, but I suddenly feel . . . oddly excited about it."

"Excited? I don't get it. You just basically said that your people are coming after you or me. You even said you know they're nearby."

"Yes, and it's like I was describing to you once . . . the bullfighter facing death."

She turned around and embraced herself.

"I find I feel more alive now that I know I could die and not at the hands of a Ghoul Bird, but because something might be happening to me. I've often tried to feel things the way you do, limited, but with a desperation that comes from knowing you don't have that much longer to go. You know, that stupid term, the 'bucket list.' Can you imagine how big my bucket would have to be."

She looked up. Her face so captured by the subdued evening light, he thought he might burst with pleasure looking at her.

"Everything . . . all this . . . the stars, the sea, the very air we're breathing is heightened. I can't wait to get you home to make love to you," she said.

"Oh great," he said. "I was having a hard enough time keeping up as it was."

She laughed.

"Do you think you understand a little of what I'm saying?"

"Sure," he said. "It's why we go to war so much and why I'm in this job. The danger is an aphrodisiac."

"Yes, only for me there was little danger, even when I was pursued recently by a Ghoul Bird. I knew I'd survive;

I'd beat him. We're far superior when it comes to that. I've been challenged enough to build my confidence, but against my own kind . . . it's like your Superman fighting Superman, I suppose."

"So I repeat . . . what do we do next?"

"Nothing. There's no way to prepare except to be alert and expect it will come."

"Can't you talk it over, negotiate?" She laughed.

"I told you. Forgiveness is not an option and compromise is forgiveness. Come on. Beika will be waiting for us."

They started back. He couldn't help looking at everyone who walked by or past them and at every dark corner. The slightest sound shook him and anyone suddenly popping up out of a gate gave him pause.

"Relax," she said. "There's no way they'll reveal themselves to you ahead of time. The taxi driver in Prague proved that."

"Lucky I was carrying that wooden arrow. I'm getting a wooden stake to wear on my belt."

They walked on. Beika was waiting just where he had left them off. They got into the car and he started back to her villa. They were a good five minutes or so into the trip when Sean sensed Opal's agitation. She felt for his hand and held it tightly.

"What?" he asked.

She started to speak when suddenly, seemingly out of nowhere, a large bat smashed against the windshield and spread its wings. Beika screamed and missed the turn. The car careened off the edge and flipped in midair. Sean flew into the ceiling so hard, it knocked the breath out of him. He barely had time to utter a cry before the car spun again and then fell toward the rocks and the sea below.

14.

He awoke in a few inches of water. His head was resting comfortably against a boulder covered with thick moss. He could hear the water crashing against the rocks. The spray splattered his face. He was afraid to open his eyes. He actually wondered if he was dead and this was how it was. Someone once told him that when you died in an accident, your soul remained at that place until its disposition was determined.

After he opened his eyes, he remained in the same position for a few moments, trying to make sense of it. Was he dreaming? He had no pain and from what he could see, no broken bones and no bleeding from any trauma. Finally, he cautiously raised his arms and moved his legs to see if everything was still attached and functioning. Then slowly, still expecting some excruciating pain, he raised his head and looked around.

He was definitely at the base of the palisades. He looked up and could see the headlights of automobiles cruising the highway a few thousand feet above. He turned to his right, wiped his eyes, and gazed around. Opal's car was over on its roof just a half dozen yards away. The roof had caved in and the windows were all shattered. One of the headlights dangled and a tire floated on the water like some child's lost swim tube. The vehicle looked caught up on some rocks and shook as the tide rushed in and out around it. One wave washing through the car, brought Beika's arm and head into view.

Where was Opal?

A movement on his right caught his attention. When he turned he saw Opal seemingly rising out of the water. She was dripping wet and looked like she was walking a few inches above the water and the shore. He wiped his eyes again. Now they were burning a little from the salty sea. She stepped up beside him. He looked up at her, focusing her in gradually. She seemed to come in waves until she was clear in his vision.

"What happened? Am I . . . alive?" he asked as she knelt beside him.

"As alive as I am," she replied. She looked back at the automobile. "Unfortunately, I couldn't do anything for Beika."

"What happened?"

She helped him to his feet and he looked around and then up at the road above again. He thought he could clearly make out the break in the guard rail.

"I don't get it. We went through that guard rail and over the side of the road. I remember hitting the ceiling and then . . . nothing."

"You passed out immediately which made it easier for me."

"To do what?"

"Pull you out of the car with me."

"In midair?"

"Yes."

He stared at her. After all he had seen her do, any skepticism quickly died, even though he had trouble imagining what she was claiming.

"Midair?"

"Get over it," she said.

"And then what happened?"

"Sean, I got us down here as softly as I could. I was able to break the fall and slip under you so you didn't hit hard. The details might give you more nightmares." She looked up the palisades. "I thought we'd be followed down, but we weren't. There's a path about two hundred yards or so off to the right. We'll take it up."

"What about Beika and the car?"

"I'd rather the authorities believed he went over himself. He was coming to pick us up and was late or something. It's better left like that. C'mon. We need to get up to my villa andput ourselves back together."

"Listen. Don't worry about me having nightmares. I'm used to nightmares. How did you do this?" he asked.

"We'll talk about it later." She started away and stopped. He couldn't help but stare at the car. The water washed Beika's arm back into the vehicle. He could see him sprawled inside, his body twisted and broken. "Sean," she snapped. "We must get out of here quickly."

He started after her.

"Can't you just float us up?" he asked as he began to navigate the nooks and crannies.

"It's complicated. For now, let's both behave like mere mortals."

"Don't worry about my feelings. I'm feeling pretty mere," he replied. A memory came flashing back. "What was that bat? I never saw one that big. I thought it had a human face."

"Figure it out," she replied. She didn't look back and it took all his energy and strength to keep up with her.

"Hey," he cried at one point, "I thought you said for now we're mere mortals. This mere mortal is exhausted."

"You mean a fashion model is in better shape than a CIA agent?" she mocked.

He cursed under his breath and dug in. Twenty minutes later, they stepped onto the road. Cars went by, but no one paused to see if anything was wrong.

"Fortunately, we were attacked close to the villa," she said. "It's only another ten minutes."

"Might as well be ten hours the way I feel. C'mon, fill me in at least. What happened? It looked like a bat spread its wings and covered the windshield. Am I imagining it? Didn't it have a sort of human face? I never saw one that big."

"You didn't imagine anything. I recognized him. It was Draegan Gambit. We haven't seen each other or crossed each other for nearly two hundred years."

He stopped walking.

"So that bat was one of you . . . that's not a joke, this metamorphosing?"

"I think we've left the joking behind us some time ago when it comes to me, Sean." She continued on.

He lingered, thinking a moment and then followed. "So you . . . you plucked me out of the car in midair?" She kept walking.

"Well, where's this Gambit creep now? Why isn't he at us again?"

"He'll pick his time. Don't worry about that. I'm sure he's quite annoyed about failing. He will face a lot of anger and disappointment. He'll come at us harder."

"That's a relief. I thought he might leave us alone and life would become boring again."

This time she laughed.

"I need a hot shower," he said.

"You need a hot bath," she corrected. "I have some bath oils that will restore you quickly. Don't ask me where I got them or what they are. I might tell you and you wouldn't touch them."

"Probably from the eyes of a newt," he mumbled. She heard him but didn't turn to let him see her smile.

They rushed on with him looking back and to the side

constantly. When they reached the villa, Mary was standing in the open doorway waiting as if Opal had somehow communicated with her.

"Are you all right, Miss?" she asked.

"Was anyone here in the last hour or so?" she asked in reply.

"No, Miss."

"No one came to the door?"

"No, Miss."

"Okay. Go up and draw a hot bath for Mr. Waters immediately. The usual drops of my oils."

"Yes, Miss," Mary said, looked at Sean as if she thought he had been changed into one of Opal's kind. She looked jealous for a few seconds and then hurried to the stairway.

"You need a drink first," Opal said and led him to the bar.

He followed, gazing up after Mary.

"What, do you think he came here first looking for us?"

"I sensed he was here, but I don't know exactly when in the scheme of events," she replied. She poured his drink and watched as he practically gulped it down. Then she poured him a little more. "Easy," she said. "You need to calm down, but not too quickly."

"No kidding. What about you? You hardly looked disturbed."

"There are few things that set my heart racing."

"And that wasn't one of them?" he asked, astounded.

"Not considering some of the other confrontations I've been in over the centuries, Sean."

"Talk about being blasé," he said sipping his second drink. "Too bad about Beika."

"He had a good life considering what I had plucked him out of years ago. I always found desperate people to be the most obedient and trustworthy servants. Gratitude cements loyalty," she added.

He looked back at the front door.

"What's to stop Gambit from simply bursting in on us?"

"Me," she said.

"It didn't stop him just now."

"He had the element of surprise. That's lost. He'll change his technique. "No sense worrying about it."

"Oh, I'm not worried. I'm too terrified to worry," he said.

She smiled and nodded at the stairway.

"Let's look after you for now."

Later, while he was having his hot bath, which Mary had prepared for him, mumbling to herself the entire time, he heard the police arrive. Opal had called to report her driver and car were missing and the police came to tell her the bad news. Sean was still in the bathtub when she came up to tell him what they had said.

"So they bought your story?"

"They certainly wouldn't suspect what had happened. What else can they believe? People drive fast and destroy themselves and others, even when they don't drink. It's this crazy avoidance you mere . . . you mortals possess."

"Avoidance? Avoidance of what?"

"Facing your mortality," she said. He nodded.

"Right." He smiled and stretched his arms. "I don't know what you had Mary put in this water, but I feel like I could get out and run ten miles."

"Don't be like your Mr. Crowman and ask me to turn over the formula."

She knelt beside the tub and began to wash his back. Then she stood up, took off her clothes and got into the water with him. She pressed the button to get the pumps on and the water circulating. She lay back against the plastic cushion and closed her eyes as the bubbles and foam rose and danced about her breasts, causing them to shake and jiggle seductively. She moaned and arranged her legs on the outside of his. After a moment of simply enjoying the sight of her, he sat up.

"You do love your mere mortal comforts," he said.

She opened her eyes.

"I'll give you this," she said. "For a self-destructive species, you at least have progressed when it comes to pleasure."

"Thanks. We need every compliment we can get."

"Although the Greeks and Romans were no primitives when it came to that. You've simply modified and enhanced what they already knew"

"You giveth and taketh away when it comes to compliments." He lifted her forward and they kissed. Then he shook his head.

"Here we are embracing in a bubble bath and less than an hour or so earlier, I was spinning in space and apparently seized out of the jaws of death just before splattering like an egg on some boulders."

"How poetic."

"As you implied, I know for you this is old hat, but for me the old fashion simple attempts at assassination are far more comfortable. I've been shot at, but not until now with bows and arrows. There was an attempt to run me down in Paris a few years ago and a car I was going to use was blown up about a minute before I got into it. You know, your standard lethal stuff, but vampire bats driving cars off cliffs, vampire taxi drivers . . . you've enriched my closet of lethal possibilities."

"I must say, you do have good training. You're handling it quite well considering."

"You forgot to add, 'for a mere mortal,' but thanks. I know it seems like I keep asking you this, but I don't have too many other questions rolling about my brain. What's next?"

"I think we'll have to cut our Capri holiday short, for one thing."

"When?"

"After my shoot tomorrow. It's the last day. I was hoping to remain for four days, but I don't think we'll be comfortable here right now."

"Where will we be comfortable? Is there anywhere safe from such an assassin?"

"We'll see."

"No," he said letting go of her hands.

"No?"

"Look, it's pretty clear they're after me, not you. This last attempt was the third on my life. Twice in Prague and now here when I'm with you, but it was also pretty clear, even though you won't describe the details to me, that this attack on the vehicle would not have resulted in your death, correct? So what was done was clearly not an attack on you, too. Maybe if we separate, if I go, they'll back off. You will take a holiday from the Company as well and possibly this will blow over."

"I don't know. They realize you know about me and therefore about them. That can't blow over, Sean. They have their concerns. Secrets have always been our lifeblood. They don't believe in taking chances. I should say, we. Look at how my use of pronouns is revealing the changes in me."

"My high school English teacher did try to make me aware of the importance of grammar. Okay. So why are they worried anyway, when you really think about it? What can I do that would bring harm to your kind? First, I can't blast your involvement on the evening news and compromise the Company, can I? And probably more important, how can I claim to believe in vampires and still have any credibility? Someone will say my work got to me or something?"

"It's a matter of insurance, Sean. Your death is the best insurance. I don't like you out there on your own."

"Not something I'm not used to or comfortable about," he said. "I admit this enemy is significantly more impressive, but I'll take my chances. I think it's for the best, at least for a while."

"You just want to leave me? Just like that?"

"Well, maybe they'll back off. Call me selfish, but I'm still fond of pizza, and from what I've heard, there isn't any on the other side. Besides, eventually they'll get to you as well if I stick around. You've said so yourself in so many words."

He stepped out of the tub and reached for a bath towel. "This whole thing was probably impossible from the beginning," he added wiping himself off and wrapping the towel around his waist.

She lay back looking up at him. The expression on her face was one he had never seen. She looked stunned, but a bit amused.

"What?"

"So you're saying you could leave me, end it just like that?"

"For a while."

"How long?

"I don't know. A while."

She looked away for a moment and then back at him with a wider smile on her lips.

"Now what?"

"You really are special, Sean. Maybe what you told me about your not being able to commit to a serious long term relationship before me has something to do with it, but as odd as it might sound to you, I admire you for it . . . as a mere mortal, of course."

"Of course."

"No man for hundreds of years has been able to walk away from me, Sean."

"Yeah, but by your own admission, none knew everything about you like I do."

"Even you don't know everything."

"But I know enough to rile up the family, right? Don't wait for the translation, Opal. Right?"

"Okay, okay. We'll try it your way for a while as you say. A while."

She rose from the tub and he handed her a towel. She smiled licentiously.

"So tonight has to be very special then," she told him. "It has to be good enough to last . . . a while. Even for me," she added.

He laughed as she sauntered past him into the bedroom. She dropped the towel and pulled back the cover sheet. Then she sprawled on the bed and turned to him, her arms out. The graceful lines in her neck called to him as strongly as her perfect breasts and shapely legs. It was as if his entire body went erect and the blood flew to the tips of his fingers, to his lips and to his chest as quickly as it did to his groin. He approached her slowly. Lying there with her hair floating around her on the pillow, her beautiful eyes working more like two sex magnets, she looked like the epitome of everyman's fantasy, the dream that followed them from puberty onward, drawing them even into the hands of death who promised sweet ecstatic peace and relief from the great struggle to keep their imperfect worldly bodies alive.

Every time he and others like him made love to an attractive woman, a woman who had some special essence, they thought this was it; this was going to be the greatest sexual experience of their lives, taking them to places they saw only in dreams. Afterward, all would admit it was good, but all wouldn't be satisfied. They had set standards far too high for what was possible. It was, however, this pursuit of the ultimate sexual ecstasy that drove them forward, almost explained the entire purpose of their lives, the reason to strive to make more money, to improve their bodies and their appearance, and to reach some level of power. It was all for this in the end, this impossible to achieve goal.

But it was meant to be impossible, for if any of them ever did achieve it, he would find the days and nights that loomed ahead devoid of the excitement, the chase, the hope that enabled him to open his eyes in the morning, to go to work, to care about anything in fact. Browning wrote it, but everyman would think it: *A man's reach should exceed his grasp or what's a heaven for.*

Tonight, this night, with this special feminine creature whose reasons for creation and purpose for life he could not fathom was in his way of thinking capable of improving his grasp. He could possibly reach heaven, if only for a few moments, and then, when it was over, what would he do? Where would he go? What mere mortal woman, as she would say, could or would possibly even come close to this? He knew that once he crawled beside Opal in this bed and kissed her and mounted her, he was doomed to be forever dissatisfied.

So he approached slowly while he battled the contradictory feelings of fear and pleasure.

"Why is it?" he asked in a voice close to a whisper, "that I know if I get into that bed with you, I will make it nearly impossible to leave you even though I know it could or will most certainly be fatal?"

"Is there any death you can conceive of that would be more satisfying for you?" she replied.

He shook his head.

"No."

"Then you have nothing to fear, Sean, nothing to regret. You were first drawn to me by your own manhood, your own male ego, but you justified your pleasure successfully by then drawing me into your love of your country, your dedication to this ideal of freedom and democracy and all the other rationalizations you mere mortals have for killing and dying. I accepted that to keep your love and even work for you to please you. You can go on knowing you achieved what no man has ever achieved with me."

She smiled.

"Why do you hesitate, my love, isn't that enough?" His answer was to get into bed with her.

Her kisses weren't hard, demanding. Nothing she did overwhelmed him overtly, but he could feel himself surrendering in ways he had never surrendered to a woman. He wasn't entering her, embracing her to draw pleasure out of her as much as he was trying to merge with her, trying to create some new androgynous creature out of the two of them, their sex binding them in some inextricable way. In the back of his mind, reeling with the continuous blasts of sensual delight, he saw himself being absorbed. She would keep him forever inside her. It was almost a maternal instinct to hold onto the umbilical cord, to hover forever over the child born within and fight every action, every person, and every sensible decision that would draw him or her away.

And why not?

Wasn't every lover a child of the one he loved and loved him? Didn't each of them give birth to a new identity, a new life for the other?

I will never be who or what I was before Opal, he thought.

I might leave her, but where will I go and who will I be?

He paused.

"Stop thinking," she whispered. "I can smell your thoughts. Stop thinking and kiss me as if it were for the last time."

"I've heard that line before."

"*Casablanca*," she said. "See? I'm a hopeless romantic after all."

He laughed and then he kissed her and released his body from any restraint. He gave himself over to her completely. He did think one more thought–the devil be damned. He believed, maybe deliberately deluding himself, that she was crying out more to build his pleasure than to express and experience her own. In the end they were singing a sexual duet, even their moans and cries were in harmony. It went on and on. Somehow, whenever she felt he was near a climax, she managed to hold him back, making him invest more and more of his energy, his very essence in the act until he burst through his phallus, emptying enough of his very soul into her to satisfy her.

The exhaustion that followed was not unpleasant. He felt as if he had lost all his weight and was literally floating. When she turned away and he closed his eyes, he settled back, his body closing in like some flower to dream only of sunshine. Moments later he was in the most gentle and refreshing sleep of his life. Later, he would wonder if some of this wasn't a result of those miraculous oils in the bath.

She was already up and gone when he woke. She had left Mary behind to prepare some breakfast for him. He wrapped a robe around himself and went down.

"Why did she leave so early?" he asked, realizing immediately he and Mary were alone.

Did she leave him with something special, sharper and keener instincts? Was he different?

"She had an early call, remember? Her photographer is an ogre when it comes to using the sunlight when and how he wants to use it."

"Oh, right. Did she leave any other instructions for me?"

"She wanted me to tell you she has arranged for the helicopter to take you to Napoli. A car will come for you in about an hour."

"That's it?"

"That's all I know, Mr. Waters. I know only what she wants me to know," she added, a slight note of dissatisfaction in her voice.

Sean sipped his coffee and nibbled on the croissant and jelly.

"Would you like something more? I can make scrambled eggs, bacon."

"No, this is enough for now. I never asked you how long you've been with her, Mary?"

"Three and a half years now."

"How long will you stay with her?" Mary looked up sharply.

"Why, as long as she wants me to stay of course."

"You have no other ambitions?"

"My time will come," she replied and left the kitchen. What the hell does that mean? He wondered. He finished the croissant and took his coffee to the front patio. The pool caretaker was working on adjusting the PH of the water and a gardener was pruning some bushes. He wondered who would look after it all since Beika was gone. Had she found someone else already? He heard Mary step up behind him.

"You should think of getting ready soon, Mr. Waters. The car will be here and the helicopter is on a schedule."

"Won't you miss me, Mary?" he asked, kidding.

"Well," he said in a low voice, "at least I know where I stand with Mary."

He laughed to himself and went up to dress and prepare for the trip. As he contemplated Opal's clothes, her skin creams and scents, he felt this deep longing for her already. It was a major struggle inside him to get himself to continue preparations for leaving. He lingered over everything like someone who was afraid he would forget a scent, an image, even the echo of her footsteps in the hall.

Mary had to call up to tell him the car had arrived. He looked out the window and couldn't help but wonder if the driver were a mere mortal. After all, he had no wooden arrows to use. For a moment he actually wondered if he should break off a chair leg or something, but decided he'd take his chances. With Opal making the arrangements, it should all go well, he thought.

"Okay, Mary," he said coming down the steps. She was standing in the kitchen doorway. "Until we meet again, take care of yourself."

"My mistress will take care of me," she replied.

"That she will," he said and hurried out to the car. The driver seemed about as ordinary a mere mortal as he had met. They talked little all the way to the heliport. Once there, the pilot helped him get his bag aboard and they took off. He looked down as they started across the water and was fairly confident he could see the sailboat on which Opal was doing the last day of her modeling shoot. The sea was a dark aqua with the sunlight dancing on the white caps. Behind them the magic of Capri reluctantly gave up its hold on his imagination. It was drifting off like a weakening fantasy, falling back into the files of his memory, housed in a drawer under lock and key.

"Can you go a little lower?" he asked the pilot. "I'd like to wave goodbye to someone on that boat."

He smiled and nodded and they descended. It was Opal. She was in a two-piece bathing suit and even from the height he was at, she looked breathtaking to him. She gazed up. Her photographer turned and looked as well. He couldn't see his face as clearly, but Sean was certain he was annoyed. Sean had no doubt that Opal with her superior senses could see him sharply.

She lifted her hand.

He pressed his against the glass and a moment later, they were climbing again and moving quickly away from the boat and from her.

"Thanks," he told the pilot.

He looked forward at the Italian coast. He'd take a plane from Napoli and head back to Washington.

It had only been a few minutes since he had left her at the most, but his heart was already aching, aching so hard that he wondered if it would ever stop. Whatever magic someone like Opal possessed (he would never refer to her as a creature), it surely included the ability to toss a spell over him. Instinctively, he thought that whatever it was, there had to be something in him that welcomed and wanted it to go on and on.

"*We are possessed only by that which we want to possess us*," Opal once told him. "It's too easy to find excuses after becoming a victim. It's why I never felt sorry for anyone I've possessed."

In his heart he thought she did feel sorry for him. She felt sorry for the danger in which she had placed him. In her heart she knew that he might be right. Breaking away could very well save him. His reasoning convinced her. That was why she was willing to let him go.

And it was also why they were special together.

To love so deeply and fully that you could even agree to end it was more than special perhaps. It was miraculous.

How, he wondered, could he ever let that go?

Perhaps, this was the biggest and most incredible fantasy of all.

He'd only know for sure after tomorrow.

ABOUT THE AUTHOR

Andrew Neiderman was born in Brooklyn and grew up in New York's scenic Catskill Mountains region. A graduate of the University at Albany, State University of New York, from which he also received his master's in English, Neiderman taught at Fallsburg Junior-Senior High School for twenty-three years before pursuing a career as a novelist and screenwriter. He has written more than forty thriller novels under his own name, including *The Devil's Advocate*, which was made into a major motion picture for Warner Bros., starring Al Pacino, Keanu Reeves, and Charlize Theron, and is in development as a stage musical in London. Neiderman has also written seventy *New York Times*–bestselling novels for the V.C. Andrews franchise. He lives with his family in Palm Springs, California. Visit him on Facebook at www.facebook.com/AndrewNeidermanAuthor.